His hand sho

…circling her wrist
whine of the telephone caused them
apart. Dana stared over at the instrument with a
mixture of relief and regret. She extricated herself
from Gil and reached for the phone. After she
identified herself, she just listened for several
minutes.

She mumbled something into the mouthpiece and
replaced the receiver.

"Dana, what is it?"

She exhaled before speaking. "The car I drove off
the cliff… It's been found."

Gil noticed the lines of fright about her mouth.
"Dana, why is this important?"

"Its location was accurately pinpointed by an
anonymous caller. They found a note taped to the
steering wheel."

Gil felt a sick foreboding. "What did the note say?"

Dana's voice was unsteady. "It said, 'I'm waiting. If
you want me, you'll have to come get me.' "

This one is for Corinne Meyer,
editor *extraordinaire*,
although I'll never be able to find the right words
to thank her for helping me find the right words

Risky Business
M. J. RODGERS

▼ SILHOUETTE

Intrigue

*First published in Great Britain in 1995
by Silhouette Books, Eton House, 18-24 Paradise Road,
Richmond, Surrey TW9 1SR*

© Mary Johnson 1992

Silhouette, Silhouette Intrigue and Colophon are
Trade Marks of Harlequin Enterprises II B.V.

ISBN 0 373 22185 1

46-9510

Made and printed in Great Britain

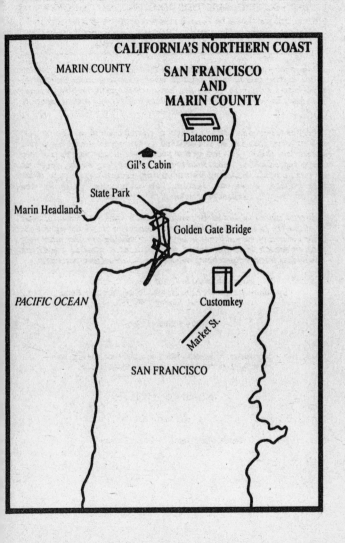

Chapter One

FBI Special Agent Dana Carmody knew something was wrong the moment she walked unchallenged into Data-comp's ultramodern steel-and-glass facility in Marin County just north of San Francisco.

Her alerted senses stretched ahead toward the unnatural quiet of the office complex while her heartbeat synchronized to the agitated rhythm of the heavy April rain at her back. Then the thick glass entry doors sibilated behind her, shutting out the noisy downpour and black of night, and ushering in a tomblike hush beneath the bright fluorescent lights. Her stomach muscles tightened.

She turned her head slowly. Large, illuminated red digits of a silent wall clock blazed 1900 hours against the vacant white wall to her left. To her right, multicolored lights glowed on a long, wood-grain panel lining an empty guard station. Two security monitoring screens sat on the high white counter.

A quick look at the screens satisfied her that the two hallways radiating out from the central lobby were empty. Dana was conscious of just one movement: the stretching of the tiny hairs along the back of her neck.

She unbuttoned her dark blue raincoat and reached into the large shoulder bag resting on her hip. The familiar shoulder bag and its contents were the same temperature as her skin, more like a living appendage than a separate compartment. Her fingers closed around the cold and comforting steel of her .38 Smith & Wesson revolver.

She took a moment to unwrap a peppermint candy and pop it into her suddenly dry mouth as she listened and watched warily.

Slowly, carefully, Dana walked over to the unmanned security position. As soon as she rounded the high counter barrier, her eyes widened at the sight of the unconscious guard sprawled on the white tile.

She dropped to the floor, her fingers probing until they found the faint pulse in the guard's neck as the water from her raincoat dripped out its own staccato beat onto his stiff uniform jacket. She exhaled in relief to find him still alive, but a sticky mat of blood on the side of his head told her he had received a recent blow. That message squirted a new shot of adrenaline into Dana's already alerted system.

She jumped to her feet and grabbed the phone on the guard's desk, punching in 911 and relaying the need for an ambulance at the Datacomp address before again depressing the switchhook and punching in Kristin Harcourt's extension. Four long, electronic rings went unanswered. A black foreboding seeped like spilled ink into Dana's thoughts as she dropped the receiver on its base.

Her eyes darted anxiously over the wall map of the complex beside the guard's station. Her index finger traced the route to Kristin Harcourt's private computer room. On the soles of her white boots, she noiselessly raced the length of the uncarpeted hallway to Room 121, stopping just short of the ajar door.

Her breath came in short little puffs. She felt the pounding beat of her heart, the automatic tensing between her shoulder blades. She stood next to the door to Room 121, listening. The quiet was absolute. She removed the gun from her shoulder bag as she carefully pushed the door inward. Within a fraction of a second, her eyes had grabbed and discarded every shadow in every corner. Nothing moved. The small room contained two computer positions. One was occupied.

Dana had never met Kristin Harcourt in person. But as she stared at the short, dark hair of the woman in the green dress slumped over the computer keyboard, she had no doubt that this was she. Dana moved quickly to the still programmer's side. The unnatural position of the woman's head and the open, staring eyes told Dana she was too late.

Images flashed on the screen before the dead programmer's glazed, unseeing eyes. Dana glanced briefly at the program that continued to add data and compute, just as though the dead woman lying on the keys was still typing away—a living program of a corpse. The thought brought invisible, frozen fingers to knead at Dana's spine. She shivered.

If Kristin had been concentrating on her monitor, she might not have noticed the murderer creep up behind her, not, at least, until the hands had encircled her neck and cruelly snapped it back.

A sudden noise shattered Dana's concentration on the imagined scenes of the programmer's death. She jerked her eyes away from the screen, straining to hear over the pounding of her own heartbeats. There it was again—the distinctive cadence of slapping leather on the outside hallway tile! She raced the few steps back to the door of the computer room, peering through a slit in the door frame so as not to expose herself. Every muscle in her body stiffened at the sight of the three approaching men.

A very tall, lithe man was flanked by two shorter men. The one on the left was stocky, casually dressed with dark hair; the one on the right was also stocky, but taller, and wore a suit. His blond hair and beard were closely trimmed. All three men held guns with silencers.

Dana's notice of the other two men and their weapons was purely perfunctory. Her eyes had locked onto the tall, sinister man in the middle—stone faced, hard muscled, silver haired—in a pearl gray suit and moving like no human she had ever seen. He had that cool and precise bearing generally restricted to one of nature's more deadly inspirations— the swooping eagle, the racing cheetah.

Dana felt her blood gushing in a sudden torrent. Quickly she drew back, quietly closing and locking the door.

Dana was sure these men were not the authorities responding to the report of a break-in. They had murdered Kristin Harcourt. She had no time to speculate on why they had returned. They were coming fast.

When she had pulled into the parking lot moments before, she had made note of only two other cars. She had mentally assigned the Ford Bronco to the guard and the BMW to Kristin Harcourt. She was sure these men hadn't seen her yet, but they must surely have seen her car. They would know someone was here.

Dana's right hand still held the gun. However, since the men were expecting to find someone, Dana knew she had lost the element of surprise. Engaging in a gunfight against three armed men would be foolish.

Then her searching eyes finally saw the dully lit red letters high on the back wall. An emergency exit! Just what she needed. The alarm she would set off by going through that door might disorient and delay the three men just long enough for her to escape.

And if it didn't?

Frantically she looked around for something to buy her time. She grabbed a chair and pushed its back up against the door to the hallway. Then she turned and raced for the emergency exit. She was shoving her shoulder against its bulk at the very moment the door into the computer room was being kicked open.

GILBERT WEBB SWAYED ABOVE the cliff at the Golden Gate National Recreation Area, staring blindly into the dark, rain-swept rocks below as his shaking hand brought the bottle to his lips. The illuminated deck span of the Golden Gate Bridge and the muted lights of San Francisco blinked at him through their soggy cloaks of rain. Officially, the park had closed at dusk, but he knew the back roads around the restricting, white metal gates.

Gil choked down the cheap whiskey in a desperate spasm of gulps, unconcerned he was spilling alcohol on his Pringle cashmere sweater and his Gianni Versace shirt and pants. Somewhere to his left, the pitiful wail of a lost and lonely sea gull echoed in his ears as though its sound was originating from the depths of his own soul.

A wave of uncontrollable shivers swept through his large frame. He decided he needed another drink. As he raised the bottle once again to his lips, his hand scraped the camera slung over his shoulder and jogged his memory as to why he had come to this ledge.

Ever since his dad had given him his first camera, photographing a spectacular display of lightning during a storm had been a goal. But the years had passed and the cameras and storms had come and gone, and he never seemed to have one in hand when the other hit. That's why when the shrieks of this storm had penetrated his numbed brain tonight, he had gotten in his old Jeep and made the trip into the hills, camera in hand.

Except fate had once again sneaked in to thwart him by unplugging the current to this storm. There wasn't any lightning left to photograph, just an ugly blanket of rain with scraping sheets of ice-cold wind. He hadn't been successful at anything else during the past six months. Why had he thought this would be any different?

Gil gulped more whiskey. The cheap, searing liquid burned his throat as the cold rain streaked beneath his clothing. The dry seat of the Jeep was just twenty feet behind him. But he stubbornly stood under the wet pelting, embracing every drop of its icy chill as a welcome diversion to the defeat burning holes in his soul.

THE ALARM SCREECHED INTO the dark, drenched night around the minimally lit parking lot of Datacomp. Dana raced for her car. She heard the emergency door being thrown open behind her. She didn't have to look back to know they were coming fast.

A whizzing bullet smashed the back window of the blue Toyota MR2 just as she jerked open the driver's door. She had the key in the ignition and the engine turned over before her body had sat fully on the seat. She closed the door as the car leapt ahead in response to her flooring the gas pedal. As she shot out of the parking lot, she saw two men scrambling into a black Cadillac Seville.

The tall, silver-haired man, who she knew instinctively must be the leader, and the stockier, dark-haired man were going to give her a run for it. She realized they had to. She had seen them. They could not afford to let her live.

As she had run for her car, she had noticed another vehicle, a light beige truck with the word Delivery painted across it, pulled up to the entrance with someone behind the wheel. One or more of the men must have arrived in it, although, clearly, the Cadillac belonged to them, too. The need for two vehicles confused her, and so did their return to the scene, but at the moment she had more pressing concerns.

She turned right, then left, then found herself on Highway 101 heading south for the Golden Gate Bridge and San Francisco. Traffic was light into the city. She floored the gas pedal, but found the Cadillac easily eating up the distance between them. As long as she stayed on a straightway, she didn't have a chance. What she needed was some winding, twisting roads where a sports car could show its stuff.

She took the next off ramp with no clear direction in mind, just aware that the straightway could not aid her es-

cape. She didn't know the area, so she followed her natural
instincts and headed for higher ground. It mushroomed up
on the road to her right. The sign flashing in front of her
headlights signaled she was entering a park as she yanked the
wheel right. She began to climb.

GILBERT GULPED DOWN MORE of the bitter drink. Prior to
today, the last time he could remember even having a drink
was the week before Thanksgiving over at Lionel's, nearly
six months before. It seemed like a lifetime ago. It was
barely a week later when Lionel's once friendly face had
become contorted in anger, when the man's tone had turned
harsh with hate.

"You're a stinking piece of traitorous trash, Webb. But
you won't do this to anyone else. I'll see you never work
again. That's a promise!" And over the past few months,
Gil had learned that Lionel could keep that promise.

But Lionel had been wrong. Gil wasn't a traitor. Still, Gil
had soon found it didn't matter whether anyone was wrong
about him, whether he was guilty or not. All that really
mattered was that everyone thought he was guilty. Everyone. Lionel, Vanessa—everyone.

He was despised and shunned, an outcast to his friends
and profession. And the worst part was, he didn't know
what he could do about it. He took another drink.

DANA'S DAMP PALMS GRIPPED the wheel of the Toyota MR2.
She had to reduce her speed in order to take the dark, twisting, slippery turns. The black Cadillac still hugged her tail.
Its flashing headlights in her rearview mirror leered at her
like a hungry cat. She tried to swallow the fear sticking in
her throat.

They had been shooting at her for several turns. She knew
it although she had not actually heard all the shots. The
wind, the rain, the car's laboring engine and the screech of
the protesting tires blotted out nearly all other sounds. For-

tunately, hitting a moving target while moving oneself was not an easy task. Particularly up a dark and winding mountain road in the rain. She had a better than even chance of not being hit at all.

About the same time she was comforting herself with the favorable probabilities, she turned a corner and was suddenly confronted with a pair of locked white gates dead ahead. She knew she didn't have time to stop. She had no time to indulge new fears, no time to lament the road taken. She had just one option.

In the instant the thought had reached her conscious mind, Dana jerked the wheel toward the jagged cliff of the mountain road.

SINCE HE WASN'T much of a drinker, Gil thought the liquor would hit him quick and hard. But the more he had drunk, the clearer had become the pain of his thoughts. He would probably need the whole damn bottle to drown them out.

"To the whole damn bottle," he yelled into the black nothingness before him as he once again raised the cheap whiskey to his lips. His toast released an unexpected memory that swirled out of the blackness to engulf him. He could hear a clink of glasses as his mind's eye once again saw his dad pouring out Gil's first drink when he had gotten his scholarship to college. The memory was etched so clearly, Gil could even make out his father's hard-working, grease-stained fingers grasped around the dusty bottle of Chivas Regal as the golden liquid bulged the sides of their glasses.

"To a future as bright as my boy," Gil's father had said, his dark eyes swimming in proud tears.

Gil squeezed his eyes shut, trying to blot out the memory, taking a large swig of the cheap whiskey in an attempt to swallow the choking lump in his throat. But although the alcohol rushed down, the lump remained, thick and suffocating. He was thankful his father had not lived to see him so disgraced.

Gil's head rolled back from the weight of the persistent memories as the rain pounded his face and the salt in his tears crystallized into grit down the sides of his cheeks.

DANA ROLLED WITHOUT control into the thick branches of the scrub brush at the side of the road. A sturdy stem brought her to an unceremonious halt as it painfully whipped into her back. She had only had time to jump from the car, not time to select her landing site. Now she looked up to watch the MR2 jump the edge of the road, arch into the air for an instant of determined flight and then plunge like a felled blue jay into the dark depths below.

Before the deafening echoes of the smashed metal had been swallowed by the rain-soaked wind, the black Cadillac had pulled to the edge of the road. Dana drew her white boots under her dark blue raincoat and huddled in the camouflage of the thick bushes, watching her pursuers make their way to the edge. They stopped less than fifteen feet from her hiding place, the strong headlights of their car illuminating the men clearly in the wet, black night.

Dana held her breath and hugged the ground. For a very long moment, both men just stood in the pouring rain and stared over the cliff into the darkness below.

"That takes care of her," Dana heard the dark-haired man say.

"We must be sure," the silver-haired man replied. Dana felt the vibration of his voice pound its way down her spine. She battled to overcome the sudden, unreasonable panic that made her want to flee.

"Get the flashlight from the car," the silver-haired man said. "We'll have a closer look."

Dana watched the physical agitation of the dark-haired man's flailing arms. "You think I'm going down there in this rain? Man, you're crazy. It's as black and slippery as hell!''

The taller, silver-haired man's voice changed neither in volume nor inflection. "Get the flashlight."

Dana watched the dark-haired man's hands as they passed the gun back and forth in a growing frustration. "Hell, the way that car sailed over the edge, it could be down three hundred feet or more! Maybe fell into the ocean!"

The silver-haired man's voice still did not change. "I know this terrain. There's a land ledge down there. It probably stopped the fall. I said, get the flashlight."

His companion glowered at him, then turned and stomped back to the car. He switched the engine off, but left the headlights on to light their way as he fumbled inside the interior.

All the time, Dana watched him only vaguely. Her real attention was on the silver-haired man, who still peered into the darkness and listened at the edge. She knew he was the real threat.

When his companion returned with the flashlight, both men began their determined descent. No sooner had they disappeared from sight then Dana crawled carefully out from the protection of the bushes. Nothing seemed to be broken, but she hurt all over. Trying to ignore the protest from her battered muscles, she got to her feet and headed purposefully for the Cadillac. The doors were locked and after a few wasted, precious seconds, she realized the hood release operated from the inside, too. They had walked off with the key.

She fought down the welling disappointment and the chill of the battering rain against her bruised flesh. She must not let the discomfort dull her brain. Since she couldn't take their vehicle, she must figure out a way to incapacitate it, if possible. Her eyes glanced down to the tires as her hand groped for something sharp in her shoulder bag. All she could find was a needle from her purse-size sewing kit. She needed a knife to slash those tires.

The seconds ticked way in her brain in an urgent refrain. She couldn't risk using the gun because the sound would alert her two pursuers and bring them on the run. They were armed, and she was outnumbered. Her efforts must be focused on escape. She stepped around the barrier of the white gate and began to run swiftly up the road.

It wouldn't take the silver-haired man long to realize that she hadn't been in the Toyota MR2 when it went over. Of course, he would notice the driver's door had been open. He might think she had been thrown clear, and he might delay further pursuit while he looked for her unconscious body in the scruffy undergrowth. He might, but she doubted he would. And she also doubted that the chain securing the white gates would prove much of a deterrent to him.

She was a quarter mile up the road when she heard a single shot. Soon she could hear the Cadillac engine laboring under the uphill climb. He was coming after her. Her accurate assessment of the silver-haired man's intelligence and diligence did not bring her joy.

GIL WAS GLAD HE HADN'T eaten all day. His empty stomach was finally helping the alcohol to take effect. Of course, he wouldn't be able to drive home, but that didn't matter. He could sleep in the Jeep or, more accurately, pass out into a painless oblivion for a while. And tomorrow? Who cared about tomorrow?

He laughed as he raised the clutched bottle, but before he could tilt the nozzle in the direction of his open lips, his unsteady hand slipped on the wet glass surface and the bottle crashed to the rocky ground.

Gil swayed above the broken glass and spilled liquid. Was there any left? As he bent over, the camera strap fell from his sloping shoulder and the camera hurtled down on top of the broken bottle of whiskey. The additional piece of broken, jagged glass swirled in front of him.

He knew it wasn't a valuable camera, not in terms of money. But it was the only possession other than the old Jeep and the cabin that his father had been able to leave him. And he had dropped it, broken it, in a drunken stupor. His act was like the final shame to his father's name.

DANA TURNED THE CORNER and stopped for a moment to listen over the rasping sound of her own labored breathing. Despite the noise of the rain and wind, she picked out the sound of the Cadillac, continuing its slow, steady pace a few turns behind her. Her pursuers were searching for signs of the woman in the dark blue raincoat and long white boots. Over the past few minutes they had gained on her as the tiredness had begun to numb her limbs. It wouldn't be long now.

She looked ahead, trying to control the desperation that swelled sick and hollow within her chest. She blinked through the steady rain, not quite believing her eyes as she saw the old, beat-up, gray Jeep parked on a shallow turnout. She ran the few feet to reach it, surprised to find it both empty and unlocked. She jerked her tired body around, but could see no one who might own the vehicle. It appeared to be abandoned, which probably meant it wouldn't start. But she had to give it a try.

When she reached underneath the dash for the leads to hot-wire the starter, however, her hands collided with the keys dangling from the ignition. For one long surprised second, she just sat there, not believing her luck. Then a quarter turn later, the engine hummed obediently beneath her fingertips. That was also the moment when the Jeep's headlights flashed on the man standing at the edge of the cliff.

He didn't even turn at the sound of the engine, and Dana realized it wasn't because the rain and wind had drowned out the noise. His bent head and shoulders and the way he kept staring down into the darkness below gave Dana a very uncomfortable feeling. Had he come here to jump?

Precious seconds passed as her mind wrestled with what she could do to save them both. Once decided, it took her less than a second to shut off the engine and headlights and reach back to loosen her long, light brown hair from its tight chignon. The men had seen her only from a distance and in the darkness of the night. They probably thought she had short hair. They wouldn't expect to be confronted with a woman with almost waist-length locks.

She tore the raincoat off, then threw it beneath the Jeep as she jumped from the vehicle. She tugged off her boots and threw them down alongside her raincoat. Now clad only in a white sweater over black slacks and black stockings, she ran to the man's side and jerked him away from the cliff's edge, wrapping her arms around him in a sturdy embrace.

The black Cadillac turned the corner, washing them in its strong headlights at the same instant that Dana urged the stranger's pliant arms around her waist and joined his lips with hers in a desperate kiss.

Chapter Two

Gil tasted peppermint and felt a sudden rush of very agreeable warmth traveling through his cold body. His lips eagerly sought more of that exciting taste. Damn, if he'd known he could get this out of a bottle, he'd have drunk up long ago!

His chilled hands happily circled the dry, soft, enticing flesh beneath his fingertips, drawing the warm, yielding body even closer. His dulled mind wondered how the enticing taste of peppermint could kindle his senses into such an agreeable scorch.

"LOOK AT 'EM, SPARR. Don't even know it's raining. And they ain't teenagers, neither. How you figure they got that Jeep through the locked gate?" the dark-haired driver of the Cadillac said.

"Obviously, Leach, there must be a back road," the silver-haired man said, his black eyes intently studying the two figures caught in the car's high beams. This woman didn't look like the one they had just chased out of Datacomp. She was differently dressed, had much longer hair and a smaller stature.

Still, there was something about the two people in the clinch that bothered Sparr. However, he couldn't believe the red-bearded, ill-kept man with the old Jeep had anything to do with the quick-thinking, fast-moving woman they had been chasing.

"Shall I find out if they've seen the woman?" Leach asked.

Sparr shook his head. "They haven't seen her if our arrival isn't breaking up their wet clinch. Besides, use your head. The fewer people involved in tonight's stupidity, the better."

Leach scowled at Sparr's words. He noisily and abusively backed the car off the soft shoulder leading to the edge of the cliff and the couple. He pointed the Cadillac's black nose up the circuitous road, irritation underlying each of his next words.

"I still say we're wasting time. She ain't alive. Nothing could of crawled out of that crash."

Sparr took one last frowning look at the necking couple. His answer to his ill-tempered companion was said with the same lack of emotion as his previous responses. "We didn't find the body."

"Yeah, but seeing in the dark with all this damn rain ain't exactly easy," Leach said. "She probably got pitched out of the car, smashed up on them rocks somewhere."

Sparr's index finger pressed into his upper lip, rubbing the sudden itching sensation in his upper gums. It was a bad sign. They only itched this way when he was missing something.

"Your wishful thinking is selling her short, Leach. She managed to delay us long enough to escape from the computer room. I wouldn't say she's a woman who would die so easily or obligingly."

"Even if she's alive, why would she climb? I bet there ain't nothing at the end of this here road but a dead end. We're going the wrong way."

Sparr's thick, silver hair shook ever so slightly. "You're forgetting the back road the couple with the Jeep must have taken. Besides, when we gained on her over the flat streets, she went instinctively for the climb. After she crashed, I think those same instincts were still at work. We'll go a few more miles before we start down again."

DANA KEPT LISTENING FOR the Cadillac to move on while she continued to embrace the wet man standing on the ledge. Fortunately, he was cooperating fully. Maybe too fully. For someone who had been about to commit suicide, he seemed to have a lot of life left in him. His arms were pressing her to him with a hungry and unmistakable message. And although he tasted like one-hundred proof whiskey, his mouth eagerly clung to hers.

Her hands sought the warmer and comparatively drier flesh beneath his drenched sweater. She was surprised to find a mass of well-developed muscles extending from waist to shoulders. He didn't have the body of a man bent on self-destruction. As his hands and arms circled her chilled body, pressing her ever closer, a quiver of warmth swept through her. For one totally mad moment, she found herself whole-heartedly immersed in the unexpectedly exciting embrace.

She regained her sanity, feeling somewhat shaken at the temporary abandonment. She marshaled her control, trying not to think about the warm lips on hers, but instead listened for the Cadillac's direction. When she was sure it was out of sight, she pulled away from the exciting kiss of the stranger, still holding securely on to his arms.

"What's your name?"

She distinctly heard the alcohol-induced fuzziness in his voice. "Gilbert . . . Webb."

Dana felt something poking uncomfortably at the bottom of her left stocking. She ignored it as she concentrated on reaching the obviously intoxicated man.

"You live around here, Gil?"

She had to repeat her question before he finally nodded.

"Okay, Gil, we need to get out of the rain. I'll drive and you'll show me the way to your place. Right?"

When he nodded again, Dana leaned down to pick up the object her foot had discovered so uncomfortably. She couldn't see it through the wet blackness of the night, but she could at least feel its shape well enough to identify it as a camera. Obviously this man must have dropped it. She swung its strap over her shoulder and then circled her arm in his and led him back to the Jeep. He stumbled beside her like someone without a will.

She sat him in the passenger's side, securing the seat belt around him, and then leaned down to retrieve her raincoat and boots from underneath the Jeep. She slipped her boots over her wet stockings. She threw the raincoat behind the driver's seat. Then, before she got in, she took some mud and obliterated the license plate on the back. She tried to forget how wet and cold and battered she felt as she started the Jeep and headed it down the twisting mountain road. She knew the chase was far from over.

AS SOON AS THE CADILLAC had gone a few turns, it finally occurred to Sparr what had bothered him about the necking couple.

"Damn it, I've been a fool! Turn the car around, Leach. We're going back."

Leach's grin was smug. "You finally going to admit she went down?"

"No, she went up, you idiot. We were looking at her and didn't even know it. Now turn the damn car around!"

Leach's forehead puckered at the sudden sharpness in Sparr's tone. He began a hurried turnabout on the narrow mountain road, ignoring the protest from the tires. His tone had retreated from its sarcasm. "I don't understand. We only saw one woman."

"Precisely."

"You're saying she was the one in the clinch with that guy? You're crazy. She ain't nothing like the woman we've been chasing."

Sparr shrugged. "I'll concede she went through a surprising metamorphosis. But it was her."

"Meta . . . What you say don't make no sense."

Sparr controlled the irritation that lay just below the deep cellar of his voice. "Didn't you see how soaked the man's hair and clothing were? They clung to his body. He'd obviously been standing out in the rain for some time."

"So what?" Leach said.

"So the woman's clothes and hair weren't clinging like his."

"So maybe she sat in the Jeep awhile."

"While her lover stood in the rain?" Sparr said. "Never compound your errors by trying to make them fit into a rational explanation. If this couple were such ardent lovers, one of them would hardly have been standing out in the rain while the other stayed seated in a dry Jeep."

"But the woman we've been chasing had to be soaked after running a half mile up hill in this downpour."

"She was dry beneath her raincoat," Sparr said. "She must have removed it and her boots and loosened her hair from however she had it tied back. That's why the ends didn't look that wet. Look, the Jeep's gone. Hurry, we must catch them."

GIL WAS REALLY ENJOYING his hallucination. The warm vision that tasted like peppermint and felt like heaven kept insisting he show her the way to his small cabin. Hell, even in his better dreams the lady wasn't this eager!

Only problem was trying to focus on the road through the pouring rain. And getting his finger to point straight. "Got to turn back. Gate up ahead. Clear road back there."

Her answer was succinct. "Hold tight!"

Gil didn't respond quickly enough. As his driver hit the brakes and skidded into a one-hundred-and-eighty degree turn, he found himself thrown against the passenger door.

He didn't feel any pain at the jostling, but he was beginning to wonder why she just didn't pull over to the side. After all, if she was in this much of a hurry—

"Gil, stay awake. Where do we turn?"

He felt the pressure of her hand on his left arm. It was warm and steady, and his right hand closed over it, luxuriating in its feel. He opened his eyes, not realizing he had closed them, and was immediately blinded by the headlights of an oncoming car. He heard the squeal of protesting tires as the car that just passed them skidded to a hasty halt.

The road undulated before him in sickening waves. He fought down a sudden queasiness and strove to regain his bearings over the dark, rain-swept path. Then he recognized a familiar landmark.

"There," he said, pointing. "Angle to the . . . right."

The woman yanked the wheel hard, turning onto the dirt road and flooring the accelerator, knocking him back against the seat. Damn, he was beginning to feel like an eloping bride with an irate daddy in pursuit! The image tickled him and he began to laugh.

He turned toward his driver and saw a light spray of water splashing off a long, light brown tendril of hair as the Jeep bounced beneath them. Lights from behind them illuminated her profile. She had a pretty face—delicate and white.

Except suddenly, he knew something was wrong. A sickness in his stomach bubbled up as though stirred by the fear he saw lining her features. Once again her eyes darted behind them to the lights flashing in the back window.

DANA PULLED HARD ON THE sluggish wheel of the Jeep as the gleaming eyes of the black Cadillac glowed hungrily in the rearview mirror. The way they were being chased left no doubt in her mind that the silver-haired man suspected who she was. She heard the whining ricochet of a bullet off the side of the Jeep's door.

"Get down, Gil. Down!"

Her passenger scrunched down obediently, albeit slowly, in his seat just as another bullet tore through the Jeep's plastic rear window. Dana yanked the wheel into the next sharp turn.

"This won't do. They're too close, and whoever is doing that shooting is far too good a shot," Dana said. She didn't even realize she had voiced the words until Gil said, "Shooting?"

From the continued slur of his speech, Dana knew he wasn't fully grasping the situation. "Just stay down, Gil. Stay down."

Dana's hands twisted around the wheel as she tightly cut the next corner. The road sign flashed a warning of a sharp U-turn ahead. An idea formed in her mind the moment she saw the sign, and a grim smile circled her lips.

"All right," she said into the rearview mirror. "Let's see how good your reflexes are."

Dana attacked the accelerator and took the turn at a dizzying speed. Just as she straightened out the wheel, however, she stomped on the Jeep's brakes, stopping in the middle of the roadway. She knew when the Cadillac came around the blind turn behind her, the driver would either hit the Jeep or swerve out of reflex. As she set her emergency brake lights flashing, she prayed he wouldn't have enough time for anything but reflex.

The rain, the racing engine and her heartbeat all competed for recognition in the fraction of a second it took for the Cadillac to roar around the turn. Dana heard the powerful brakes squeal in panic. Then just when it seemed the car was about to ram the Jeep, the driver yanked the wheel, heading the big car over the edge.

Enormous sharp rocks tore at the underbelly of the powerful machine, crunching the steel with its tenacious jaws.

Dana turned to watch pieces of sheared metal fly in all directions like plucked feathers. The front tires of the Cadillac ripped apart and melted like black licorice over the boulders lining the top of the ridge.

But despite the beating the car took from the rough and jagged terrain, it had been those huge chunks of roadside granite that had saved it from sailing into the sea. When the car finally came to a rest, its engine stalled, its front end tottered precariously over the cliff's edge and its headlights stared blindly into blackness.

Even the noise of the wind seemed to die down as the final reverberations of the tearing metal were replaced by an unnatural deafness beating against Dana's ears. After a moment of silence, she began to hear the crescendo of loud cursing coming from the wrecked Cadillac, floating over the renewed roar of wind and rain.

A satisfied smile circled her lips as she gunned the engine, heading the Jeep down the mountain and out of shooting range.

To GIL, EVERYTHING HAD become a blur but the woman's voice asking him directions to his cabin. Sometimes he realized she asked more than once as his brain was slow to process her questions and as he fought with the sickness that swelled in his stomach.

Finally, they arrived. She drove around the back, parking the Jeep behind a clump of trees. Gil knew it didn't make any sense since there was a covered carport in plain view, but not a whole lot was making sense at the moment. He stumbled up the back steps to the cabin, fumbling in his pocket for his key. He tried to hurry as the fire broke out in his gut.

Once inside, he made directly for the bathroom, where he got thoroughly sick. Afterward he felt weak, but mentally more aware. He peeled off his wet clothes and stood underneath a hot shower. The heat penetrated, easing his shakes and restoring some semblance to his perceptions. He came out of the bathroom a few moments later, dressed in an old, faded blue terry bathrobe.

He looked toward the kitchen to see the woman smiling at him, and suddenly he felt like a lost ship that had just spotted a lighthouse. He had forgotten how good it felt to be on the receiving end of a flash of white teeth.

"I've heated some soup."

The smell of food filled Gil's nostrils, and he eagerly sat down in front of the chicken soup and sourdough bread. As the bowl before him emptied, he began to feel somewhat human again.

He looked up to see she was coming out of the bathroom, a white towel wrapped around her head. She was wearing a long, dark blue raincoat, obscuring everything but her legs below the knees. She laid the rest of her wet clothes and a pair of white boots to dry in front of the fireplace.

He sat back, still feeling a bit shaky and fuzzy. Images were drifting back to him, but he wasn't sure which were real, which imagined. He watched the woman's pale face, small and fine boned. Her skin was delicate and almost translucent, like an expensive porcelain.

"How are you feeling, Gil?"

"About fifty percent conscious, which is a forty-nine percent improvement. I'm afraid I had a lot to drink earlier."

She sat across from him on the other side of the small kitchen table. "I gathered as much."

He thought her gray eyes were the color of a summer rain. As he gazed into them, his mind began to swim aimlessly until he forcibly brought it back into focus. "At the risk of being rudely direct, who are you?"

She extended her hand. "My name is Dana. What were you doing on that ledge?"

He took her offered hand, then directed his attention back to her eyes. There was a tenderness in her look. He continued to hold her hand, having no desire to let it go.

"I think that should be my question, Dana. There were people following us and shooting at us . . . weren't there?"

She withdrew her hand and gaze from his. "Tea will be ready in a minute. I managed to get a pretty good fire going to take the chill off, but I've found there is nothing like hot food and drink to really warm the insides. Don't you think so?"

He recognized her evasion, and it both surprised and confused him. "Why aren't you answering my question?"

Her eyes met his again in a direct look. "Why aren't you answering mine?"

Dana got up and walked into the living room to check her clothes spread out before the fire. They were dry enough, but she felt reluctant to put them on and leave this man. He was a bit of a mystery. As she glanced over at him now, she could see his blue bathrobe wrapped a solid frame with powerfully built forearms and calves. And he had that rare shade of hazel eyes that picked up specks of gold when the light hit them in a certain way.

Ordinarily, she wasn't one fond of long hair and full beards, but the thick consistency and reddish hue of his hair reminded her of a ruggedly handsome Viking. As her eyes followed the reddish, bold strands on his powerful chest, she watched them disappear down the deep apex of his terry-cloth belt toward the sharp outline of a flat stomach. She tore her eyes away as the sudden memory of the feel of his hard body returned in a warm wave.

She rested her thoughts and eyes on the expensive label inside the collar of a cashmere sweater draped across the back of the living-room sofa. He certainly seemed to have the basics for success. Why would such a man want to end his life?

She moved about his spotlessly clean cabin, looking for the clues that would tell her who he was, but everywhere she found contradiction. Sitting on a cheap old card table was a very expensive collection of classical tapes, but nowhere could she see a tape deck or sound system of any kind. He had no television or VCR, yet the chipped shelves of a rickety, imitation-wood bookcase were well-polished and the background for some very expensive volumes. Many were about computers. She reached for one, newly intrigued.

Gil watched his visitor, perplexed and concerned at her earlier evasions of his questions. She wasn't tall, maybe five-five, with small bones and a slim, nonmuscular frame. He thought he remembered she had long, light brown hair, but the towel around her head obscured it now, so he wasn't sure.

Her graceful, almost effortless movements combined with her white skin and delicate structure made her appear very soft and feminine. He had always liked soft, feminine women. He remembered the warmth of her body as he had held her to him and the sweetness of her kiss as her mouth—

"Is this your cabin away from home, Gil?"

Her question brought him back to reality. He wasn't grateful. "This is home. All there is."

As he watched her eyes taking in the small, neat cabin that had once been his father's, he felt more and more depressingly sober. Its kitchen, living room, bedroom and bath comprised only eight hundred square feet, and its furniture was old castoffs of chipped wood and worn upholstery. He had tried to keep it clean, but it certainly wasn't much to look at.

This is all she'll ever know of you, a voice inside him said. He swallowed a bitter lump collecting in his throat, hardly noticing the crunch of gravel beneath the tires of an approaching car.

Dana hurried to the front window. She peeked through the edge of the cotton curtain, feeling relief as a small pickup clattered by. Fortunately the cabin was on a side road that didn't seem to be frequently traveled. Still, it would be unwise to let her guard down.

It would also be unwise to stay much longer. The cabin was close to the park where she had managed to strand the two men in the Cadillac. If they were still stranded. She doubted it would take the silver-haired man much time to extricate himself from this last delay.

She had counted on using Gil's phone, but it was dead. If it had been just her, she would have headed for the airport directly. But this man was involved now. She felt a professional responsibility for him and a curiosity about the contrast of prosperity and despair she found around her. And considering where and how she had found him, a definite concern.

Gil watched Dana turn from whatever had interested her at the window and collect the faded, chipped stoneware that had held their meal. She took the dishes to the sink to wash them.

It was such a homey, companionable act that it almost brought him pain. For months, no one had been in this cabin but he. Gil hadn't realized how much he missed human company. For whatever reason she had come, he was glad she was here.

Gil watched her bring the cast-iron pot from the stove, and he picked up the cup she had set before him. As she poured the hot water over the tea bag, Gil felt the cup warming his hands. He also caught the unmistakable scent of peppermint. She was sucking on a mint. He knew then that his blurred memory was correct. She had kissed him on the edge of that cliff. At a moment when he had felt so cold and alone, she had appeared out of nowhere—warm and alive.

"Why did you kiss me, Dana?"

She sat across from him. Gil felt the assessing look in her light eyes chaining his attention as she swayed the tea bag like a pendulum through the hot water in the delicate cup.

"I understand despair, Gil. A year ago, someone who meant the world to me died. And I wasn't there for him when he needed me."

Gil was surprised at the sudden sadness in her voice. "You blamed yourself for his death?"

She nodded. "Enough to contemplate suicide."

He heard the seriousness in her tone and got an uncomfortable chill up his spine. "But you didn't go through with it."

She looked intently into his eyes. "I didn't because in my heart I knew that suicide doesn't give anyone a chance to correct life's mistakes. It just adds the last big one."

Gil pushed his cup of tea away untouched. Her meaning became clear. "Dana, I wasn't thinking of jumping from that ledge, just getting a picture of some lightning. Not a particularly bright thing to do since there wasn't any lightning, but as you've no doubt already determined, the liquor I've consumed today didn't exactly sharpen my wits."

Dana sat back. He saw the tightness in her shoulders relax and her lips curve into a small smile.

"I'm glad to hear it, Gil. But something unpleasant must have occurred to have caused you to drink so much and to recklessly stand on the edge of a cliff in the pouring rain. There are no empty liquor cans or bottles in your trash, and no full or partial ones on your shelves. That tells me you're not normally a drinking man."

He blinked at the message in her words. "You searched my shelves and trash?"

She shrugged, seeming to take no notice of the redress in his tone. "I just happened to notice while I was fixing us something. What's troubling you, Gil?"

He liked the soft, almost hypnotic quality of her voice. After she had seen the way he lived, he was surprised she still wanted to know about him. But she did, and suddenly, he wanted her to. Perhaps if she understood who he had been, she would see his present circumstances did not define him.

"I used to be a developer of computer programs."

She nodded. "I noticed your advanced books on the subject. How long ago?"

"Six months," Gil said, still having a hard time believing so much had happened in such a short time.

"And you stopped?"

"Not voluntarily." He put his hands to his temples and rubbed them. His head had begun to throb. "It seems such a jumbled mess sometimes. I hardly know where to start."

Her voice was encouraging. "Back far enough to give a beginning to your story, if there clearly was such a time."

He reached for his discarded teacup and recognized it as one of his father's. He brought it to his lips, clutching it reverently. "Actually there was. I won a programming contest in high school."

"And that started your career in the field?"

Gil nodded as he sipped some more of the hot tea, enjoying the warmth of the liquid and the happy memories flowing through him.

"I took every computer-science and programming-language course offered in college. Still, the real challenge and experimentation came after class, when I could sit in front of the computer screen and see what I could create."

"And after college?"

"I got a job at Computech."

Her look was questioning.

"It's a Silicon Valley computer company that was just getting started about ten years ago. There were only about five employees then, and I was the only programmer. A year ago, it employed more than five hundred. I was vice president by then, second in command only to Lionel Cobb, the president."

Dana straightened. "Wait a minute. I remember reading about a computer-software genius by the name of Webb from the Silicon Valley. Let's see, *Fortune Magazine*, maybe three years ago. That was you?"

Gil nodded. "Actually, closer to four years ago."

"'The software wizard,' they called you," Dana said, the focus in her eyes sharpening. "'The master of programmers, capable of the most amazing computer feats, but human enough not to be able to get his tie straight.'"

Her quotation from the article was almost exact. It made him enormously pleased. Her next question evoked a different response. "Gil, what happened?"

He put his cup down, exhaling as though he carried a heavy burden strapped to his shoulders. "It started when Lionel and I had a fight late one Friday afternoon about six months ago. We had begun to argue more frequently because of our differing philosophies."

"How did you differ?"

"I thought the company should continue to reinvest its profits in expansion. Lionel wanted out. He had had a difficult time raising a brilliant but rebellious son, and now that the boy was finally on his own, Lionel wanted to put the company up for sale and retire. He told me my five-year contract with him would be sold to the new owner. I told him I wasn't one of his computers that could be sold, and stormed out, taking an unscheduled skiing vacation with my fiancée back in Vail. I thought I'd let Lionel sweat."

"Did he?" Dana asked.

"Much more than I had intended. The following Monday, he found the company's new-product-line computer data base wiped out. Lionel and the others could do nothing. Six new software programs representing revenue in excess of five million dollars vanished."

"Who did it?"

Gil exhaled. "Investigators analyzed the data base and decided it had been invaded by an ingenious virus program that left no trace. After evaluating the expertise of all personnel, they decided I was the only one who could have devised such a virus."

Dana shook her head. "Why couldn't this virus have been sent over a telecommunications connection by a competitor through a trapdoor, you know, a fault in the security programming?"

"No," Gil said. "Industrial espionage had long ago caused us to protect the new-product-line data base by severing telephone datalinks to it. No one could have picked up a phone and dialed into our system. It had to have been someone using a terminal hardwired to the mainframe computer, and those terminals are only found in Computech's high-security building."

"Then someone broke in and used a terminal."

Gil shook his head. "That possibility was checked. The security system for Computech is state-of-the-art. Only employees are permitted on the premises, and each is computer-identified by their hand print. No unauthorized entries occurred."

"Any security system can be breached," Dana said.

"Maybe. But even if someone broke in, they would not have been able to gain access to a terminal without a key. And in addition to a key, all terminals have secret passwords that are changed daily by their individual users so that they cannot be breached. It had to have been an employee with access to a terminal and its security password who infected Computech's system with that virus."

"So that's why they decided it had to have been you?"

Gil exhaled a deep breath. "Yes. That, plus the fact that they traced the last entries into the system before the database wipeout. They pinpointed the originating terminal."

"And?"

Gil turned to watch her light eyes, wanting to see the effect on them as he detonated the last bomb of his story.

"And it was my terminal that sent the virus program through the system."

Chapter Three

Dana's white forehead sprouted a small gray frown. "Your terminal?"

She watched Gil's head nod as his hazel eyes held a guarded hope. He obviously wanted her to believe him, and yet had steeled himself against the disappointment of her possible disbelief. She'd give him neither false reactions nor premature ones. Her training demanded she get all the facts. They were what she sought now.

"What about the radio waves that your system unit emits?" she asked. "Did you know that those waves can be picked up by interception equipment outside a building?"

"Yes. Reports of industrial espionage in the computer industry kept us aware of the various eavesdropping techniques. But our terminals are new, encased in metal shields to prevent wave interception...." Gil stopped. He had been talking as though he still belonged to Computech, which of course he didn't.

Dana munched on her lip. "It must have been someone who looked over your shoulder when you were entering your password. From everything you've told me, only someone at Computech who used your terminal to initiate the virus program could be responsible."

Gil shook his head. "Except I'm positive no one looked over my shoulder while I was entering my password. Two months after the disaster, I convinced my lawyer to give me an opportunity to get back into the data base. I thought I might be able to reclaim the data."

"And?" Dana prompted.

His look was both perplexed and defeated. "It was completely gone. I still can't figure out who could have done it."

She nodded in understanding. "Were you prosecuted?"

"Not criminally. Not yet, anyway. Civilly, my lawyer advised me the case was open and shut and we should settle out of court. You see, even he believed I had done it."

Dana watched Gil shake his head as though he might be able to dismiss the painful memories before he went on.

"That was okay with Computech. They didn't want the disaster broadcasted and have customers lose faith in their security. That would have caused even more financial problems."

"How did you settle out of court?" Dana asked.

"I had to turn over all my stock in Computech, sell my home in Hillsdale, my investments, my Ferrari, my furniture. Everything I had was turned over to Computech in restitution for the damage I was accused of causing. I'm thirty-two years old, and what you see around you is what I have left."

Dana looked surprised. "You've measured yourself by the possessions you own?"

He shook his head as he leaned forward in his chair. "No, Dana. My life was synonymous with my expectations."

And I don't have any more expectations. He didn't say the words, but they hung in the air just as though he had. Disillusionment dwelt in his hazel eyes. She had seen the same look in the mirror.

She glanced away. "I would have thought with your expertise that you could have gone into business for yourself?"

He shrugged. "I tried. But with my ruined reputation, no financial group would trust me with a start-up loan. And since most of my possessions had been turned over to Computech, I had no capital to finance myself even on a small scale."

She nodded. "What happened today?"

"I had a job interview with the last computer-software firm on my list, a borderline operation barely making their payroll. They told me what all the rest had. I was a security risk."

She rose and began to pace, feeling angry at those who had sentenced him without trial. "Can you get another type of job?"

He tried to keep an even tone in his voice, knowing as soon as the words were out that he hadn't succeeded. "I've been blacklisted for all computer work, and only computers claim my passion. Working in anything else just has no value for me."

She nodded. "Of course. It wouldn't. No one stood by you?"

He shook his head.

"What about this fiancée you spoke of?"

"Vanessa is a beautiful woman with a large bank account her wealthy father maintains. She immediately broke off our engagement because her father 'no longer approved.'"

Gil watched Dana retrieve her cup of tea from the chipped wooden kitchen table as she considered his words.

"Someone must have benefited by what happened to Computech because of that virus," she said. "Are you sure a competitor didn't infiltrate the company's new-product date base?"

"Competitors try to steal, not destroy."

He watched in curious fascination as her tongue wet the pinkness of her lips before offering her new idea. "But if a competitor was duplicating some of your new-product lines and wanted to get the jump on introduction, wouldn't destroying Computech's data base work to their advantage?"

"Maybe," Gil said. "But I can't think of any particular company. None have come out with anything similar."

Dana's comments told Gil she knew a lot about computers. He was just about to ask how when she spoke up again.

"Your boss and the others behaved stupidly. On the one hand, they thought you genius enough to have devised a devastating computer virus to wipe out your company's new-product line. On the other hand, they didn't give you credit for the basis logic of not devising a scheme so blatantly attributable to yourself."

A hard, tightened knot of anxiety and tension that had been balling in his stomach relaxed into an audible sigh. Gil didn't know why it had been so important for this woman to believe him. He only knew her belief gave him a new feeling of hope. He watched the indignation light her clear eyes and felt his heart smile.

"Is that why you think I'm innocent?"

Dana glanced away from the open warmth of his look, trying to ignore the tingle it caused down her spine. "It would be foolish to think you guilty. Everything about your work in computers is based on logic. You wouldn't initiate a program from your own terminal that implicates just you. Didn't it occur to anyone that you couldn't gain from that devastating virus?"

"They thought I did it because I wanted to try to coerce Lionel into reinvestment instead of his planned pullout."

"Again, not a logical motive," Dana said. "Ruining someone's data base makes them angry, not amenable to negotiation. Your accusers can't have it both ways. Either you're logical or you're not. No, the accusations against you don't make real sense. Although I admit that from what you've told me about the execution of this virus, finding out who really did it would be a difficult job."

Gil stared at the certainty in her eyes, feeling mesmerized by their power to look at him and see everything so clearly. Lionel had supposedly been his friend for ten years. Vanessa had known him for three years, been engaged to him for the past year. Neither had believed him. Yet this woman, this stranger, had listened and understood and seen the truth.

He leaned across the table to grasp her soft, slim hand. "Dana, please tell me who you are."

Gazing into the sudden intensity within Gil's eyes left Dana breathless. She felt the pressure of his hand pulling her. Of its own accord, her body began moving closer to him across the small table. Then suddenly she realized what she was doing and extricated her hand from his as she got to her feet.

"I have to leave."

"Please, not yet," Gil protested as he rose quickly. Suddenly the blinding pain of a horrendous headache pierced him like a dagger. He stumbled, one hand grasping the back of the couch for support as the other reached for his temple.

"It's the additives they put in the alcohol," Dana said as she circled her arm about his waist and helped him to the couch. "Stuff is as poisonous as the alcohol itself. It'll take at least a day for it to work out of your system."

Gil opened his eyes, but the pain was so bad, he couldn't see. He hated to feel so damn weak and incompetent!

"It's okay, Gil. Lie on the couch, and I'll massage your head. I had a girlfriend who used to get migraines. I know how to take away the pain."

He wanted to argue, but the promise of relief was too great an inducement. As he stretched out, the stabbing in his head was almost unbearable. He closed his eyes against the wave of pain. She lifted his head into her lap.

Her soft, cool fingertips gently circled around his hot, throbbing temples, gradually working their way to the back of his head. Her fingers were like magical pied pipers playing a soothing song through his brain, drawing out the pain.

The last thing he remembered was her gentle voice telling him it was time to sleep.

DANA PARKED GIL'S JEEP in the labyrinth of the San Francisco International Airport lot and looked around carefully before taping the ignition key onto the inside frame of the front left tire. When she was sure no one had seen her, she made a note of the Jeep's location and then headed for the nearest phone.

She popped another peppermint into her mouth and checked her address book for Jerry Talbot's home number. After the phone still went unanswered after the second ring, uncomfortable thoughts that he might not be home began to nag at her mind. She checked her watch—11:00 p.m. Could he be asleep already? Finally the ringing stopped and a distracted female voice said hello.

"Jerry Talbot, please. Special Agent Carmody calling."

The woman repeated Dana's message to someone in the room with her, and then Dana heard a male voice in her ear.

"Talbot here."

"Talbot, it's Dana Carmody."

"Dana Carmody? I thought my wife had gotten the wrong name. It's been almost two years. Where are you?"

"Your neighborhood."

"San Francisco?"

"Yes. Sorry for the hour, but this isn't a social call."

Talbot sounded surprised. "You're working here? I thought your beat was still the Capital. Wait a minute. Are you the agent they sent to check out that possible computer infiltration of a sensitive defense program at Datacomp?"

"That's me."

"I had no idea, Carmody. I only got back to the office today after a couple of weeks on the spring ski slopes. Metcalf, one of my agents, received the communiqué that someone familiar with computers would arrive to do the initial interview, but no name was attached. So they flew you out from Washington. How did it go?"

"Not exactly as I expected. Someone knocked out the guard and murdered the computer programmer I went to see." Dana related the facts of her attempt to meet with Kristin Harcourt and the subsequent events of her escape.

"Unbelievable!"

"I need you to contact the local police and find out as much as you can about the evidence collected from the crime scene. Only you'll have to be discreet. Don't let it be known that the FBI is officially interested and involved."

"I'm happy to assist, but I don't understand," Talbot said. "It's our case, and it sounds like you've got the bruises to prove it. Why don't we just take over and get their cooperation?"

"Under normal circumstances, I would," Dana said. "But I don't understand what's going on, so I don't want to tip our hand. The men who chased me don't know I'm FBI. I'd rather they thought just the local police were involved until I have time to figure things out."

"All right," Talbot agreed. "Anything else I can do?"

"Yes. Check out the California registration on a late-model, black Cadillac Seville, license number 2SLK001. You'll probably find it still on that ledge in the park, if you can get someone up there tonight. I'd like it dusted for prints."

"Right. When do you need the license identification?"

"I'm on my way to catch a plane to D.C. How about if I call you from Washington around nine in the morning Pacific time?"

Talbot sounded doubtful. "I may not have too much by then."

"I'll still call at nine," Dana said. "If things go the way I expect them to, I may have a few more favors to ask tomorrow when I call. I need to get an okay from the boss first."

"The boss?"

"Lew Sargentich, my squad supervisor. And speaking of supervisors, I heard you had been promoted. A belated congratulations. I knew you were destined for good things when we worked together those first two weeks of mine on the job. I couldn't have had a better agent to show me the ropes."

Talbot cleared his throat and sounded embarrassed. "It was just my time, Carmody. So, it's still Lew heading your squad? I remember when the three of you got assigned to D.C. after your class was graduated out of the academy. Lew took one look at you, Liz and John and asked the SAC if there were any openings in the Alaskan office."

Dana smiled. Lew Sargentich always reminded her of a bullet-proof jacket with scratchy seams.

"What did you say, Talbot? My mind wandered."

"I was just asking how's Washington's three musketeers?"

"Just Liz Bennett and I are left."

"Just you and Bennett? Where's John Archer? I remember hearing a little over a year ago you two had become engaged."

Dana's immediate silence brought a response from Talbot. "Carmody, what is it? Did I say the wrong thing?"

Dana forced her voice to remain even with the message. The initial shock was gone now. So were the sleepless nights. Still, no matter how many times she said it, it never seemed to get any easier. "John died in a shoot-out almost a year ago."

She heard Talbot exhale a long breath on the other end of the connection. "Damn, I'm sorry, Carmody. I hadn't heard. What a rotten break. What kind of a case was it?"

"They'd gotten a tip on a bank robbery. John was stationed at a teller's position when one of the gunmen unexpectedly began to fire."

"You weren't part of the action?" Talbot asked.

"No. Everyone else in the squad was sent, but Lew made me stay behind. He doesn't think I can handle the physical part of the job. Nothing much has changed since we rode together two years ago."

"Is it still the size thing?" Talbot asked.

"Size and lack of muscles. Lew's from the old school that believes all agents should be big, brawny men. He thinks paperwork is all I'm capable of handling."

"Being big and brawny didn't seem to help John dodge the bullet with his name on it," Talbot said. "Besides, Liz Bennett isn't a man. I don't remember Lew hassling her."

"Liz is over six feet and built like a fullback," Dana reminded him. "I don't think it occurs to Lew she is a woman."

Talbot chuckled. "You know I don't share Lew's attitude. I've seen you work. You're a good, thorough, consistent agent."

"Thanks, Talbot. And Lew's not a bad sort, as you know. It's just that he's afraid I'm going to get hurt and that fear puts me in a Catch 22."

"You mean it's a little hard for you to prove you can take care of yourself if he never gives you a chance?" Talbot asked.

"Yes. That's exactly what I mean. John and I had agreed that each would cover the other if we found ourselves in a tight spot. I should have been part of that stakeout team. If only Lew had put me into the action, maybe I would have seen—"

"No, Carmody," Talbot said. "Don't get tied up in that dead-end if-only scenario. It's unproductive and debilitating. I've engaged in enough of it on my own to know what I'm saying. If you had been there, nothing would have changed."

Dana sighed. "Still, I live with the fact that I'm not considered good enough to take my chances with the rest of them."

"You are good enough, Carmody. Hell, you know the FBI isn't looking for any Dirty Harrys. If we're going to recruit any fictional characters, we'd be much more likely to take a Sherlock Holmes. Being a good agent means using your intelligence, ingenuity and training. You've got all three in abundance. Maybe your real problem isn't convincing Sargentich, but yourself."

Dana found a loud ring of truth in Talbot's words. "It's good to talk to you again, Talbot. I've got to hurry to catch my plane now. I'm not calling Lew. This is one report I've got to give in person. I'll contact you tomorrow."

But after she hung up, Dana still clutched the telephone receiver for a moment, as the tough beginnings of an earlier plan started to marinate in the added seasonings of Talbot's words. It was time she tested her abilities and found their true limits.

NIGEL SPARR'S BLACK EYES never wavered as he studied the massive frame of Irwin Vogel, his employer, as the large man sat across from him consuming his five-course meal and rich dessert at the Carnelian Room at the top of the fifty-second floor of the Bank of America Center.

No matter how much Vogel ate, however, Sparr knew the greedy man would soon be coveting his dessert, too. He had learned Vogel was never satisfied with just his own share of anything.

"So you wanted to talk," Vogel said between mouthfuls. "Talk."

Sparr related the evening's events, finishing with his final dig. "You should have contacted me earlier, Vogel. Leach has the IQ of a lug wrench, which is why the killing of the Harcourt woman was bungled."

Vogel's expression clearly said he resented being told he had made a mistake, particularly when he had. "I don't have to explain myself to you. Harcourt had accessed the computer while my programmer was making changes on-line. Leach was just a block away in the delivery truck. He got the job done."

"Yes, Leach got the job done, leaving the corpse to be found on the premises and opening up Datacomp to a homicide investigation."

Sparr knew the sarcasm of his words could only be inferred by the context of their presentation. Long ago he had learned that a lack of displayed emotion was always more effective. Now he smiled internally at Vogel's reddening face as the man went on the defensive.

"Okay, so maybe it could have been done better. Don't you think I realized that? Why do you think I called you in to fix things up?"

"But too late, Vogel. We've got a witness now."

Sparr watched Vogel fidget uncomfortably out of the corner of his eye as he stared out the window at the fantastic view of San Francisco's bright lights and fog tails just below them.

"So who is she?" Vogel asked.

Sparr leisurely brought his eyes back to the large man's face. "Her tactics are not those of local law enforcement. She may be a private security cop that Datacomp's hired. But if she is, she's not from any big company around here, otherwise I would have heard about her."

"Could she be an amateur or a friend of the Harcourt woman?"

"She doesn't move or think like an amateur."

"What does she look like?" Vogel asked.

"Maybe thirty. Medium height. Small-to-medium build."

"Is that all you know?" Vogel asked.

"When I first saw her, she had short brown hair and was wearing a dark blue raincoat and white boots. The next time I saw her, her hair was long and she was sans raincoat and boots and dressed in a white sweater and black slacks. At seven-thirty at night in what should have been a deserted park, she found some bearded guy with an old Jeep to use as a cover."

Vogel frowned. "Why didn't you get her then?"

"She tricked Leach into driving off the road."

"What? How could she possibly do that?"

Sparr shrugged. "A little ingenuity and guts. Leach damn near lost control of the car and ended up in the Pacific Ocean. Fortunately, the car phone was undamaged. I had what's left of the mess towed. It's been pretty well totaled, so the good news is you can write it off your income tax. Any more questions?"

Sparr could tell Vogel didn't like his familiar manner. That was the reason he used it, of course. As far as he was concerned, Vogel was too enamored with his own importance.

"Yes, I have another question," Vogel said. "What exactly do you plan to do about her?"

Sparr didn't immediately react to Vogel's irritated tone. Instead, he purposely moved his plate of chocolate-cream pie closer and then slowly cut out a chunk with his fork. All the time he could feel Vogel's greedy eyes.

"There's not much I can do until I find her, is there?" Sparr said, after he had deliberately and slowly savored each morsel of the chunk of pie on his fork before the sweating man seated opposite. He watched Vogel dab a napkin at the oozing corners of his wet lips before he spoke.

"She knows the Harcourt woman is dead. She's seen you. If she goes to the police—"

"We'll know, won't we?" Sparr interrupted. "Besides, if she tells them what she saw, they're not going to believe her. I left Thiel and Brine behind to clean things up. They had everything under control before the police arrived."

"But she was there when the program was running—"

"Relax, Vogel. Worry is an unproductive emotion. It can cause mistakes. You've got me on the payroll because I'm the best. Even if she knows something about computers, whatever she saw on the Harcourt woman's computer screen wouldn't have made any sense to her. Besides, I'll find her. I've put out feelers throughout California. I'll know soon."

"What about the guy she was with? Could he be working with her and not have been a pickup at all?"

"The odds are too small to even consider."

Vogel's index finger darted in to catch a glob of cream falling off Sparr's piece of pie. He brought it to his lips. "What did he look like?" he asked as he licked the cream off his fingers.

Sparr purposely moved his pie farther away from Vogel's reach. "Not much to tell there."

Vogel watched the retreating pie as new irritation laced his voice. "Well, tell me what you know. I don't have all night."

Sparr lifted the coffee cup to his lips, just as though he couldn't care less what Vogel's time constraints were. He purposely paused to savor the taste of the coffee while he watched Vogel's irritation turn his fat neck red.

"Tell me, damn it!"

Sparr smiled as he placidly began his description. "The man was a little over six feet, casually dressed, long reddish hair, similar shade in his full beard. I got the license-plate number of his Jeep on our first pass, before she smeared mud on it. I imagine she used him and then dumped him, but I have Leach cruising the neighborhood in an old pickup, checking around the houses and apartments in the vicinity for a sign of the Jeep just to be sure. I'll have our friend check out the license number through the Department of Motor Vehicles."

"It could be too late by then," Vogel said. "She's probably already gone to the cops. You should have gotten her tonight."

Sparr fed the major source of Vogel's irritation by taking another large chunk of chocolate-cream pie onto his fork. He watched the perspiration bead on his companion's face.

Slowly, he brought the pie to his lips, enjoying Vogel's growing discomfort.

Vogel took out his handkerchief and wiped his brow. He acted as though the excess saliva in his mouth was about to choke him.

"Damn it. First that Harcourt woman and now this other one. So far everything you've touched tonight has turned into garbage."

Once again Sparr kept his face an unemotional mask as he returned the full fork to his plate. "I hope not. Otherwise that certain something you've been looking for might not be in the best condition for a position in your office display case."

He watched the curiosity in Vogel's eyes and knew he had selected just the right time for his surprise. Sparr reached into the bag at his feet and brought out a large white box. He handed it to Vogel.

It took the man less than a second to tear off the top and reach in to grasp the porcelain statue. His voice rose perceptibly. "It's *Antique Car,* the Lladro limited edition I've been looking for to round out my collection. I can't believe you found it!"

"Not exactly found, Irwin. My bid set a record among the two hundred offered lots at the Universal City Lladro Festival and Auction last weekend. But you did say price was no object, didn't you?"

Irwin Vogel swallowed uneasily. "How much was it?"

Sparr knew his employer hated to pay for anything. He ignored his question. "It should go well in your office along with the rest of your Lladro porcelain collection. Reconsider and let me in to see them someday. The best part of collections is showing them off."

Sparr saw the flickering suspicion cross Vogel's face. He knew the reason Vogel didn't invite him to his office was because he was afraid Sparr would bug it.

"It's hard for me to think of you as someone who appreciates art," Vogel said.

Sparr's expression did not change. "Varied tastes are what sweeten life. And speaking of sweetening things, why don't you finish this piece of pie for me?"

Vogel seemed startled at Sparr's suggestion. He looked down at the plate eagerly and grabbed it as though he expected Sparr to change his mind.

Sparr watched Vogel's unmasked greed as the man loaded up his fork. He knew the heavy man would enjoy this piece of pie even more than his first because this piece had belonged to someone else.

With his mouth partially full, Vogel tried to articulate his next words. "Where do you think the woman will go?"

Sparr took another sip of coffee. "Hard to tell. I underestimated her tonight, and I almost ended up bathing in the waters just outside of the Golden Gate. She's clever."

Sparr heard Vogel's improved disposition in his changed tone. "Underestimated her? You're admitting to a mistake?"

Sparr's right index finger carefully circled the rim of his coffee cup as he considered his response. "Her strength lies in her unpredictability. She sent a car off the edge of a cliff to mislead us. Then she managed to change her appearance sufficiently to confuse me. Still, next time I'll be ready for her."

Vogel swallowed his mouthful of pie and shoved his fork out for more. He managed to spit out his next words before he packed his mouth full with more chocolate cream.

"You sound like you're happy she's a challenge."

Sparr shrugged. "An intelligent adversary always quickens the pulse, makes the game more interesting."

"Don't enjoy it so much you forget the woman is dangerous. We can't let her live, no matter how 'interesting' she is."

Sparr looked across at the weak, greedy man before him and masked his revulsion. He had always thought power should never be in the hands of people too quick to slaughter, especially when a slow and careful dissection could yield so much more.

Still, sometimes he had to placate the Irwin Vogels of his world. That is until he found out the man's full plans and decided how best to eliminate Vogel from the picture. The bug he had planted in the antique-car figurine should help to clear up the details. Until then, Sparr knew he would continue to wear his placid mask.

"Well, Sparr?"

"Well what?"

"I said you'd best remember we can't afford to let this woman live," Vogel repeated.

Sparr's hard black eyes found Vogel's muddy brown ones. "Don't worry. She's dead already."

Chapter Four

Dana studied Lew Sargentich for a moment as she leaned against the jamb of the door into his office. His dishwater blond hair scraped the upper edge of his beige, no-nonsense glasses as he sat forward in his chair studying some papers on his moderately tidy desk.

He was a moderate man in many respects. Moderately tall, moderately trim, moderately tough, moderately sober. His only excess seemed to be his dedication to his work. And in that excess, he went completely overboard. He must have realized someone was there because he looked up suddenly and her light gray eyes met his dark blue ones.

"Hi, boss. So how's your day so far?" she asked as she plopped heavily into a chair facing the front of his desk.

Lew flew to his feet. "Carmody, what's wrong? You were supposed to call your report in from San Francisco. Why are you back in D.C.?"

"Well, a funny thing happened on my way to meet with Kristin Harcourt. You know, the computer programmer at Datacomp who thought she might have found evidence of a computer infiltration in her company's programs?"

"I haven't forgotten who Kristin Harcourt is," Lew said.

"Who she was," Dana corrected. "When I got to Datacomp, she was dead."

Lew's voice rose in obvious concern. "Dead? How?"

"A broken neck—and before you ask, it wasn't an accident."

Lew sank into his chair. "Is that what the coroner said?"

"No. That's what this highly trained special agent of yours discerned within the few seconds before the murderers came back to the scene of their crime."

Lew rose out of his chair again. "The perpetrators were there? Why didn't you call me about this right away?"

"I would have just awakened you."

Dana watched Lew look down at his clenched hands. He unclenched them as though he had only then become aware that he had clenched them in the first place.

"Okay. Let's have it," he said.

Dana gave as clear and complete an account as she could of the events leading up to and following her discovery of Kristin Harcourt's body in the computer room at Datacomp. While he listened to her story about the car chase up the dark mountain road, Lew removed his sturdy glasses several times to wipe away some unseen debris. Dana knew it was a controlling mannerism that helped him to appear calm no matter what he was thinking and feeling. He employed it freely now as she described her narrow escape from the men who pursued her. She could see he was surprised at her success. It gave her a warm feeling of satisfaction.

"After Webb told me about his experience at Computech, he fell asleep on the couch. I took his Jeep and drove to the airport."

After Dana's final comment, Lew walked around to the front of his desk and sat down on the edge. "This should have been just a routine interview."

Dana nodded. "Well, now it isn't, and that poses a problem. Since you've always told me never to come to you with a problem unless I have a solution..."

Lew didn't look as though he wanted to hear her solution. "Why would the Harcourt woman have been murdered? Even she wasn't sure what it was she was seeing. Do you suppose she found something else after she informed York?''

Dana nodded. "Possibly. In any case, we now know that whatever is being done to the computer programming at Datacomp is serious enough to commit murder for. What I'm really interested in at the moment is how they found out about Harcourt's suspicions."

Lew frowned. "What do you mean?"

"Well, since you and the president of Datacomp, Wayne York, and the local FBI personnel were the only ones aware of the fact and reason for my meeting with Harcourt, I can't help wondering who was in back of the murder of the programmer?''

Lew nodded. "What about York?"

"If he had wanted to silence Kristin Harcourt, he could have done so the moment she brought the problem to his attention. He didn't. Instead, he contacted us and immediately set up my contact with Harcourt. I believe he's acted in a manner that removes him from suspicion."

"Who does that leave?" Lew asked.

"Our local FBI field agents, and that, of course, is absurd. There's got to be another explanation."

Lew shook his head as he slipped his backside off the edge of his desk. "Maybe it's just as simple as Kristin Harcourt told someone else."

Dana's head shook away the possibility. "With all the precautions the programmer took to inform only the president of the company of the security breach? No, her disclosing the information intentionally or unintentionally to someone else seems unlikely."

Dana paused to put some drawings on Lew's desk. "I had the artist draw up a fairly accurate representation of the silver-haired man and the other two I glimpsed. I've searched the records. I was hoping I could bring you an ID. I didn't have any luck."

Dana watched Lew glance at the drawings in a perfunctory manner. She knew he was really watching her tired body hugging the chair. She tried to sit up straighter.

"You didn't sleep on the plane, did you?" he asked.

Dana shrugged. "I was thinking about my case."

Lew circled around to the back of his desk and looked at her directly. "This is not your case. California is not your territory. Get to your desk and get your written reports prepared. The California agent I assign to take over will need your information right away. Then you can get home and start those two weeks of annual leave you're supposed to be on."

Dana didn't react immediately. She knew her calmness was probably confusing Lew. Normally she would have immediately argued with him about taking her off a "dangerous" case. But not today. She had had all night to think through her approach. She felt him watching her as she reached into her shoulder bag and retrieved two pieces of peppermint candy. She popped one into her mouth and offered the other to him.

He took it, but laid it on his desk, as though it was a gift with strings. He looked uncomfortable, apparently sure something was coming. But for the next half minute, Dana let him sweat as she just sat and savored the peppermint in her mouth.

"The way you suck on that stuff, I'd hate to see your dentist bills," he said, finally breaking the silence.

"I have cavity-resistant teeth."

"Now maybe. But one day they'll probably—"

"I'm going to handle this case."

Lew seemed to recognize this new, subtler stubborn streak with some internal irritation. She guessed he had been hoping she was too tired to fight.

He frowned. "You're supposed to be on annual leave."

"It's already been postponed a couple of days," Dana said. "It can be postponed a few more."

Lew scratched the palm of one hand with the well-manicured nails of the other. "Since Kristin Harcourt is no longer around to pump for information about what happened to the computer system at Datacomp, I'm going to need to send out a computer expert to check the program thoroughly."

"You already checked the technical list before you sent me in. No one was available. The San Francisco field agents know nothing about computers. Why can't I just continue with the assignment?"

"Look, Carmody, I'll grant you know something about computers, but you're hardly an expert."

"Agreed. That's why I've identified a computer expert to assist on this assignment."

Lew's voice rose in surprise. "You've found a free computer expert?"

"Not exactly free. More like rentable."

Lew's deep blue eyes turned even darker behind the lenses of his light beige glasses. "Who are you talking about?"

"Gilbert Webb."

Lew shot around his desk as though pushed. "What? The Gilbert Webb whose company kicked him out for wiping out all their new-product software with a computer virus?"

Dana leaned forward in her chair. "No. The Gilbert Webb I'm talking about is the man whose company unjustly kicked him out when their software mysteriously disintegrated in their data base."

Lew paced rigidly around his desk. "Don't talk rubbish. We're the highest, most prestigious law-enforcement agency in the country. I'm not going to recruit a felon for the FBI!"

Dana frowned. "'Felon' is inaccurate. The civil suit was settled out of court, and he's never been criminally prosecuted."

Lew stopped pacing. "An oversight on our part, no doubt."

Dana's blood pulsed as she stood up to face her boss.

"It's not like that at all. Look, Lew, I've told you the story. I've talked with him. He didn't wipe out his company's programs. He had absolutely no reason to, and he lost everything when it happened."

Lew studied the unwavering look in Dana's eyes for a moment before speaking. "All right, maybe he didn't do it. Maybe he lost everything. But even if his treatment was unjust, we were not involved. What do we owe him?"

"How about a chance to work again?" Dana asked.

"We're not a second-chance employment office."

Dana fought to keep her tone cool and controlled. "No, we're an investigative agency trying to stay a step ahead of a growing white-collar computer crime wave more sophisticated and complex than we're presently equipped to handle. At the moment, we're in over our heads, and you're much too savvy and honest not to admit it. Gilbert Webb is a born hacker. He's got more programming smarts than probably all of our experts put together. We need him to understand what's going on at Datacomp."

Lew waved his hand in a negative sweep. "We can use the other programmer at Datacomp, that Riley woman."

"No," Dana said. "Kristin Harcourt told Wayne York that Linda Riley might be responsible for the data shadows."

"It was only a suspicion."

"Even so, it doesn't make sense to involve her."

"Explain," Lew said.

"If she's guilty, it could compromise our entire investigation. If she's innocent, it could place her in danger. Remember what happened to Kristin Harcourt."

Lew frowned. "What makes you think Gilbert Webb wouldn't be placed in the same danger?"

Dana exhaled a tired breath. "I'm sure he would be."

"Then how can you condone—"

Dana's hand came up as a barrier to Lew's further comments. "He'll be one of us—an FBI employee. We all accept the responsibilities and the possible risks."

"Yes, but the Bureau is our career. Webb will only be offered a temporary assignment. Why should he put his life on the line?"

Dana shrugged. "Frankly, I don't see he's got anything to lose. Gilbert Webb can't get another job in his field."

Lew turned away in obvious frustration. "Great. We use him because nobody else will. This is impossible, Carmody."

"No. It is the only possible solution—for us and Gil Webb. What's so wrong about giving the man a second chance?"

Lew pivoted on the carpet in his shiny, black leather shoes to face Dana. "What if you're wrong about him? What if he really is guilty of sabotaging his company's programs? What if he pulls something like that with us?"

Dana sat even straighter in her chair. "You've never had any confidence in my physical abilities, Lew, but I always thought you respected my logic and instincts. Are you telling me now that you don't?"

Lew went back to cleaning his glasses, obviously embarrassed by the truth in her words and the question. Dana recognized his next comment was a side step.

"We don't have time to give him even a basic orientation," he said after replacing his glasses on the bridge of his nose.

"What does it matter?" Dana asked. "He only needs to concentrate on what he knows best—computers."

Lew circled his desk and sat down. "We could dig up another computer expert. If I put out a priority—"

"You'll never get anyone as good as Gilbert Webb."

Lew studied her face. "Why are you so interested in this man?"

Dana was uncurled and out of her chair in one fluid movement, belying any semblance of fatigue. "Webb was convicted and sentenced without trial for a crime he didn't commit. And as a result, his livelihood has been taken away from him. Do you know how unjust that is? How maddening? How disheartening?"

"Dana, I understand the situation. It's regrettable but hardly tragic. After all, the guy hasn't been jailed."

"Hasn't he, Lew? The mind and spirit can be imprisoned as well as the body. When I joined the FBI, I swore to uphold the Constitution of the United States—the only legal document in our land that proclaims the right of all citizens to the pursuit of happiness. How can I turn my back on a man whose reach for such happiness has been barred by a lack of due process?"

Dana suddenly heard and felt the anger in her voice. Until now, she didn't realize how deeply Gil's predicament had registered on her outraged sense of justice. She sat down again, carefully folding one leg beneath her and trying to regain control. She felt Lew's eyes on her averted face.

"Carmody, I expect you to act like a professional. No matter what happens, you can't let yourself become personally involved with this man or his problems, whether I agree to let you recruit Webb or not. Do you understand?"

Dana nodded at Lew's chastisement. He was right. Her effectiveness would diminish with every ounce of emotion clouding her judgment. She inhaled and got a firmer grip over her feelings before she spoke again.

"Yes, I understand and agree. But totally aside from the unjust predicament the man finds himself in, Gilbert Webb has a superior mind. Let's give him a chance to use it again while we reap the benefits of his expertise. It won't hurt us to give him a chance."

Lew didn't sound at all persuaded as he continued to pace around his office. "Except that everything you've told me about these men who murdered the Harcourt woman indicates they're professionals. Webb wouldn't have a chance against them.''

''He'll have me,'' Dana said.

Lew took off his glasses to wipe some more imaginary dust away. Dana watched him studying the lenses as he continued to fight for control. ''I can't send you in alone.''

''I won't be. Jerry Talbot works out of Field Office Fifty-two in San Francisco. He could swing some investigative support my way, if you can get it okayed with his special agent in charge. I need him to gather evidence against those men who chased me. Which reminds me, I need to call Talbot and have him approach Gilbert Webb right away. I'd also like Talbot to pick up Webb's Jeep from where I left it at the airport and let me know what the local enforcement agencies have about the murder.''

''Now just a minute, Carmody—''

''I can be back out there on tonight's flight.''

''I can't—'' Lew began.

Dana stood, putting every ounce of determination she had in her voice. ''You can, Lew. You must. It's my case. I've earned it. I'm not giving it up. Not this time.''

Lew took off his glasses and began to clean them again. He wouldn't look her in the eye. ''Those men saw you. They know you can identify them. I'd like you alive to take the stand at their trial.''

Dana stood her ground. ''It was dark. All they really saw was my back. I can alter my appearance sufficiently to pass.''

''You can't be sure. You might still be recognized.''

''I can be sure. I'll give them what they won't expect.''

Lew looked up. ''What would that be?''

Dana watched Lew fold his arms across his chest as though he was determined to stand tough. Today he would find her even tougher.

''I'll gray my hair, put on thick, tinted glasses, wrap a brace around one of my legs and lean on a cane.''

Lew looked at her as though she had lost her mind. "That's crazy. You're talking about disguising yourself as handicapped."

Dana sat down again, slowly and deliberately.

"Lew, do you know anything about the Arctic wolves?"

"Arctic wolves?"

"Yes. An extremely interesting and clever breed. They're pure white and so fastidious that even when they're ravenous, they insist on cleaning themselves before consuming their food. Yet, before a hunt, they've been known to roll around in rancid fish carcasses in order to mask their own scent."

Lew undid his arms to impatiently drum his fingers on his metal desk. "For God's sake, Carmody, what do Arctic wolves rolling around on dead fish have to do with your pretending to be handicapped?"

"Quite a bit. Those hunting preparations illustrate the most important reason for any pretense—to catch your prey off guard."

Lew was still shaking his head. "I don't understand."

"Then let me explain," Dana said. "If you're a musk-ox roaming about the tundra and you hear a rustle in the grasses, you might think, 'ah, a white wolf could be lurking there.' So your muscles tense, your nostrils flare, but lo and behold, the only scent that registers is dead fish. You relax and go back to grazing because what musk-ox in its right mind is going to run from a dead fish?"

Lew leaned back. "You're saying these men won't feel threatened by a small, handicapped woman and so will let down their guard?"

Dana smiled. "That's exactly what I'm saying."

She watched Lew try to repress a smile. She could tell his interest had been piqued. There was a new, speculative light in his eyes. "How do you know you can pull it off?"

Dana sat up straight and tall before answering. "Because I possess the right instincts of how best to use the handicap of relative weakness. After all, I have intimate knowledge of how people overrate size and muscle.''

Lew grunted uncomfortably as her jab hit home. ''Carmody, you can't deny—''

''That I'm small? I'm not trying to. I'm trying to tell you I can use it to my advantage. By playing up physical limitations, I can gain the edge I need.''

Lew recleaned his spotless glasses, and Dana saw the conflicting emotions cross his face. He was stubborn and pigheaded. But he was also logical, and she knew his primary concern was the successful completion of FBI business. She had a chance. She waited anxiously for his response.

His next question told her she had won. ''What do you plan to do with Webb?''

She smiled in relief. ''He'll have to have a different name. The computer community knows Gilbert Webb. I'm also planning changes in his appearance since the killers saw him briefly.''

''And after you accomplish these changes?''

''I'll have Wayne York hire Webb as his new programmer.''

''All right, that gets him inside. But you're not forgetting Kristin Harcourt got it while sitting in front of her computer?''

''That's not an image I'll forget easily,'' Dana said. ''But I'll be right next to Webb, posing as his assistant as he gathers the information to make our case against these men stick in court.''

Lew watched her for a moment in speculation before leaning forward in his chair. ''Okay, I'll agree on one condition.''

''Which is?''

''Keep Talbot nearby and report to me every day. I want to know exactly what's going on.''

''Agreed,'' she said.

Dana felt him studying her face as if he noticed something new there. Whatever he saw, he could never know how important this case was to her image of herself. She must succeed.

"You seem very sure about this Gilbert Webb accepting our offer of an employment filled with possible danger. What if he refuses?"

Dana's smile was small. "I'll make you a deal. If he refuses, I'll back off the case gracefully."

Lew Sargentich shook his head. "Fat chance from what I've seen today."

"You're right," Dana said. "But that's how sure I am of Webb. He'll join us as soon as he convinces himself the offer is real. You see, he's got nothing to lose."

Lew smiled sarcastically. "Just his life, you mean."

Dana looked at her boss very directly and seriously. "Yes, there is that possibility. But sometimes, I don't think facing possible death is nearly as difficult as facing the certainty of an empty life. Gil's passion is all wrapped up in his work. Without that work, how can he know happiness? We all have to pursue where our passions lead us, Lew. All of us."

"NO WOMAN WITNESS reporting a murder? Are you sure, Thiel?" Sparr said as he stood behind the polished oak of his desk in his office at CustomKey on Market Street in San Francisco.

The big blond man with the thick beard standing before him nodded. "Just the anonymous call for the ambulance."

Sparr frowned as he looked at his watch. It was half-past noon. He stroked one of his silver sideburns and frowned. "I wonder why she didn't go to the police."

Leach shifted about in his chair positioned diagonally from Sparr and ran his dirty fingernails through his greasy black hair. "She's probably scared. She'll never talk."

Sparr looked over at the food-stained shirt and torn jeans of the dark-haired man, thinking his reasoning power was equally in need of tidying, but said nothing. He redirected his attention back to the blond man in the three-piece suit, who still stood as though at attention.

"All right, Thiel. What did you find out from the Department of Motor Vehicles?"

The man nodded as he pulled a piece of paper from his pocket. "The Jeep was registered to a Theodore Allen Webb, 414 Dusty Road, Marin City."

"Theodore Webb?" When Sparr said the name, he rubbed his smooth forehead at the same time, as though he might be able to massage it into bringing up an elusive memory. He wasn't successful.

"Is that all you could get on him?"

Thiel nodded. "Just the Jeep registration. No current driver's license for anybody by that name."

Sparr shook his head. "There's something familiar about that name. What are the possible variations of Theodore?"

Thiel supplied them. "Theo Webb. Ted Webb. Teddy Webb. Allen Webb. Al Webb. Or maybe he even used initials—T.W., T.A.W., A.W...."

"No," Sparr said, rubbing his upper lip as he tried to relieve the sudden itching of his gums. "There's no pull on any memory cord. Thiel, get me the files."

The big, bearded, blond man moved obediently to a file cabinet in the back of the office, which he opened with a key. After a moment's search, he brought out several folders and relocked the cabinet. He brought the folders to Sparr's desk and handed them to the silver-haired man.

"I don't believe you guys ain't on computers yet," Leach said.

Sparr's voice sounded distracted as he read through the files. "Computers can be invaded, as Vogel and his programmer are proving so aptly, Leach. Besides, file organization is really the key to information retrieval, whether it's on paper or in a computer data base. This file is an alpha-betical list of the names of everyone we've impacted. Here it is.''

"What?" Leach asked.

"The name Webb, of course. Not Theodore, but Gilbert. We have run into a Webb before. And now I remember where."

"I don't remember no Webb," Leach said.

Sparr avoided looking at the unkempt man, as though the sight was just too disagreeable. "Gilbert Webb was the programmer at Computech when the data base was destroyed."

"It's not the same name," Leach said. "This guy is Theodore Webb. Probably just coincidence."

Sparr shook his head. "Except that Theodore Webb doesn't have a current driver's license. Something's wrong with that. Thiel, I want you to get me everything we have on Gilbert Webb. Leach, get to this address in Marin and see if anyone's home at Theodore Webb's place."

The dark-haired man rose. "And if I find someone there?"

"Be discreet, but bring him to me. Without a ruckus and without bruises. Is that clear?"

"Yeah, it's clear. Anything else?" Leach said.

"Yes. Move it. I suddenly have the very strong feeling that we've entered a race, and the hot breath of pursuit is blowing at the back of my neck."

Chapter Five

Gil awoke to a spinning ceiling and a softly throbbing head. Light framed the drawn shade that covered the one window of the small living room in the cabin. He closed his eyes and opened them again, almost expecting the sight to fade.

The thumping in his head became differentiated from the thumping on the heavy wood of his front door. He realized the urgent knocking must have been going on for some time and had been the reason for his awakening. Gradually he rose to a sitting position, feeling some surprise as he looked down to find himself wrapped in his old bathrobe and lying on the living-room couch. Why wasn't he in his bed?

His question went unanswered as the thumping on the front door continued and he got up to answer it.

What he found there caused him to blink in surprise. Two men stood on his doorstep in dark blue suits so straight and uncreased that they looked as though the coat hangers were still in them. Both men had short, dark brown hair, were around six feet and had medium builds. The man on the left had blue eyes and a larger assortment of facial lines and the kind of a raccoon-type tan that said he skied a lot. The younger, dark-eyed man on the right had a natural curl to his hair and a deeper cast to his skin that probably resulted in a punctual three o'clock afternoon shadow. The younger man held a large white bag. Neither smiled.

They looked official and a sudden sinking feeling in Gil's stomach told him he should have just let them pound away.

"Gilbert Webb?" the one with the raccoon tan asked.

Gil nodded. No point in denying what they undoubtedly could find out if they didn't already know. They each reached into a pocket and brought out identification. Gil's eyes focused on the FBI designation and felt his worst fears materialize. He was going to be criminally prosecuted after all.

"I'm Agent Talbot," the one with the raccoon tan continued. "This is Agent Metcalf. May we come in, Mr. Webb?"

They were asking? Would they ask to put the handcuffs on, too?

"Yeah, sure. Close the door behind you. I'm just going to get on a pair of pants."

Gil almost expected one of them to follow him into the bedroom while he took a clean pair of jeans from a hanger in the tiny closet. As soon as he had zipped them up, he returned to the living room. His visitors were standing, patiently waiting.

"Sit down. Sorry, but I can't offer you coffee."

Agent Talbot looked at the threadbare couch as though he expected something live might crawl out of it at any moment. He finally overcame his obvious foreboding and sat down. As though receiving a silent signal, Agent Metcalf took three take-out cups out of his white paper sack. He handed one to Gil.

"We've brought our own coffee. Have one. There are plenty of donuts, too," Agent Metcalf said. His brown eyes suddenly looked almost friendly.

Gil was more than surprised by the offer of coffee and the half dozen donuts that materialized on a paper plate before him. He was so surprised that he just drank the offered coffee and helped himself to a large donut. It turned out to be filled with cream that melted in his mouth. He was on his third when he looked up to find Agent Talbot's blue eyes watching him.

It was an appraising look, neither friendly nor hostile. Gil's curiosity eclipsed his appetite. He put down the half-eaten donut, deciding that whatever was to come, he had to know the worst without further delay. He took a gulp of the hot coffee. It burned his tongue.

"Why is the FBI bringing me breakfast?"

"Breakfast, Mr. Webb?" Agent Talbot said. "It's one-fifteen in the afternoon."

Gil looked down at his wrist, but his watch was missing. His brow filled with lines until he remembered he had taken his watch off just prior to getting in the shower the previous night.

Then suddenly, memories of the previous night flooded his thoughts. He had driven into the Golden Gate Recreation Area. He had drunk too much. A woman tasting like peppermint had kissed him. They had been chased. He looked around the small cabin as though he hoped to see Dana standing in her raincoat, checking her clothes drying in front of the fire.

"Is everything all right?" Agent Talbot asked.

"Just got a bit of a headache," Gil said. "It's afternoon?"

Agent Talbot continued to direct the conversation as the younger Agent Metcalf sat quietly and sipped his coffee. "We need your help, Mr. Webb. We'd like you to work with us."

"Us?" Gil said.

"The Federal Bureau of Investigation."

Gil repeated the words that had reached his disbelieving ears. "You want *me* to work for the FBI?"

Agent Talbot nodded. "The FBI is in need of your skills. We are offering you a temporary clerical position."

"A clerical position?" Gil was beginning to feel like a parrot.

Talbot nodded. ''There are only two types of employees at the FBI—special agents and the clerical people who support them. Don't let the label mislead you. Our clerical force can be anyone from a secretary to a scientist.''

''Which label do I fit?'' Gil asked.

''We'll find a specific title for you if you require one.''

Gil looked at Agent Talbot's face and waited for the punch line to this joke. The FBI did not offer jobs to people, and even if they did, they would never approach someone like himself.

He laughed uneasily. ''I'm finding this hard to believe.''

Agent Talbot didn't even blink at Gil's reaction. Gil began to think that it would be impossible to read this man's mind. No emotions changed the consistent bland expression on his raccoon-striped face.

''Call the information operator and ask for the FBI director in Washington, D.C. He will authenticate the identity of Agent Metcalf and myself and the seriousness of our job offer.''

Gil took another sip of coffee as he shook his head. ''My phone was disconnected months ago.''

Agent Talbot reached over to the old dial instrument sitting on the chipped wooden coffee table. He picked up the receiver with two of his neatly manicured fingers. ''We had it reconnected this morning. Your overdue bill in the amount of $367.86 has been paid. Please go ahead and make your call.''

A loud dial tone filled the silent space between Gil and his guests. Gil hesitantly took the phone from Agent Talbot's hand, aware that the agent's quote of his overdue telephone bill was accurate down to the penny.

The local directory-assistance operator gave him the area code and number to call for Washington, D.C. information. Gil got the number of the FBI office and punched it in, but even before anyone answered, he knew the information

Agent Talbot had given him would be verified. It was. He hung up the phone.

"Well, Mr. Webb?" Agent Talbot asked.

"I believe you," Gil said.

"Good. Now I am authorized to offer you a temporary position with the Federal Bureau of Investigation, commencing immediately."

Gil shook his head. "Do you people know who I am?"

Talbot's tone did not change. "We know why you were fired from Computech. Is that what you're concerned about?"

Gil felt a sudden foreboding. "Can it be you want me to inform on Computech? Is that it? Do you want me to tell you about their confidential computer systems?"

"Why would confidential computer systems at Computech interest us, Mr. Webb?"

Gil shook his head. "I can't think of one reason."

Talbot nodded complacently. "Then you can rest assured that your assignment with us has nothing to do with Computech."

An excitement began to course through Gil, causing him to sit up straighter. The caffeine in the coffee cleared his mind, and the import of this conversation was starting to sink in. Could the FBI really be offering him a job?

"What do you want me to do?" Gil asked.

Talbot shrugged. "We need your computer expertise."

A job in computers with the FBI? What an unbelievable opportunity to come his way! Gil tried to control his mounting excitement. "What will I be doing with computers?"

"The details of your specific assignment are not known to me. I am charged, however, with telling you that should you choose to accept this position, you must keep silent regarding all matters pertaining to your activities."

"Will they be legal?" Gil asked.

For the first time Gil saw Agent Talbot's jaw clench. His normally precise articulation was now honed so sharply, Gil felt the man's words slicing through his eardrums. "We enforce laws, Mr. Webb. We do not break them."

"Sorry. Okay, I can keep quiet."

"You should be aware that physical danger is a possibility. We're not up against Boy Scouts. However, there will be a fully trained agent working closely with you. Every reasonable attempt to assure your safety will be taken. Do you accept the conditions of this temporary position?"

Of course, Gil knew he was going to accept. But he mustn't appear too eager. "What will I be doing?"

"As I told you before," Talbot said, "the specific information concerning your assignment will be given to you at a later time, pending the acceptance of our offer."

"You said the assignment is temporary. How long?"

"That information will be given to you at a later time, pending the acceptance of our offer. Do you accept this temporary assignment?"

Gil was still stunned by everything he was hearing, but he knew Agent Talbot's repetition of "pending the acceptance of our offer" signaled the time for reluctance was over.

"Yes. I accept."

Agent Talbot got to his feet immediately. "Good. Again, the specific case parameters will be discussed in detail by the agent assigned to work with you."

"Who is this agent?" Gil asked.

"Carmody. You met last night. You'll need some casual clothing, but keep your selections to a minimum. We'll be going shopping for some new stuff this afternoon."

Gil didn't mask his surprise. "Wait a minute. Last night? You said I met this Agent Carmody last night?"

"Yes," Talbot said. "As she described the situation to me, you were instrumental in helping her out of a tight spot."

A light was coming on in Gil's brain. He sat forward as the eagerness invaded his voice. "Her? Her first name is Dana?"

"Yes," Talbot said. "However, Webb, I think you should understand that we all go by last names. That helps to maintain a professionalism among us. As you work with Agent Carmody..."

Talbot went on, but Gil wasn't listening anymore. He was still trying to get over the shock of learning that his mysterious woman visitor of the night before was an FBI agent. It was now obvious to him that she had been instrumental in having him recruited to work in his field of computers. First, she had believed him, and now, she had gotten him a job. If she were here now, he would hug her. Then suddenly another thought brought up less desirable images.

"Excuse me, Talbot, but you said earlier that there was a possibility of physical danger on this assignment. Will you be issuing me a gun to protect Dana...I mean Agent Carmody?"

"Webb, Agent Carmody is assigned to protect you, not vice versa. Besides, your job position does not authorize your use of a weapon."

"But—"

"Look, Webb, I realize this has been all quite sudden for you, but your questions will have to wait. We can't linger here. I must insist that you gather some basic clothing."

"This minute?"

Agent Talbot nodded. "We need to leave as soon as possible and get you sent to a barber and fitted for new clothes. There are minor alterations that must be accomplished before your briefing tomorrow morning."

Gil nodded, rose and went into the bedroom to get some socks and T-shirts. He felt still in a daze, not quite believing what was happening. But he could also feel a mounting exhilaration pumping into his body.

It was while he was putting some of his clothing into a shabby suitcase that Gil noticed his camera sitting on the dresser. For a moment he just stared at it in welcome surprise.

Had his memory of dropping it from his shoulder on the edge of the cliff the night before been a dream? Elated he had not lost it, but still confused over how, he reached for the camera to put it on the shelf in the closet. Then he saw the broken lens and the piece of peppermint candy within the leather strap.

So Dana had picked it up, just as she had picked up the broken man who stood on that cliff ledge. He inhaled deeply as the memory of her smile drifted back soft and sweet. He owed her a lot. Somehow he'd find a way to pay her back.

"You ready, Webb?" Agent Talbot called from the doorway.

Gil turned and smiled. "For just about anything."

"LOOK, I COULDN'T DO nothing! Get off my back!" Leach said, rubbing his dirt-storing fingernails through his greasy hair.

Sparr sat back in his tightly upholstered chair at CustomKey and stared at the untidy man who sat in front of his very neat, fine-grained oak desk between two healthy ficus trees. The glare of the late-afternoon sun filtered through the large window in back of Sparr's head to shine uncomfortably into Leach's eyes.

"Who were the three men who left the cabin?"

"I don't know. A late-model green Olds was hugging the curb in front of the dump when I drives up so I parks up the street and waits. So then after some time goes by, three guys come out of the cabin and get into the Olds," Leach said.

"What did they look like?"

"One was the bearded guy we saw last night with the woman."

"Did you see the gray Jeep?"

"Nope."

"Did you get the license number of the Olds?"

"Yep. I gave it to Thiel when I got back."

Sparr looked over at the blond man expectantly.

"It's registered to a San Francisco real-estate company called Professional Properties," Thiel said.

"Yeah, those dudes were get up like business stiffs," Leach said. "They must've took the bearded guy out to see some property."

Sparr stared at the stocky man's dull face.

"Webb is that 'bearded guy,' Leach. And since he's living in that shack, I very much doubt he has the wherewithal to buy a trash can much less property in San Francisco. No bonafide real-estate agent would waste two minutes' time driving him anywhere."

Leach squirmed under Sparr's steady gaze. "So why were those guys carting him around?"

Sparr responded more out of a need to voice his thoughts than to answer the unkempt man's question. "They're obviously not real-estate agents."

"But Thiel said the license—"

"Leach, I think for your continued health and my continued patience, you'd best stop asking questions and just concentrate on listening and answering a few. The registration on that Oldsmobile is no doubt for a dummy company. They sound a lot more like plain-clothes cops to me. Did he go willingly?"

Leach shrugged. "Yeah, I guess. No handcuffs, if that's what you're getting at. Yeah, now that I think about it, they probably were detective cops. Had that short-haired scrubbed look, if you know what I mean."

"I know what you mean. Maybe they're some special task force. Maybe that's how the woman ties in. Where did they take Webb?"

"Beats me. I kind of lost them going south on the bridge."

Sparr's dark eyes narrowed on the face of the man, but he said nothing to him. Instead, his next comments were clearly directed at the bearded blond man in the back of the room.

"Thiel, we must learn everything we can about this real-estate company, and we must learn it fast. Use your contacts at the banks and the local precinct. Get over to Professional Properties and look for a green Olds."

Thiel didn't say anything. He just got up and left. Both actions satisfied Sparr. But as he looked across the desk at Leach again, he seemed quite a bit less than satisfied.

"I want you to go back and stake out the cabin in Marin."

"Ain't gonna do no good," Leach said.

Sparr frowned. "What do you mean?"

"Webb was toting a suitcase."

"As though he might be away for a while?" Sparr asked. "Why didn't you mention this before?"

"How was I to figure what was important? And anyhow, you didn't ask."

Sparr rose agilely, effortlessly, and circled his desk to stand in front of Leach. His smooth face was expressionless except for a small squinting at the corner of each eye, as though the sight he was seeing was giving him eye strain.

"How long have you been with Vogel?"

Leach shifted uneasily in his chair. "Maybe seven months. My cell mate said he hired cons for odd jobs. I looked him up."

"Been good to you?"

"Real good."

"Do anything he says?"

"Anything."

Sparr stared at Leach with dark, stone eyes. "Since Vogel pays you, you can follow him around from now on."

Leach leaned forward in surprise. "Vogel told me to follow you. I mean to do what he says."

"And what I say is go back to Vogel. Now."

"What's I supposed to tell him?"

"Tell him you belong together," Sparr said, unsmiling.

"Vogel ain't going to like this."

"Leach, if you're not out of here in five seconds, I'm going to do something to you that you're not going to like."

"I DON'T BELIEVE IT, Talbot," Dana said into the phone.

"You've got to, Dana. No one was found injured or murdered at Datacomp last night. There wasn't even a sign of a break-in."

"There had to have been! I set off the alarms myself!"

Talbot exhaled loudly. "The local police station got a call from the security company a few minutes after seven. When the police arrived about five minutes later, the guard on duty said that there must have been a short in the alarm system somewhere because no one was in the building. The police naturally checked it out by doing a thorough room-by-room search, but they found no one. Case closed."

Dana tried to think of an explanation. "You say the guard on duty greeted the police and claimed a security-system malfunction?"

"Yes."

"What was this guard's name?"

"Uh…I've got it somewhere in my notes. Yes, here it is. Gordon Mercer. Leasehold Security Systems. They're the security company who supplies twenty-four-hour guards for the Datacomp Corporation."

"Have you called the company?" Dana asked. "Checked to see if he works there? Gotten a description?"

"No. What I'm giving you is all from the police report. Are you sure we've got a murder?"

"Positive. I saw the body. The way I read this situation, this phony guard put the dead woman and the real, unconscious guard in the delivery truck that had been brought into the parking lot. Then he put on the guard's uniform and greeted the police."

"Yes, that's possible," Talbot said. "But why go to all that trouble and possible exposure? Was postponing knowledge of a murder that important?"

"Apparently. Although, I must admit, I still don't know why. I'm going to need you to do some investigative work following up on that guard's identity."

"Lew Sargentich's boss called the special agent in charge here and cleared my time and Metcalf's. I can also pull others out of my squad if we need them. We're at your service."

"Thanks, Talbot. I'll be keeping you busy. We've got to locate Kristin Harcourt's body. You might want to see if her BMW is still in the parking lot at Datacomp. Your records should show her home address. Then we've got to find the real guard."

"What's wrong with letting the local police in on our knowledge of the crimes? They could help."

"No," Dana said. "Keeping things quiet at a local police department just isn't manageable. I don't want the murderers alerted. If they know we're on to them, they might disappear. They don't know who I am. I want to keep it that way. I want them to feel safe enough to proceed with whatever they're doing to the software at Datacomp. That's the only way we're going to catch them. Any luck yet on the license for the black Cadillac?"

"Yes. Its legal owner is CustomKey, a computer-accessory manufacturing company operating out of the Bay Area. Main office is in San Francisco on Market. They're relatively new. There's nothing on them in the files."

"CustomKey? Sounds like we need to start a file. Let's find out who they are, what they market and to whom."

"I'll assign Metcalf to it first thing tomorrow while I start trying to locate the programmer and the guard. He can check the business-licensing agencies in the area."

"Good," Dana said. "How did it go with Gilbert Webb?"

"Pretty much as you predicted. Metcalf is with him now at the San Francisco hotel. You know Marin has a few that would be much more convenient to Datacomp."

Dana shook her head. "And much easier for my pursuers to pick out Webb and me. No, I go with the old adage that a large city is the best place to blend in. With all the hotels in San Francisco, we should fade into the woodwork. Have you told Webb when and where to meet me?"

"Yes. We've accomplished the physical alterations you directed. He's full of questions, mostly about you."

Dana smiled to herself as a familiar memory of Gil's warm hazel eyes and strong arms came to mind. She had found herself thinking a lot of Gil over the past twenty-four hours. "What did you tell him?"

Talbot's voice filled with speculation at the wistfulness in her tone. "Nothing, Carmody. What did you want me to tell him?"

Dana felt her cheeks getting warm and sought to refocus the conversation. "What did you do with his Jeep?"

"It's in a private garage. Should I return it to Webb?"

"Under no circumstances," Dana said. "I'll be his chauffeur from now on—or, more precisely, a taxi driver will chauffeur us both, since parking in the city is the pits."

"You still want to leave that MR2 where it is?"

"Yes," Dana said. "We might cause too much attention dragging it out. Besides, it might be staked out."

"That silver-haired man looking for you?" Talbot asked.

"Exactly. Frankly, I think he's responsible for Harcourt's body disappearing. He's not a man to miss much."

"I haven't been able to identify him from the artist's drawing you faxed," Talbot said. "Of course, it's a little difficult since I can't be too open with local enforcement."

"Keep trying," Dana said. "I don't like the idea of that man lurking about in the shadows. I don't like it a lot."

Talbot's voice sounded concerned. "You seem afraid, Carmody. What is it about this man that has you so on edge?"

Dana tried to think through Talbot's question to examine her fear. "I don't know if I can put it into words. There's something absolutely cold and calculating about him that gives me the shivers. I've never met a human being who struck me as so coolly controlled."

"You mean he's without fear?" Talbot asked.

"No," Dana said. "Something much worse. I think he's without conscience."

SPARR LOOKED AT HIS WATCH as the tape was rewinding in the player on his office desk. It was getting close to midnight. Thiel should be back anytime. His information would be important. But nothing could eclipse what Sparr had just learned over the past couple of hours from the bug in Vogel's office.

His two-month search for the Lladro porcelain figurine had already paid off. The meeting he had just taped using the bug within the figurine made so many things clear, the most important of which was why Vogel had targeted the WCTS software program at Datacomp.

The two sharp knocks at the door interrupted Sparr's racing thoughts. He called for Thiel to come in. The big blond man did so quietly and approached Sparr's desk.

"I trailed the green Olds when it left Professional Properties and I think I know where they took the Webb guy."

"Where?" Sparr asked.

"Holiday Inn, downtown San Francisco."

Sparr frowned. "Curious place for cops to take him. What's the banking arrangement for Professional Properties?"

"It's a corporation," Thiel said. "Went into business about four years ago. Nothing spectacular, but doing okay."

"Yes. That's exactly how it would look if it were used for undercover work. Has your contact at the precinct come through on Professional Properties?"

"He won't be able to get back to me until tomorrow morning. They've got him out on some PR assignment."

"Did the two guys from Professional Properties just visit the hotel or are they spending the night?"

"The desk clerk doesn't remember anyone of their description checking in, but he only came on duty at ten. They could have registered earlier. The car's still there, so I would guess they're spending the night."

"Good work. Check the restaurants and bars within the hotel."

"And if I don't find them?" Thiel asked.

"You can get a room for the night and stay close. If they've checked Webb in, then there's a possibility they'll use the coffee shop for breakfast or call room service. Check both in the morning. If neither of those pan out, wait near the car. They have to come back to it sooner or later."

"Right. By the way, Leach has been following me. Vogel must have put him up to it. Should I do something about him?"

Sparr shook his head. "Not unless he gets in the way. I don't want to alarm Vogel unnecessarily. Not yet."

Thiel nodded knowingly. "Should I grab the Webb guy if I can?"

"By all means. But don't hurt him, Thiel. And don't get caught."

"What if these guys really are undercover cops?"

Sparr massaged his upper gums through his thick skin. "I'm sure they are and that the woman is in back of Webb being picked up. The fact that she's been able to go to the authorities so quietly bothers me. We're missing something. You've got to bring this Webb guy to me. He's our only lead to the woman, and I want her. I want her bad."

Chapter Six

Dana took her small steps interspersed with the tap of her walking cane as she slowly made her way across the coffee shop toward the dark-haired man in the far corner booth. Uniformed waiters zipped by her on their way to wait the busy breakfast tables. They paid her no heed outside of the cursory glance needed to identify an obstruction that must be avoided.

She was a few minutes late. She'd had trouble putting her long hair into a tight bun at the back of her head with all the stiff gray spray-on paint coating it. Still, with persistence, it had finally come together.

But right now all her attention was focused on limping correctly, on remembering all the little things that would make her role effective.

At least she didn't have to pretend to move stiffly. She had taken a nap after her flight and had awakened to feel soreness everywhere. It had always fascinated her that exertions were always felt so much more acutely on the second day. And today marked her second day after the jump from the MR2. She concentrated on negotiating the leg brace through the aisle.

It was because of her concentration that she almost missed the big blond man with the beard who stood over in the corner, studying the faces of everyone in the coffee shop.

She was almost at her destination when an automatic eye sweep finally included him. Stopping dead in her tracks, she held her breath as he looked directly at her.

His eyes scanned past her, and she exhaled thankfully. The first thought that raced through her mind was, *How did the silver-haired man know where to find them?*

"Lady, you're blocking the aisle," an impatient voice said suddenly from behind her. She turned to see the abused look of one of the waiters, his hands full of a loaded-down tray of hot, steaming dishes. Then she noticed his changed expression as he looked down to see the brace on her leg.

"Sorry," he said, his expression becoming one of shame.

Dana limped out of his way, feeling guilty. "My fault."

With one eye still on the blond man, Dana continued on her way to where Gil sat in the corner booth. If the watching man remained, she would have to pass the booth where Gil sat and find another way to contact him. But to her relief, the blond man made one more survey of the room and then turned. As he pivoted, a stiff white piece of paper slipped from his pocket, landing noiselessly on the thick carpet.

Dana immediately changed her direction. She waited until the blond man was out of sight before she made her way over to where he had been standing and reached down for the piece of paper. A quick reading told her it was a room receipt made out in the name of E. Thiel. She slipped it in her oversize shoulder bag and slowly made her way back to Gil.

She was comforted by the fact that apparently, no matter how the silver-haired man knew to send the blond man to the Holiday Inn, he didn't know enough to recognize her and Gil.

GIL HEARD SOMEONE CALLING his name and looked up expectantly, only to have his mouth drop open in disbelief. What he saw in no way matched his remembered vision of the woman in his cabin on Monday night. And she definitely didn't look like anybody's perception of an FBI agent.

Her gray-streaked hair was drawn into a tight, unattractive bun at the back of her head. Her small, pale face was obscured by a pair of large-framed, lilac-tinted glasses. A much too large, long-sleeve, 1950s vintage, lilac-print dress hung off her small frame. Heavy support hose wrapped both of her legs, which peeked out of a white pair of orthopedic shoes. Her left leg was supported by a brace that stretched from her ankle to her knee, and she was leaning on a sturdy black cane.

Gil stood up, feeling embarrassed because the exciting woman he had expected looked very unexciting and because he could only achieve a wedge position in the booth. "Dana?"

Her lips drew a small smile. "Good to see you, Gil."

Despite her unexpected appearance, her voice was as soft and sweet as ever, and he felt heartened by its unchanging melody. "Please. Sit down. Did you injure your leg Monday night?"

Dana carefully tried to maneuver her leg brace into the booth. Her sore muscles were making her even more clumsy than her role dictated. She landed with a small sigh. From the look she now saw on his face, she could tell why Gil was really sorry. He thought he was seeing her true appearance. He must have been less aware Monday night than she had thought.

She shook her head. "I'm a little sore from Monday night, but not really injured. Actually, Gil, this leg brace is not worn for injury. I bought it at a shop that specializes in supporting prostheses for people with weak limbs."

He looked even more distressed. "I'm sorry, Dana, I didn't realize what the situation was. Monday night is still rather fuzzy in the area of details. I wasn't trying to be so insensitive as to draw attention to your . . . leg."

Startled, Dana finally realized that Gil thought she was really handicapped. She hadn't expected that mistake. It tickled her that he hadn't tumbled to the fact that if his appearance could be altered with a few minor adjustments, so could hers.

And she had to admit, his appearance was quite altered. His beard and long hair were completely gone and a dark rinse over his now-short hair had totally eliminated the prominent red cast. His muscular body was downplayed in a dark, conservative, three-piece suit. He also wore a pair of large-framed, blue-tinted glasses that obscured both his true eye color and the shape of his face. And although the minor changes had greatly changed his appearance, she found him still handsome, maybe even more so.

He removed his glasses for a moment and looked at her with those warm hazel eyes of his. She wasn't sure how much direct contact with those eyes she could take. Perhaps it would be best if he continued to see her as handicapped and plain.

He smiled as his hand reached across the table to cover hers. "Dana, it's so good to see you again."

He sounded as though he meant every word. Of its own accord, her body began to move closer to his across the table.

Then Lew Sargentich's warning against involvement with this man repeated itself in her mind. If she was to maintain her wits about her, she must keep their relationship on a professional basis. This assignment was her chance. She had to let it claim all her attention. She eased her hand out from under Gil's and took a firm grip on her emotions.

"Gil, I'm sorry I had to leave so abruptly Monday night. I wanted to explain, but I had to get an okay from my superior first. You understand, don't you?"

Gil smiled. "Of course. You convinced him to use me on this assignment. I'll never be able to show my appreciation."

"There's no need," Dana said quickly as she moved uncomfortably in the booth, feeling the warmth of his words still curling around her. Keeping her mind on business was not going to be easy in this man's company. She was more than thankful for her disguise now.

The waiter approached and they gave their breakfast orders. Gil studied the delicate bone structure of Dana's face. The alcohol had obviously distorted many things about her, but he was glad that at least some things were as he remembered them.

He found many questions springing to mind about her past. He remembered her telling him about someone special in her life who had died. He wanted to know more. But as soon as the waiter left, she forestalled any such personal questions by plunging right into business.

"While our breakfast is being prepared, we'd best discuss our assignment. There's not a lot of time. We must leave here in twenty minutes. What did Talbot tell you?"

Gil consciously directed his thoughts away from the pinkness of her lips as they strummed out the melody of her words. "Talbot told me you would explain everything."

Dana nodded. "Have you ever heard of Datacomp?"

Gil laced his fingers before him on the tablecloth and waited until the returning waiter had poured coffee and left.

"Yes," he said. "It's a medium-sized software company that writes and supports programs geared to the banking industry."

"Only not just the banking industry," Dana said. "It is also currently under contract to produce a Defense Department software related to weapon costs."

Gil felt confused. "That doesn't make sense. Datacomp's strength is in banking programs. What could it possibly be doing for the Department of Defense?"

"A few months ago, Datacomp won the bid to devise a sophisticated financial tracking system for new and existing weapons. The finished software will track initial weapon costs and accurately evaluate the weapon's life span based on all existing and proposed firepower."

"You mean the program will compare weapons?" Gil asked.

Dana nodded. "Through all departments of the military. It will interface with defense programs, pointing out redundancies and fire-power gaps. It will also track all costs relating to their maintenance for ten years, factoring in projected rises in living expenses, gross-national-product fluctuations in key industries and at least a dozen other economic indicators all impacting on the production of weapon systems."

Gil was trying to take in all the information. "I don't understand. Datacomp is not that large or sophisticated a company that they could produce so intricate a software program."

Dana nodded. "Ordinarily, you would be right. But while enhancing software for international banking, they built in enough sophistication to mirror most of the functions required for the weapons cost-tracking system. WCTS for short. Their president recognized its other possible applications when he heard of the Defense Department's need. Because the basic program was already there, the bid was low enough to win."

"So they got the contract," Gil said. "Something wrong?"

"Yes," Dana said. "Monday morning, Kristin Harcourt, the lead programmer for WCTS, contacted Wayne York, the president of Datacomp, to tell him that while she was working over the weekend, she saw data shadows on her screen. She thought the program might have been attacked by a virus. York contacted us."

"Data shadows? What did she mean by that?"

"Unfortunately, I didn't get to her in time to find out," Dana said. "I found the programmer's dead body in the computer room at Datacomp on Monday night."

Gil swallowed his surprise. "She had been killed?"

Dana nodded. "Two of the men involved were pursuing me when I came upon you in the park."

Gil felt anything but calm. He tried to appear so for his companion's sake. "You outran them in the Jeep."

Dana nodded. "However, when the local police arrived a few minutes later at Datacomp, the bodies of Kristin Harcourt and an unconscious guard had both disappeared."

"Disappeared? You mean there was no sign of a murder?"

"None," Dana said. "And Harcourt's car had been removed from Datacomp's parking lot. Someone identifying himself as Kristin Harcourt's doctor called in yesterday morning to say Harcourt had a serious case of the flu and wouldn't be in for a couple of weeks."

"Only he wasn't Harcourt's doctor?" Gil asked.

Dana nodded. "We checked with her regular doctor. He advised us he hadn't seen her in over six months. Harcourt was a single woman, twenty-nine, no family, living alone. A search of her apartment yielded missing clothes and suitcases. Several love letters between herself and the missing Datacomp guard, Gordon Mercer, had been left on her dresser. The last one spoke about their running off together. Gordon Mercer's wife said he never came home after his shift Monday."

"I'm confused. I thought you said you found Kristin Harcourt dead. How could she have run off with the security guard?"

"She couldn't have, Gil. But I think someone has gone to a lot of trouble to leave a false trail in that direction."

Gil shook his head. "But why? Surely the truth will have to come out sooner or later."

"A missing-persons case can go on for months, particularly if the bodies have been disposed of and with the kinds of false clues that have been left. The people behind this

probably figure they've got two weeks until people start
getting wise that Harcourt isn't returning to work and
doesn't really have the flu. Then they are no doubt counting on the love letters and missing luggage to further confuse a trace of her whereabouts.''

''But you think this Kristin Harcourt found out what was
infecting her program and someone killed her to shut her
up?''

Dana shrugged. ''She may have found out what it was or
maybe who was behind it. In any case, yes, I believe she was
killed because of what she knew.''

It was a disturbing thought. Gil pondered it as the food
arrived and he began to eat his omelet.

''Was anyone else working on WCTS?'' he asked between bites.

''Kristin Harcourt had an assistant, Linda Riley. Harcourt feared that her assistant might be involved in infecting the program, so she said nothing to Riley about
contacting us. Logically, Riley seems to be the only likely
suspect. You see, this case is not unlike what you faced at
Computech.''

Gil put down his fork. ''How do you mean?''

Dana swallowed a bite of toast. ''The infiltration of the
computer system at Datacomp seems to have been accomplished as mysteriously as the infiltration of the software at
Computech. Technically, no one but the two programmers
had access to WCTS.''

''How were others kept away?'' Gil asked.

''Well, because of the sensitivity of WCTS, as soon as the
bid was awarded to Datacomp, a special computer room was
cordoned off for the exclusive use of WCTS programmers.
The minicomputer containing the WCTS software was
hardwired to only two terminals—Harcourt's and Riley's.
Neither Harcourt's terminal nor Riley's communicated with
any others. Both programmers had personal passwords only
they knew.''

Gil nodded. "So what you're saying is that since no modems were hooked up to the terminals connected to the minicomputer, a data-communication's computer virus couldn't get in. Just like such a virus could not have gotten into Computech's new-product data base."

"Exactly, Gil. Kristin Harcourt's death tells us something has infiltrated WCTS. Whatever it is must have entered through one of the two terminals."

Gil continued chewing his food without tasting it. Dana's description of what they were up against engaged all his senses. "Who else at Datacomp knows about the WCTS system?"

"According to Wayne York, no one but Harcourt and Riley were involved. And York, Harcourt and Riley all passed FBI security clearances."

"Which means?" Gil asked.

"They're probably in the clear."

"Probably?"

Dana put her coffee cup down. "Gil, we're thorough at the FBI, but not infallible. However, finding out who's behind this is my problem. What we need you to do is to get into WCTS and look for the infiltration. Once you find it for us, you can assess what harm it's done to the program and then remove it."

Gil read the division of their responsibilities from her words. And it was immediately clear to him that his area was definitely one cut off from any possible action. Despite his disappointments over the past six months, he had kept himself in good physical shape. He sat up straighter.

"Dana, I can be handy if there's a fight."

She shook her head. "You're not trained, Gil. Besides, your value to this assignment is as a brain, not a brawn. I will do my best to keep us out of any physical confrontation, but should one occur, you must let me handle it."

Gil leaned forward and put a hand on her arm. "Dana, you're not physically equipped to deal with trouble. Frankly, it seems rather foolish and unorthodox for the FBI to have given you this case. How can they place *you* in such a position of danger?''

Dana felt a sharp, sudden heat. She snatched her arm away from Gil's hand. The last thing she needed was someone else doubting her abilities.

''Gil, I'm the agent. I call the shots. I carry the gun. Believe me, I can use it.''

Gil tried to see Dana's eyes through the lilac-tinted glasses. They seemed shielded with more than just glass. He looked skeptically at her slight frame swallowed in the oversize dress and then down at the brace on her leg and shook his head. ''Dana, surely you don't expect me to believe—''

Her hand reached out to grab his arm and prevented him from continuing. ''Don't just see me with your eyes, Gil. Use your other senses. Focus on the brain in this body and the determination behind that brain. There are many kinds of strengths.''

Gil studied her face for a moment. ''Dana, do you think I'm the kind of man who'd hide behind a woman?''

She gritted her teeth. ''You didn't hear a damn thing I just said!''

His face turned equally dark. ''And you didn't hear a damn thing I just said!''

Dana ripped her hand away from Gil's arm. Her teeth tore at some buttered toast, which tasted awful in the souring saliva of her mouth. She gulped down coffee, working to get her anger under control.

When she looked up again, Gil was frowning into his coffee cup. The heightened color in his face told her he, too, was working at containing his emotions. His hands gripped the knife and fork in his hands as the food on his plate got cold. His well-built shoulders straightened in a line as unyielding as the set of his jaw.

Stubborn. Obstinate. Just as Dana was assigning those labels, she caught sight of the lopsided job Gil had done tying his tie.

There he sat—a brilliant, powerfully built, angry man capable of so much, but one who couldn't get two ends of a piece of silk to behave.

When Gil looked up at Dana again, he was flabbergasted to find her smiling. His anger swarmed into frustration. This woman was an infuriating mystery. How could she think she could protect them? Did she really think he was physically useless?

Dana controlled her voice. "Any other questions, Gil?"

Once again he tried to see through her tinted glasses, to read the expression in her eyes, but failed. There was something about that lilac tint that hid her eye color and shape almost completely.

He quit straining and sat back, wishing he could understand. She told him to see past her appearance. Well, handicapped people needed a sense of accomplishment just like everybody else. Perhaps because they were handicapped, the drive was even stronger. And surely the FBI wouldn't have assigned her to this case if they really thought there would be serious trouble, would they?

A frown of doubt dug into his forehead as he thought of the murder of Datacomp's programmer. If that wasn't serious trouble, what was? No matter what she said, he planned to stay close and be ready. Now he tried to project a calm he was far from feeling.

"Well, bodyguard, since you've gone to all the trouble of getting these glasses for me, removing my beard and spraying what's left of my hair dark, I assume you don't want me to use my own name at Datacomp. Who am I?"

"I've told Wayne York you're Lief Gilson. The unusualness of your first name will allow me to still call you Gil, as short for Gilson, without the personnel at Datacomp thinking it odd. If I'm unsure of someone there, I'll just introduce you as Lief. They won't know if it's a first or last name.''

Gil nodded. "What do I call you?"

"Dana or Carmody should be all right. Changing my name isn't necessary since I'm unknown here. After breakfast, we'll drive to Datacomp and assume our roles as new employees. I spoke to York by telephone, and he will cooperate fully. I haven't told him about Kristin Harcourt being murdered. I was afraid he wouldn't be able to carry such information confidentially. He believes she really is out with the flu. Why are you shaking your head?''

"This is nothing like I expected."

Dana heard the disappointment in Gil's voice and fought down some of her own. "You mean *I'm* not what you expected."

She watched him trying to peer through her glasses again, as though he was trying to see her better. She was tempted to remove her obscuring lenses, but she knew stripping away any part of her disguise at this point wouldn't make much sense. She had to keep a professional distance between them if she hoped to keep her concentration on the successful completion of this, her first real assignment. But it gave her heart a little tug as she saw his handsome head shake in obvious disappointment.

"Let's just say that I feel like I've gotten into the cowardly lion costume by mistake, and because I'm already on the road to Oz with the Good Witch by my side, there's no time to change."

Dana blinked at him for a moment, a little surprised and amused at the characterization he had selected for them. She smiled as she laid her hand on his arm.

"Gil, if it's really Oz we're entering, as far as I'm concerned, you're the wizard. And as the wizard, you hold the key to the success of this operation. That's why your safety must be maintained at all costs.''

He felt the warmth of her hand and the assurance of her words. His other hand covered hers and he found his eyes resting on the natural pinkness of her lips as they contrasted against the paleness of her skin. "Dana, that wizard in Oz proved to be a fake."

She shook her head. "Not at all. He was an extremely intelligent man who tried to help those around him see the truth of their own worth without ever realizing his own."

Gil smiled as he stroked her hand, enjoying its smoothness beneath his fingers. Then he felt it begin to tremble beneath his ministrations and he looked up to see what her eyes might tell him, but once again their expression was obscured. Next he felt her hand retreating from within his.

He didn't know if it was his imagination, but her tone seemed a little less even as she spoke. "And just so you'll know, I'm planning on keeping my wizard in that separate computer room designated for WCTS so he can channel his efforts toward discovering the infiltration. It won't be easy. You've got a lot of magic to work and you don't have much time in which to work it."

Gil was still trying to catch her eye through the lilac-tinted glasses. "How much time?" he asked.

"I think the delivery date on WCTS is next week," Dana said as she concentrated on watching the cup in front of her and purposely avoided returning his direct look. She was still trying to control the racing of her pulse that his warm touch had started. "We can check that with York when we get to Datacomp. Since this is already Wednesday, if I'm right about next week being the delivery date, that means you have just a few days."

Gil sat back and smiled to himself. Her trembling hand and avoidance of his eyes told him she was not as physically ambivalent to him as her words conveyed. It was the one cheering thought in his otherwise bleak knowledge of her doubts about him. On some level, however tenuous, she cared for him. And because she did, he knew he would find a way to prove himself. For now, all he could do was bide his time. "What will you be doing?" he asked.

"Lending any technical assistance I can. My basic knowledge of computers was the initial reason I was given this assignment."

Gil smirked. "Really, bodyguard? I thought it might be for your physical prowess."

Dana didn't crack a smile. There were some attempts at levity she didn't want to encourage. "Of course, there was that, too. Any other questions?"

Gil heard the new tone in her voice and backed off. "Just one. Isn't the other programmer, that Riley woman, going to get wise as to what I'm doing?"

"York has temporarily assigned Riley elsewhere. She shouldn't be anywhere near the computer room for the next few days." Dana took a moment to lace the strap of her bag over her shoulder. "Don't worry about Datacomp's personnel. Your job is evaluating the computer software for tampering. And speaking of your job, it's time I got you over there."

Dana rose, carefully maneuvering her leg brace out of the booth and reaching into her shoulder bag for the money to cover their meal. Gil rose, too, and stood beside her. Dana kept her eyes averted from Gil's face and tried to ignore the clean, exciting smell of his skin mixing with his after-shave.

"What happened to my Jeep?"

"It's in storage. Our pursuers on Monday saw it, so we've had to keep it undercover. We'll make do with taxis."

Gil nodded as he tried to tell himself not to feel odd about Dana automatically paying for breakfast. She was his colleague, not a date. And she obviously held the purse strings on the expense account. But still, it gave him an uncomfortable feeling.

The morning had been full of uncomfortable feelings. Despite her overall plain appearance, Gil felt himself being physically and emotionally drawn to Dana. He wanted to touch her on as many levels as she seemed to be touching him. As he stood next to her now, he could smell the peppermint of her after-breakfast mint.

Gil remembered his dad telling him once that a woman could be felt more accurately than she could be seen. Although Gil had thought it an interesting statement at the time, he had never really understood his father's words until now. For now, as Dana moved through his thoughts, he found she was not a perception of feature and form, but one of emotion—like a fresh summer day warming him from the inside out. She felt beautiful.

As they walked out the front doors of the Holiday Inn into an overcast day, he wondered whether her eyes really were that clear, spring-rain gray he remembered. Sometime today, if he did nothing else, he was going to get her to remove her glasses so he could see.

The thought of removing her glasses made him frown in sudden memory as he realized she hadn't been wearing glasses on Monday night. Had she lost them trying to get away from the men who chased her? And why was it that he remembered her with long, light brown hair unstreaked with gray?

While the fragmented images of Monday night continued to cloud his mind, he watched Dana limp ahead to signal for one of the waiting taxis. The driver didn't seem to see her waving hand. Gil was just about to step forward to assist in gaining the taxi driver's attention when suddenly he felt something hard poking into his back. He tensed in shock at the whispered words near his ear.

"Get the broad back here quick or I'll blow a hole through your liver and then through hers. I'm not kidding."

Chapter Seven

Dana had started toward a cab to get the driver's attention when she heard Gil calling her name. She turned around and immediately froze as she saw the irritable, dark-haired man who had driven the black Cadillac out of Datacomp Monday night standing behind Gil.

The sudden, loud pounding of Dana's heart almost drowned out Gil's repeated call. He was obviously being threatened. Slowly, she limped toward the two men.

"Okay," the dark-haired man said. "Now, nice and easy like, I wants you to walk ahead to my car. We're going to go for a little ride. Come on, broad. I don't got all day."

Dana shuffled along, leaning heavily on her cane, trying to make herself appear as feeble as possible. When they turned the corner to the parking garage, she was glad to see the large underground structure was empty of all save them. She caught a glimpse of the gun in Gil's back. Their abductor obviously thought Gil was the real threat. The dark-haired man hardly glanced at her. Still, she would have to get in closer. She began to fake a wheeze.

Gil slowed his pace and spoke over his shoulder to the man with the gun. "Can't you hear how much trouble she's having breathing?"

Their abductor jabbed Gil with the gun barrel. "She ain't known trouble till I gets through with her. It's the broad here who I saw picking up after Thiel. You I ain't that anxious to talk to. Give me stress, you get a bullet. Now move it."

With those harsh words, the dark-haired man poked Gil and reached over to shove Dana. She was ready.

She kicked him hard with her steel brace at the same time curling the end of her cane around his ankle and yanking him off his feet. He buckled, grunting in surprise, the gun flying from his hand.

Gil shifted just in time to see the man reach out his hand to shove Dana. With all his might, Gil wheeled his forearm toward their abductor's gun hand. His arm crashed into the forehead of the falling man. With a sickening thud, the man's head cracked against a concrete pillar of the underground garage structure and his body slumped to the pavement floor like a stringless puppet.

Dana scrambled to pick up the dropped gun. Then she approached the man's unmoving form cautiously, stretching down to feel for a pulse. There wasn't one. "Damn!" She forcibly swallowed the queasiness working its way into her throat and began to search his pockets.

As soon as Gil's muscles were released from their shocked immobility, he dropped down to a knee beside her. His voice was anxious as he put an arm around her shoulders. "Are you all right?"

Dana moved away from the warmth of his arm and let out a frustrated breath. "Of course, I'm all right. And this man would have been all right, too, if you hadn't interfered."

She got to her feet holding the man's wallet and keys, examining the driver's license she had found, seething in anger.

Gil sat back on his heels, his face darkening.

"The guy had a gun pointed—"

"You don't have to tell me what happened," Dana interrupted. "I was there, remember?"

"You were having trouble walking. You could barely breathe!"

Dana's teeth locked. "I faked the damn wheeze." She gestured toward the body on the pavement. "I needed him to underestimate my threat and not see I was getting behind him as we walked. It worked. When he reached over to shove me, I tripped him and he dropped the gun. I had everything under control."

Gil blinked. "You planned to knock him out?"

Dana let out a frustrated breath. "I'm a trained FBI agent, Gil. When are you going to accept that?"

Dana's matter-of-fact tone gave Gil a bit of a jolt. He found himself watching her with new eyes. Her tripping their abductor explained why his forearm hit the man's head and not his gun arm. Had her success against this hoodlum been a fluke, or had she really known what she was doing? Well, whatever the case, it didn't look as though she had needed him at all.

He studied the straightness of her shoulders and the steadiness in her hands as she read the information from the man's wallet. There was nothing about the nervous amateur in her demeanor.

Dana turned to Gil as she slipped the man's gun into her shoulder bag. "The name on his driver's license is Julius Leach. Local San Francisco address." She turned and looked down the row of parked cars. "That's it, I'll bet."

Gil felt subdued. "That's what?"

Dana was already moving forward. "Leach's car. These keys are for a Toyota, and there's a maroon Toyota fifth car from the right. That's the direction he was herding us in. Let's see if they fit."

She walked over to the driver's side and slid the key into the lock without resistance. "Let's get him into the back seat."

"You mean move the body?" Gil asked. "Shouldn't we be calling the police or something?"

Dana shook her head as she leaned over the driver's seat to unlock the back door. "I am 'the police or something,' remember?"

Gil heard the forced civility in her tone. She was obviously still angry at what she termed his interference. A man abducts them, threatens them with a gun, they end up killing him and she coolly goes about making arrangements to move his body.

"Are you ready, Gil?"

Feeling newly stunned, Gil walked over to the dead man and tucked his arms under the man's shoulders. Dana squatted next to the man's knees, ready to lift. "I can do it, Dana."

Dana looked over at the frown on Gil's face and read the new discordant note in his voice. She left the body to him. By the time Gil had maneuvered the dead weight into the back seat of the maroon Toyota, he was perspiring, but at least he felt he had contributed something. Dana covered Leach's body with a blanket from the trunk.

"I'll call Talbot, and then we'll get that taxi for Datacomp. Talbot can run a check on Leach and find out what he was doing at Datacomp Monday night and why he was here today."

Dana headed toward the garage's exit. Gil followed, but found her words disturbing. "This man, Leach, was at Datacomp Monday?"

Dana nodded. "He must have seen me pick up a room receipt his partner dropped in the restaurant and came after us."

Alarmed, Gil stopped and took hold of her arm. "There was another one of these murderers in the restaurant? My God, Dana, why didn't you tell me? And why didn't you call Talbot then and have him arrested?"

Dana exhaled. "Gil, I can't arrest these men yet. Harcourt's body is missing. I don't even know why she was killed. I need answers and evidence that will hold up in court."

"But this man tried to kill us. What if the other—"

Dana interrupted. "He didn't recognize us, Gil, just like this man Leach didn't. We'll be okay. It was just bad luck that Leach saw me pick up the room receipt. Now, I think we'd best not linger."

Gil tightened his grip. "It's those other men you're concerned about, isn't it? They're the reason we moved Leach. You don't want to draw attention to the fact that he pursued us and is now dead."

Dana extricated his hand from her arm. "Right on all counts."

Understanding her urgency now, Gil followed Dana out of the garage structure. However, he found himself still feeling upset at their close call. She had said she'd handle it, and he had to admit, she'd caught Leach unawares. Counting Monday night, this was the second confrontation she had managed to emerge from unscathed. And the second one in which he hadn't been of help.

It was his lack of help that ate at Gil. As they walked toward the phone, he remembered the fear that had stuck in his throat when Leach had threatened to harm her unless Gil complied with Leach's demands. Gil was finding both his ineffectiveness and his fear for her left extremely unpleasant aftertastes.

"WE'VE GOT TROUBLE," Thiel said to Sparr as he entered the silver-haired man's office at CustomKey without his usual knock.

Sparr didn't fail to notice Thiel's unusual behavior. He was also instantly alert to the heightened color of the blond man's fair skin. He put aside the paperwork he had been studying.

"It's the real-estate office, isn't it?"

Thiel nodded. "It's a front for the feds. My contact at the precinct gave me this picture of the guy with a green Olds. He's Jerry Talbot, the FBI's squad supervisor for white-collar crime."

Sparr took the picture from Thiel's hand. His black eyes glowed. "She's FBI."

"She?"

"The woman, Thiel! She's an FBI agent. Who would have thought that that bastion of the big and burly would have allowed a small woman in their ranks? This puts a whole new light on the matter."

"What do you mean?"

"Don't you see? Harcourt contacted the FBI. This woman agent must know about the infiltration attempt at Datacomp."

"You think the Harcourt woman told her?"

"I think Leach told her when he killed the programmer. Damn idiot! Odds were that Harcourt woman would never have figured out the significance of the data shadows. Vogel's programmer cleared up the problem the next day. It could have all been handled smartly if Vogel hadn't panicked and called out that imbecile Leach."

Thiel frowned. "The programmer cleared it up? I thought Vogel kept everything his programmer did a secret. How did you find out?"

"Let's just say a little bug told me."

Thiel smiled knowingly. "So you think she's an FBI agent?"

Sparr nodded. "I'm sure of it."

"What are we going to do?"

"No," Sparr said, shaking his head. "The question is, what are they going to do with Gilbert Webb?"

"Gilbert Webb?" Thiel said.

"Yes, Gilbert Webb," Sparr said. "I've been doing some very interesting reading this morning from the information you provided. You see this obituary? It's for Theodore

Webb, the registered owner of the Jeep, and it's dated about two years ago. It says he's survived by his only son, Gilbert. Theodore Webb must have left the Jeep to his son. Gilbert Webb obviously never had the registration changed.''

"Then the bearded man in the park was Gilbert Webb," Thiel said. "How did the FBI woman link up with him?"

Sparr shook his head. "At the wrong place and at the wrong time for us. He's a dangerous person for them to have."

"What makes him dangerous?"

"Gilbert Webb is a computer genius, one of the few programmers in this world who could find our programmer's virus."

"But don't they think he's a criminal?" Thiel asked. "I can't see the FBI trusting him to help them."

Sparr got to his feet. "Yes, I've studied the FBI very carefully in the past and I agree. If we were just dealing with the local agents, I'd tell you they'd never let Gilbert Webb near Datacomp. But the woman is involved. And I've got a feeling about that woman, Thiel. She'll bring Gilbert Webb in. She'll find a way."

"How can you be so sure?"

Sparr began to pace. "The way she escaped us. The way she disappeared. The way she had Webb grabbed before we could get to him. She's smart. She's quick."

Thiel shrugged. "How can we stop her?"

"By anticipating her next move."

"You know what it will be?"

"Yes. She's got to get Gilbert Webb into Datacomp so he can check out the data base. Call our contact right away and tell him to keep us apprised of what happens in that computer room. I want him to call me directly the minute a change occurs."

"How can you be so sure that's her next move?"

Sparr's dark eyes shone as he turned to look directly at Thiel. "Because it would be mine."

DANA HAD TOLD DATACOMP'S president, Wayne York, not to be put off by her appearance when she spoke to him by phone, but apparently nothing she said had prepared York for her disabled-person disguise. Embarrassment eroded all over his face the moment she limped into his office. He ignored her outstretched hand, gave Gil's a hardy shake and then beckoned them both to sit.

Dana took a moment to study York, a tall, thin man with lots of salt-and-pepper hair that continued to shake up and down from nervous energy. His blue suit didn't look as though he ever sat in it long enough to get creased, and his hands were nomads, roaming through the office air, never alighting for very long.

"Good to meet you, Agent Gilson, Carmody." Dana thought the smile that accompanied his words didn't look good at all.

She took her time sitting down, carefully studying his office. It was a shrine to the air force, with model planes all over his walnut desk and pictures of various combat planes in flight formation across its walls. A framed portrait of four male members of the York family posed in uniformed splendor next to his telephone. Two were full colonels. With such prominent connections, she was beginning to wonder if it wasn't just a low bid that had gotten Datacomp its contract to do WCTS.

"Look," York began, "I understand you have to investigate, just as I had to inform you. But as I told you this morning, Agent Carmody, Kristin's doctor called. Bad case of flu. Double vision. If she was that ill last weekend when she saw all that nonsense on her screen, well, I think you understand what I'm trying to say."

"Of course," Dana said. "But as you pointed out just a moment ago, we have to investigate."

Her response caused a small frown on York's forehead. His next words pinpointed why. "WCTS's due date is next Monday, when the Defense Department opens for business. If you don't find anything, you understand you have no authority to jeopardize my delivery date?"

Dana didn't reply, but instead asked, "Mr. York, I understand your company got the contract to develop WCTS approximately four months ago?"

York barely glanced at Dana in answering. "Five months ago. We guaranteed to deliver in five, and that's what we're going to do. I run a tight squadron here."

Dana acknowledged the enthusiasm in York's voice, even if she couldn't appreciate other parts of his personality. "May we have the system documentation that your programmers prepared?"

York was already back on his feet, operating the combination on a small safe in the corner of his office. When he closed the safe and returned to his desk, he automatically handed everything to Gil and addressed his comments to him.

"The passwords and the key to the computer room are included. How long do you think it will take to check on this 'data shadow' business and give WCTS a clean bill of health?"

Gil recognized York's hesitancy to deal with Dana directly. It irritated him that the president of Datacomp was dismissing her so blatantly. He knew why, of course. In York's mind, Dana was a handicapped woman and far from his idea of an authority figure. Gil deliberately handed the file and key to Dana without looking at them.

He kept his voice very matter-of-fact. "I'm just along for the ride, Mr. York. Agent Carmody is in charge."

Dana smiled in welcome surprise at Gil's words. Despite the reservations he had about her abilities, he at least supported her position in front of Datacomp's president.

"Has the programming been completed, Mr. York?" she asked.

"Last Friday. Kristin ran a basic test on Sunday afternoon. That's when she *thought* she detected the data shadows."

Dana knew York had convinced himself now that whatever Kristin saw was in her head. He had to believe that in order to feel safe that his contract would not be jeopardized. He was one of those men who accepted only the facts that supported what he wanted to believe. She had met others like him. There was no way to reach them with logic. She looked over the system documentation briefly and then handed the file to Gil after pocketing the computer-room key.

"Do you have any suspicions as to who might have tried to invade the program or how?"

York straightened his already straight tie, still clumsily avoiding a direct look at Dana. "No. As I told you, my call to the FBI was purely a step of caution. Other than Kristin, Linda Riley was the only one with access to the data base. But if Riley had tried some mischief, Harcourt would have found it."

"You're sure?" Dana asked.

"Absolutely. Riley doesn't have the kind of... well, discipline needed."

Dana unsuccessfully tried to catch York's eye. "Is there anyone who knew you were working on WCTS and was angry or envious or viewed your opportunity in a less than positive manner?"

York circled his desk and sat down again, leaning over to straighten the already straight picture of his air force family.

"You mean outside the company?"

"Yes."

"No. Uncle Phil was part of the decision committee. He assured me the appropriations staff selected the WCTS software unanimously."

"And Uncle Phil is . . . ?" Dana asked.

York's hands glided over the silver-framed photograph. "Colonel Philip Ramsey. Defense appropriations staff. Even if Uncle Phil had not voted, we still would have gotten the contract. Our bid was lowest and our software showed the most promise of interfacing with existing defense-software configurations on weapon systems. WCTS is going to have to draw data from a lot of sources. Defense Department programmers will make those software connections. Datacomp has a contract to deliver the WCTS software only."

Dana nodded and started to get to her feet. "Well, I think we have the picture now, Mr. York. Gil and I will get to work. Don't bother showing us to the computer room. I know the way."

DATACOMP EMPLOYEES hustled by them as they made their way down the hallway. Dana paused as they reached the door to the computer room and looked at it carefully. A faint odor of new paint was the only evidence she could detect that repairs had been made to the door frame. Such attention to detail by Harcourt's murderers left her feeling even more uneasy. She dug inside her pocket for the key to the door.

"I've arranged for the locks to be changed today," Dana said as they entered the room.

Gil closed the door behind them. "In a building full of people, we should be safe, shouldn't we?"

Dana shrugged. "I wouldn't count on it." She placed her large shoulder bag on a small table, aware of the deep hum from the minicomputer. She knew most computer people thought turning them on and off more wearing than just letting them run. In any case, it being on now would save her time.

Gil watched Dana reach inside her shoulder bag and bring out a strange-looking metal saucer.

"What's that?" he asked.

A slim finger found its way to her closed lips in the gesture of silence. She reached back into her bag and quickly scribbled something on the back of an envelope. Then she handed it to him. It read, Electronic sweep. Don't say anything until I've checked the room.

Gil watched as she went over each inch of wall space, the two desks, the separate small table in the corner, the chairs beneath it, the telephone on top of it, the laser printer and even the minicomputer and the two terminals. When she was finished, she placed the device back in the shoulder bag.

Gil pointed to her bag. "David Copperfield's magic hat?"

His light tone elicited a smile from her lips. Gil liked its warmth and was happy they seemed to be on friendlier footing after the tension of their earlier disagreement. "No bugs?"

She shook her head. "They're not responding to the microwave signals from the sweep. But that could be because they're not transmitting."

"You mean there could be bugs that have been turned off?"

"In a way. Some of the newer types can soak up data for a while and then when their capacity is full, transmit what they have gathered in one quick burst. Unless the sweep is focused on them at that microsecond, they're not detectable."

"Then there could still be bugs in this room?"

"There could be."

"Why don't we buy a loud radio and turn it on while we talk?"

Dana smiled. "You need to watch more recent spy movies. If there were several bugs scattered about in this room, a computer could compare all sounds from different angles, pick out the voice vibrations and edit out other noise. What would result is our voices clearly and unmistakenly reproduced without any background noise."

"Then someone might be listening to us now?"

"Someone might be, but I doubt it. Data transmissions, not human conversations are what computer intruders are generally after. If a bug is here, I believe it's one that can transmit data from one or both of these two terminals."

"But these terminals are metal-shielded and hardwired to that minicomputer," Gil said. "And look, no modem connections. Where could a bug be planted?"

Her brow wrinkled, Dana studied the setup quietly for a moment. "Yes, it is a totally closed, self-contained system, isn't it?"

"Which means it had to have been one of the programmers. And since Harcourt is dead—"

"You want to hang Linda Riley," Dana finished. "Just like Computech wanted to hang you?"

Gil grimaced. "Good point. By the way, was it just me or did you get the impression that York was sorry he'd called the FBI?"

Dana shrugged. "He didn't do it because he wanted to, that's pretty obvious. But it does get him off the hook."

"Off the hook?" Gil repeated. "I don't understand."

"Well, if we don't find anything, it hasn't cost him. If we do find something, he'll be applauded for saving the day. Whatever else he may be, he's not dumb."

Gil stepped closer to her. His voice was deep and sincere. "I'm sorry for the way he treated you back there, Dana. If I thought he'd learn any respect by it, I'd punch him in his pompous mouth."

Dana smiled up at Gil. She found his type of chivalry warming her modern woman's heart. She reached up to kiss his cheek.

In delighted surprise, Gil quickly wrapped an arm around her before she could retreat. He felt the startled tenseness of her muscles as he held her, but was encouraged by the fact that she didn't immediately try to pull away. His pulse had begun to quicken as her nearness invaded his senses. He raised his free hand and removed her tinted glasses so he could see her eyes more clearly.

They were beautiful, that same clear gray he remembered. But filling in the outlines of their expression were confusion and apprehension. He had obviously taken her as much by surprise as she had taken him. But her body language signaled neither retreat nor advance. He had to know what she was thinking.

"The first time you kissed me it was to save my life, Dana. What was this kiss for?"

His voice was deep and breathy and Dana felt alarm at the way his arm held her so possessively, and even more alarm at the way her own body was responding. Warmth raced into every organ and limb, and she longed to just let go and cling to him. With an effort, she fought to regain her senses and pushed out of his circling arm.

She was irritated to find that her face felt hot. She reached for her glasses still in his hand and put them on.

He hadn't resisted her attempts to withdraw from his embrace, but he was determined she would not withdraw from his question. "Dana? The reason for the kiss?"

Dana was irritated at the hesitancy in her voice and the fact that she found she had to look away before she could speak. "I always appreciate the signs of real chivalry."

Gil reached for one of her hands. He brushed the back of it with his lips and bowed in the way of an old-fashioned salute. "Always at your service."

Dana looked back to the warmth in his eyes. She should still be angry at his doubts of her physical capabilities, but the anger wouldn't surface. Her unattractive disguise should be keeping him away from her, but for some reason it wasn't. The importance of this assignment to her own self-worth should be keeping her away from him, but for some reason it wasn't, either. When she was close to him, she found a lot of "shoulds" falling by the wayside.

She removed her hand from his touch, confused and searching for conversation on a more professional level. "Was there anything else about York that you noticed?"

Gil recognized the conversation switch for what it was. He had expected it. Everything about Dana's retreat told him that she was uncomfortable with the attraction between them. How could he blame her? Why would she want to get involved with someone who had nothing to offer and didn't even seem capable of taking care of himself? He had a lot to prove.

He stuck his hands into his pockets and considered her question. "Well, one thing that struck me as odd was why York was so down on Riley. If he thought poorly of her, why was she assigned to WCTS?"

Dana nodded. "Yes. That concerned me, too. I think we should have a talk with Linda Riley at the earliest opportunity."

"And now?" Gil asked.

"Now we get to work," Dana said.

Gil looked at the two terminal positions. "They're so far apart. I suppose that was to give each programmer as much privacy as possible. Which one was . . . hers?"

"Harcourt's was the one on the left. It has better lighting. There's a slight glare from the overhead fluorescents on the other. But you have your choice. Wherever you'd feel more comfortable."

Gil didn't like the idea of sitting at the dead woman's position, but if he didn't do it, he knew Dana would be forced to. So he boldly headed for where Kristin Harcourt had been murdered.

Dana watched him, smiling. There were a lot of different ways to be caring toward someone, and she was finding she liked some of the ways Gilbert Webb chose very much. She turned toward the terminal that used to be Linda Riley's, thinking about the day when she could take off her disguise, and wondering what she would see in his eyes then.

Exasperated at her unprofessional thought, she deliberately forced herself to study the position before her, finding it a cluttered spot with computer reference books stacked in every available inch. She glanced back at the position on the other side of the room.

She couldn't help noticing that Harcourt's work station looked stark and pristine compared to Riley's. They were obviously two very dissimilar personalities. She interpreted a different message to their well-separated positions than Gil had ascribed.

Dana turned to Gil. "I'd like to watch what you do while you're on line, if you don't mind. Is there a way I can observe while sitting at this screen so I'm not staring over your shoulder?"

Gil looked at the cable connections briefly and nodded. "I can put these two in tandem. Then anything typed on one will appear on the other. Just give me a minute."

Dana followed his assured movements as he worked over the cabling. His big hands were deft as they handled the intricate rewiring with confidence and speed. She remembered the feel of his own special current for one stolen moment more.

When he was finished, she lowered herself onto the padded chair and reached over to turn on the monitor. She entered the password from the documentation file and punched out some practice keys. They clicked back at her confidently.

Gil's deep voice gave her a bit of a start when she heard it right next to her shoulder. Apparently he had been watching to be sure her unit would function before trying his own.

"Now that the terminals are in tandem," he said, "only one of us should be typing at a time, otherwise we will be typing over each other's keystrokes."

Dana nodded. "You go ahead. I'm here to watch and learn."

Gil put his hand on her shoulder just for a second before he turned and moved over to the far side of the room where the other position was. Dana felt the lingering warmth of his brief contact. She watched him carefully ease himself into the chair that had so recently belonged to Harcourt, and she wondered what he was thinking.

Gil was trying to tell himself to get his mind back on business and stop dwelling on his preoccupation with Dana—how she sounded, how she felt, how she smelled, how much he wanted to see if her lips were as soft as they seemed. She was counting on him, and he couldn't let her down. He fought for the discipline of concentration.

But a sudden swish of the door being swung open behind them found Gil jumping out of his chair as a rush of adrenaline battered his heart against the wall of his chest.

Chapter Eight

Gil jerked around to see a slim man standing in the doorway. He was short, in his early twenties with dark, wavy hair and a face full of bold red pimples. The young man squinted over at Dana and then back to Gil uneasily.

"Who are you?" he asked in a raspy voice.

Dana twisted in her chair, being careful to hide the data on her monitor before she cleared it. "Who were you looking for?"

Since she had responded, the man turned his attention to her. "Linda Riley."

"Ms. Riley's on a special assignment for Mr. York," Dana said. "We've pushed her out of her nice quiet room, I'm afraid. This is Lief, and I'm Carmody, his assistant."

Gil thought the young man took Dana's quick explanation without too much surprise, but his head kept bobbing back and forth between them, almost as though he was trying to fix their images within his mind. "I'm Lakoff. I work in procurement."

Dana used her sturdy black cane to stand up on her slightly unsteady braced leg and turned to Lakoff, smiling as she held out her hand. "How do you do, Mr. Lakoff?"

Lakoff stepped farther into the room to limply shake her outstretched hand and then walked over to take Gil's. Gil felt the excess moisture of the man's palm and noticed the perspiration that circled the numerous red domes on Lakoff's forehead. There was something about him that looked familiar, but Gil couldn't decide what.

"What are you working on?" Lakoff asked Gil.

Gil tried to sound nonchalant. "Not much of anything yet. Just sort of getting used to things. We should be getting our specific assignment by tomorrow."

Lakoff looked back at Dana as though for confirmation. She nodded, then asked, "Are you in computer programming, too?"

Lakoff's dark head shook. "Naw. They turn me off like a switch. Particularly after a computer screwed up my bank account a few months back. Still haven't been able to get it all straightened out with the right amount of interest and all."

Gil's eyebrows rose. "Really? That's unusual. Most computer banking transactions are much more accurate than human processing."

"Yeah, well, you'll never convince me," Lakoff said. "Everyone keeps complaining about the shape the world's in. They think people make too many mistakes. But they don't know what screwed up is until they put a computer in charge. And they will, too. You wait and see. And when that day comes, all our human programming will be wiped out in one big global reformat."

Gil chuckled. "You might be right. Problem is, if you are, no one will be around to remember you predicted it."

Lakoff had begun to back his way out the door. "Yeah. Well, no credit for what I do. That's the story of my life. I'll be leaving you to it, then. Later."

He swooshed out the door just as abruptly as he had swooshed in. And in the second the door closed behind him, Gil experienced that sensation of familiarity again.

"What do you make of that?" Gil asked, looking over at Dana. She still watched the door as a small frown pierced her forehead.

"I think it's time I had a look around. Lock the door after I leave. There might be others here who don't feel it's necessary to knock. A locksmith will be arriving sometime this morning. If he gets here before I'm back, make sure he gives you the name of Talbot before unlocking the door. I'll knock three times when I return before I let myself in."

She was already at the door. Gil closed the distance between them. "Dana? You'll be careful?"

She was ready to take exception until she saw the tight lines of concern radiating from his lips. "Okay. You, too."

His eyes traveled with her as she limped down the hall, but he found he was really feeling an image of her that materialized inside him, a warm, exciting image that made him feel good.

When she passed out of view, he closed the door and locked it as instructed. Then he approached the computer terminal and sat down. His fingers felt for their positions over the keys and he began to type. Confusion poured through him when he didn't hear the accompanying click of the keys. Then he looked down and noticed the designation of "Quietkey" under the larger "CustomKey" product label. He exhaled in relief.

Everything was all right. Unlike Dana's, his position had one of the silent keyboards. Actually, he preferred the placement of the alphabetical keys on this QuietKey board. As a matter of fact, he had used one just like this at Computech.

With almost no effort, he accessed the WCTS program. The computer screen flashed back at him with its warm and friendly amber light. It felt so good to be entering its familiar world again. He felt like he had come home.

DANA HURRIED DOWN THE sparsely peopled hallway, keeping Lakoff in sight. She followed him to the entrance, where he yelled to the guard he'd be right back and pushed through the glass entry doors.

Three public telephone booths with inadequate human cover stood in gray drizzle under the overcast day about twenty feet away. Still standing within Datacomp's glass doors, Dana watched Lakoff make his way to the first of the booths and reach for some change.

From where she stood, Dana couldn't make out the digits, but she was sure he punched in seven numbers. When he didn't put in any more change, she concluded his call was within the local zone. Why would someone brave a drizzle to make a local call in a public booth when there were company phones everywhere?

Lakoff's conversation was fairly short, just a couple of minutes. Most of the time, he had the back of his head to her. It was a shame. Her deaf mother had taught Dana to lip read even before she had learned to articulate her words. Toward the end of the conversation, she saw Lakoff's head shaking up and down in agreement.

Lakoff hung up and jogged back toward the entrance. Dana unobtrusively shuffled into a nearby ladies' room before he passed through the lobby.

She emerged a moment later to watch him enter a room with a designation above proclaiming it as the Procurement Division.

Dana went back to the security guard to let him know she was stepping out briefly to make some calls.

"It's begun to rain. Why don't you make your call from my phone? Mr. York doesn't mind as long as it's local." The guard lifted his instrument and placed it in front of her on the counter with a big smile on his full face.

Dana smiled back, knowing she didn't want a guard standing in front of her, listening to any of the several calls she was about to place. "Thanks, but they're long-distance."

"WHAT IS IT, SPARR? What did he say?" Thiel asked.

Sparr sat back in his chair and looked up at his assistant, trying to get his thoughts together.

Beside Thiel stood Brine, the bald-headed man who had stayed with the delivery truck outside Datacomp Monday night. He was shorter than the blond giant, Thiel, and had a dark, Dijon-mustard tinge to his thick skin.

Sparr spoke in the direction of his two employees, but not with the expectation that either could provide an answer. "They've made their move. But I don't understand the people involved. I wonder if some higher-up overruled the woman?"

"They're not using Webb?" Thiel asked.

"Doesn't look like it. Wayne York has just 'employed' a new male programmer and his female assistant. Lakoff has seen Webb, and he says this guy isn't him. I thought the woman might be our elusive FBI agent, but he says this one is older and handicapped."

"Who's the programmer?" Thiel asked.

Sparr leaned back in his chair. "I doubt the man's a real programmer. Calls himself Lief or something like that. His description doesn't ring a bell, but his grooming is in keeping with the FBI image. He's probably an agent. If they've assigned the case to him, that means he's playing bodyguard to the woman and she's the real programmer."

"Couldn't the woman and man both be agents?" Thiel asked.

Sparr shook his head. "FBI agents don't work with partners. They generally only bring in extra agents when backup is needed. Besides, the woman is handicapped and the FBI would never employ a handicapped agent. She's got to be a noncombatant employee. That means she's the programmer."

"So where's Webb and the FBI woman agent?" Thiel asked.

Sparr frowned. "You're sure Webb didn't leave with Talbot and that other agent this morning?"

Thiel nodded. "Positive. Brine and I watched them drive away." Thiel turned to the bald man on his left. "Right, Brine?"

"Yeah," Brine said. "Talbot has two rooms reserved. When they left, Thiel and I searched them. Clothes were in the closets, so they must be coming back. Otherwise the rooms were empty."

"And just to be sure we hadn't missed them somewhere else," Thiel said, "I checked the coffee shop. Webb just wasn't in the hotel. He's vanished."

"Just like the woman," Sparr said. "Curious. I wonder how."

"Something else I think you should know," Thiel said. "You remember I told you Leach was following me? Well, it looks like he's gotten himself lost. Haven't seen him since this morning."

Sparr didn't look concerned. "Considering his overall ineptitude, it doesn't surprise me."

"What are we going to do about the man and woman at Datacomp?"

Sparr raised his arms above his head in a relaxed, leisurely stretch. "Lakoff will tail the woman when she leaves Datacomp tonight and find out where she's staying. Then I'll take a look at her. There are less than a handful of programmers in this world who could cause us a problem. From her description, she doesn't sound like she's one of them. However, I'll take a closer look to be sure."

Thiel nodded his understanding. "Do you want one of us to follow the man?"

"No," Sparr said. "If he's an FBI agent as I suspect, he'll be hovering around the woman. If we follow her, we'll always have him in our sights. And a sighted target is always an easy kill."

"I'M STILL HAVING TROUBLE believing we've been located at the Holiday Inn," Jerry Talbot's voice said in Dana's ear. She inched forward in one of the half-sized telephone booths in front of Datacomp, trying to stay out of the rain.

"Me, too. Were you able to take care of Leach?"

"Yes," Talbot said. "Metcalf drove the car quietly away without arousing attention."

"Have you found out anything about who Leach was?"

Dana heard the rustle of papers. "Julius Stanley Leach was a thirty-eight-year-old ex-con, paroled eight months ago from San Quentin. Served fourteen years of a twenty-five-year sentence for second-degree murder. Beat a guy to death because he said he cheated him in a card game. He had a couple of other priors for assault."

"Any local employment, friends?"

"His parole officer said he's been employed by a local house painter. I drove over and checked the guy out. He was drinking heavily even this early in the morning, and he gave me some pretty vague answers. I think he's been paid to lie about Leach working for him. Given time, I might get him to talk straight."

"Time is one thing I don't think we have. Did you learn anything about an E. Thiel?"

"I verified that he was registered at the same Holiday Inn where we stayed last night, but other than that, I haven't been able to learn much. I'll keep on it, though."

"Thanks, Talbot. Any ideas about how we were found there?"

"Only thing I can think of is someone followed Metcalf or me from Professional Properties," Talbot said.

"But the only way they would know to go there was if they saw you around Webb's cabin," Dana said. "Did anyone seem inquisitive about where you stashed the Jeep?"

"Just my wife. It's in an old shed we've got in the backyard."

Dana shook her head. "Obviously no possibility there. Did you see anyone when you picked Webb up at the cabin?"

"I didn't notice anyone," Talbot said. "Of course, I wasn't really looking."

Dana bit her lip in growing frustration. "It doesn't seem possible that they could have located Webb so quickly, but they must have. And the only way was through the Jeep's registration.''

Talbot didn't sound convinced. "But how could they check on a vehicle registration so fast?"

"Law-enforcement help. A friend on the inside."

Talbot's voice held a twinge of defeat. "I can alert my contacts at the precincts, but digging out that kind of an informant takes time. And even beginning an investigation of police-department personnel might alert the mole. Should we take a chance?"

Dana found herself shaking her head as though Talbot could see her. "No. Not now. Our poking around might lead them to us. I feel confident Harcourt's murder was not a planned affair."

"I'm not sure I follow," Talbot said.

"Whoever killed Harcourt obviously left Datacomp to report to someone that the woman had been killed. That person must have decided the murder had to be covered up, so the silver-haired man was sent to do it. Otherwise it would have been done right away."

"Yes, I see. And being so eager to cover up the death, you can be sure they're now just as eager to get hold of you."

"I know, Talbot. I'm sorry about the Jeep-registration angle. My error. I should have anticipated that possibility."

"None of us is clairvoyant. You'd better let Metcalf and me stay close from now on. We'll keep the rooms at the Holiday Inn just in case they're being watched. I'll get our stuff switched over to adjoining rooms at the Hyatt. It's right off Market."

"Put Webb in the middle room."

"Right. Anything else?"

"What about the company that owned the black Cadillac?"

"They reported it stolen over this last weekend."

"That's convenient. Do the police have the report?"

"Yes. Doesn't look like the company personnel were involved."

"Maybe," Dana said. "Still, if there is an inside contact at the police, a stolen-car report wouldn't be that difficult to dummy up. What did you learn about the company?"

"CustomKey? Not a whole lot. It's a relatively small California firm specializing in peripheral computer equipment."

"Peripheral computer equipment?" Dana repeated. "Like what?"

"They make keyboards to fit any desired specifications."

"You mean they'll put the keys on the board anywhere the customer wants?" Dana asked.

"Yes. There are a lot of people unhappy about the one-hundred-and-one key enhanced keyboard with the separate number pad because it squeezes all the alphabetical keys to the left side. They give a person who types all day a backache by making them constantly lean to the left," Talbot said.

"So CustomKey will design a keyboard with the alphabetical section in the middle of the keyboard to ease text typing?"

"Or any other configuration that a customer may require. Their most popular model balances the alphabetical keys in the middle and has the added feature of being absolutely silent so as not to disturb others in the office."

"Are they getting a lot of orders for these custom keyboards?" Dana asked.

"I'm not sure. I've yet to run down their sales figures. Frankly, it's been hard to even find out who owns this company. Its stock is privately held."

"Are they located outside California?"

"No. They've got only one office location, an entire floor of the Shaklee Building on Market."

"That's in the heart of the financial district, isn't it?"

"Yes, as a matter of fact," Talbot said. "The tone of your voice says that bothers you?"

"Well, I think it's rather expensive lease space for so new a company. Their venture capital must be substantial. Can you find out where it's coming from?"

"With some time."

"Does it have a San Francisco director?" Dana asked.

"Manager. Name of Irwin Vogel."

"What do you know about him?"

"Nothing yet. I only got the other information on CustomKey a few minutes ago. Are you sure this is worth pursuing?"

"Yes. They're a company that deals with computers."

"Only keyboards."

"Still computer related," Dana said. "I don't believe it's a coincidence. The silver-haired man I've described to you is not the car-thief type. I just can't swallow CustomKey's claim that the Cadillac was stolen. I think it more likely that someone who works for them is lying and tied in to the business at Datacomp Monday night."

"Okay, I see your point," Talbot said. "We'll take a good, close look at CustomKey, including its board of directors and financial arrangements. Anything else?"

"Yes," Dana said. "Any sign yet of Kristin Harcourt's body or the whereabouts of the real Gordon Mercer?"

"Not a trace of either. Or their cars. Mrs. Mercer has filed a missing-persons report, but local law enforcement isn't taking it seriously."

Dana bit her lip. "Damn. We've got to find these creeps, Talbot. I don't like the idea of a wife having to wait for her husband's body to float to the top of the bay."

"You think they've killed him, too?"

Dana exhaled, trying to ease some of the tension in her spine. "This silver-haired man is very thorough. I can't see he'd think there was any advantage to keeping the guard alive. Which reminds me, I need you to check up on a guy working at Datacomp called Lakoff."

"What do you know about him?" Talbot asked.

"He's in the procurement division, somewhere in his early twenties. In addition to a complete background check, I want him followed when he leaves Datacomp tonight. I'm going to drop in on York now for Lakoff's personnel file. I'll call you back with his Social Security number and other particulars."

"You think this guy Lakoff might have a part in this business?" Talbot asked.

"Yes, although his role may be just a minor one. Still, even the bit players sometimes exchange dialogue with the stars. Let's hope that holds true for our little drama."

"THE FBI? I DON'T LIKE this, Sparr. You were supposed to be my insurance against this sort of thing," Vogel said as he propelled his large frame toward Sparr's office window, seeming to prefer to watch the indefinite gray sky to the determined and confident face of the man who sat so at ease in his desk chair.

"Insurance only works in cases of accidents," Sparr's deep voice said. "Hiring Leach was a conscious move on your part."

Vogel turned, a sneer curling his lips. "He's loyal."

Sparr's smooth face did not react. "Dogs generally are."

Vogel turned to face the window once more. He swallowed several times, but Sparr could see the frustration still stuck in his throat.

"You've asked me to come here and listen to this news for some reason," Vogel said. "What do you want?"

Sparr sat back leisurely, as though he had all the time in the world. "I'm confident we're safe until WCTS is ready."

"So?" Vogel asked.

"So nothing goes on forever, Vogel. As soon as WCTS is in place, you'll be leaving the country in order to be in the right position for pulling the strings on this deal. I think it's about time we made the arrangements for the payment of my promised bonus."

Vogel backed away from Sparr in alarm. "What do you know about the deal? How can you possibly know about my plans?"

Sparr shrugged. "It's my job. Tonight is your run-through. After next week, one telephone call and you can demand anything."

Vogel looked caught and a little frightened. His large, sweaty hand grasped the edge of Sparr's desk. "You've been spying on me!"

Sparr almost laughed. "What did you expect? It's what I do for a living. Now relax. You've got nothing to worry about as long as you plan to live up to your promises. You do intend to honor our agreement, don't you?"

Sparr watched Vogel squirm, knowing full well the large man had had no intention of making good on the promised bonus, but was now in no position to do anything else.

"Of course. But—"

Sparr leaned forward in his chair, his relaxed pose suddenly shed as he glared at Vogel's sweating face. "No buts. Have it ready for me tomorrow morning before your little plane trip or you won't have any fingers left to dial up anybody next week. Am I making myself clear?"

Vogel nodded nervously, not seeming able to find his voice. Sparr leaned back in his chair. "And one more thing..."

When Sparr paused, Vogel seemed almost afraid to hear the second condition. He waited, the perspiration pouring off his face.

"Don't involve Leach in this business anymore," Sparr said finally.

Vogel reached across Sparr's desk for a tissue to soak up the unhealthy glow on his face. "What have you done with him?"

Sparr looked over at the nervous man, feeling distinctly uncomfortable at his question. "Nothing yet. Why do you ask?"

The large man's legs didn't seem capable of holding him any longer. He sank heavily into one of Sparr's side chairs. "Return him to me, Sparr. I need Leach to drive the delivery truck to Datacomp tonight. He knows—"

Sparr's voice was calm, belying his racing thoughts. "Are you telling me Leach has disappeared?"

Vogel swallowed, but he couldn't seem to clear his throat. He nodded in reply.

"Since when?" Sparr asked.

"Today," Vogel said. "He was supposed to call me this morning. I tried to get him at his apartment. He didn't answer. He was . . ." Vogel's voice trailed off.

"He was following Thiel," Sparr finished for him. "The last Thiel got a glimpse of him was early this morning. I wonder . . ."

Vogel was perspiring heavily now. He seemed both relieved and newly upset at Sparr's words. "If you don't have him, where is he?"

Sparr's mind raced. "The FBI woman, Vogel. She must have been there at the Holiday Inn, after all. Only she could have recognized Leach. She must have had him picked up."

"Picked up? You mean the Feds have Leach?"

Sparr leaned forward in his chair, his forehead unfurrowed despite the content of his words. "It's a logical reason for his disappearance. Still, if she was there, I wonder why Thiel didn't spot her?"

Vogel didn't seem to have heard Sparr's rhetorical question. He was rubbing his heavy hands together as though he was trying to hold onto something. "Leach'll talk if the Feds go to work on him. Maybe not at first, but with pressure, with promises."

Sparr refocused his attention to the nervous man before him. "Relax, Vogel. Leach's been in the joint. He knows the score. If he's really been taken, he won't answer questions without a lawyer. And without a body, the FBI is going to have difficulty making anything stick. He'll call you, I presume."

Vogel nodded, obviously relieved at Sparr's reassurance. "Yes, of course. That's right. He knows the score. I'll tell him to keep quiet. I'll make it worth his while."

"Then I suggest you stay by the phone and make yourself available," Sparr said as he rose.

Vogel shook his head as another thought seemed to occur to him. "I counted on Leach driving the truck to Datacomp tonight. What am I going to do?"

"I'll give you Brine."

Sparr watched Vogel's flickering eyes. He didn't look too pleased to have one of Sparr's men with him.

Vogel shifted uneasily in his chair as his tone suddenly went on the offensive. "I'll do the driving myself. I thought you were going to find that damn FBI woman and take care of her?"

Sparr's dark eyes deepened even more at Vogel's peevish tone. He leaned back again in his chair. "She's been hiding from me. But she won't be able to hide much longer."

Vogel looked over at him. "You have a plan?"

Sparr nodded. "My error has been trying to find her. What I really need to do is let her find me."

Vogel frowned. "You can't be serious."

Sparr smiled. "Why not? It will be the last thing she does."

Chapter Nine

Gil was so mentally engrossed in his work that when the unexpected shadow crossed his screen, all he had were instincts left for reaction. He swung around and grabbed, tumbling with his intruder to the floor.

Recognition and relief poured through him at once when he found it was Dana he had tackled. She was trying to gasp for the breath he had succeeded in knocking out of her. Her glasses had fallen away, strands of hair had been jerked out of the bun at the back of her head and her face had never seemed so pale. Gil felt his heart being squeezed inside a vise in his chest.

"Dana, I'm so sorry. I thought—"

A strange gurgling sound was coming from her throat. New horror struck at his soul as he circled his arm about her and tried to raise her to a sitting position, aware her body jerked in spasms. Then suddenly, miraculously, she opened her spring-rain eyes and he saw them dancing above the moist smile on her lips.

Confusion immobilized his muscles and his thoughts as he sat there holding her, trying to understand the conflicting messages to his senses. And then in immense relief, he sighed as the strange gurgling sounds and the body spasms finally began to make sense. She was laughing!

"Damn it, Dana. I should drop you right back on this floor for finding this funny," his words said, but his smile, the relief in his voice and the way his arms had tightened about her told her he intended no such thing.

She brought her initial, unrestrained merriment at being so unexpectedly flattened by Gil's powerful arms under control and tried to get her voice to behave. "I'm sorry, too, Gil. But I did knock three times, and I made all the noise I could opening the door. I wasn't trying to sneak up on you."

He nodded. "I was so engrossed, first thing I was aware of was a shadow on my screen. I'm afraid I just reacted."

As her eyes still danced into his, he found himself inhaling the enticing, warm whiff of peppermint on her breath. The fragrance continued to bring back all the tasty memories of their first kiss, and he felt his body responding to the way she felt now in his arms.

Dana finally became aware that Gil was holding her, staring at her. The laughter in her heart shifted swiftly into a new emotion as she saw the warmth of his look, noticing for the first time that he had removed his tinted glasses to work at the computer.

Her quickening pulse told her it wasn't the only change in his appearance. He had taken off his suit jacket, loosened his tie, unbuttoned his collar and rolled up his sleeves. His muscular forearms flexed beneath the forest of reddish hair covering them. He looked very handsome, very male, and the message in his tight hold and in the deepening gold flecks in his hazel eyes made her feel instantly jumpy and excited.

She looked away and put out her hand to locate her fallen glasses. With her other hand she tried to push herself to her feet, but she felt the pressure of his arms keeping her immobile, telling her he was not ready to relinquish his hold.

She knew she was in a dangerous position, but the warmth traveling through her body at his insistence felt very good, and she was so tempted to just relax in the strong arms holding her and to give herself up to the exciting promise she read in his eyes. Then thoughts of reality turned that promise into a threat as she tardily remembered she wasn't supposed to be getting involved with Gil.

With renewed effort, she made the attempt to extricate herself from his arms. He read the changing expression in her eyes and felt disappointed that the initial excitement he had generated in her by his insistence to maintain his hold had been successfully overcome. Reluctantly he helped her up.

Although on her own two feet now and away from Gil's disturbing touch, Dana still couldn't seem to shake the warmth generated by his embrace. For her own peace of mind, she knew she had to get back to business. She replaced the glasses on her nose.

"I began to worry when I saw you so glued to the monitor, Gil. Is everything all right?"

"Fine. I was just totally absorbed. Ever feel that way?" He took a step closer.

Dana stepped away. Gil knew she was uncomfortable, and he knew why. She was fighting the attraction between them, trying to ignore it, maybe even hoping it would go away. But he didn't want it to go away. Since she had kissed him on that cliff ledge in the park, he had never felt so alive. She was the focus of that feeling, its center around which hope had evolved. He was not willing to let that feeling or her go. He smiled at her knowingly.

Dana saw his smile and looked away, concentrating on the inanimate objects in the room, trying to allow her mind to break away from the racing emotions that invaded it. She selected the lighted computer screen in front of his chair and the reams of printouts sitting on the table beside it.

"I see you've been working hard. It's just as well I interrupted. It's time you had a break."

Gil felt surprised at the suggestion. "A break? Already?"

"It's twelve-thirty," she said.

Gil checked his watch in disbelief. "You're right. Well, that just goes to show you how absorbed I become. Most of the time, you could set a bomb off next to me and I wouldn't flinch."

Dana smiled. "A shadow across your screen seems to get a rise out of you, though."

He grinned. "I am sorry. For knocking you down, that is."

Dana found herself flushing under the purposeful stare of Gil's eyes. She looked away and quickly plunged into a subject change, hearing the small quiver in her voice with irritation. "What have you learned about the WCTS program?"

Before Gil could answer, a sudden knock at the door caused them both to start. Dana recovered first. Gil watched her slip her right hand into her shoulder bag as she went to the door. After ensuring it was the locksmith, she briefly discussed what he was to do.

Gil saw the man nod and heard him say something about going back to his truck for some supplies. Dana turned back to Gil as soon as the locksmith had left.

"Have you found anything?" she asked.

"No data shadows. But I understand the logic behind the programming after reviewing the design parameters and running some input data to see how it's processed."

"And?" Dana prompted.

"And it's taken most of this morning to run a hardcopy of the complete listing of the program on that high-speed laser printer over there. The next step is establishing my own personal variation on a checksum formula against the programming to see if I can monitor changes in the files."

"A checksum formula?" Dana asked. "How is that done?"

"I assign a numerical value to each byte in the current programming. If the answer is, say three hundred, then all subsequent runnings of the checksum formula should also be three hundred."

"And if a subsequent running of the checksum formula is something other than three hundred?" Dana asked.

"Then I'll know the software program has been changed. I also have a checksum on each line and will be able to pinpoint where the data has been changed."

Dana frowned. "That will tell you if the programming is altered in the future. What if the programming has already been altered?"

Gil shrugged. "First I need to establish this checksum formula to be sure that I continue to work with unchanged data."

"How long will it take?"

"I've already written another program to convert the data in WCTS into checksum. I can run it against WCTS anytime."

"Why don't you start it now?" Dana said as the locksmith returned. "It can be running while we go grab some lunch."

Gil nodded and moved over to the terminal and began the checksum program. Then he refastened his collar, adjusted his tie, slipped into his suit jacket and replaced the tinted glasses on his nose.

All the time, Dana watched the effortless sensuality in every movement of his muscular, well-conditioned body and felt the heat rising into her neck. In the second before he looked over at her again, she glanced away, afraid her thoughts might be too plain.

"We should be on our way to the employee cafeteria," she said. "I'm told they'll stop serving in a few minutes."

He gestured for her to precede him through the doorway. "Where have you been all this time?"

"I've been checking on our inquisitive visitor."

Gil felt confused. "That guy, Lakoff? Seemed harmless enough to me. Why would you be checking on him?"

"The door to the WCTS room was closed. He didn't knock."

Gil shrugged. "So he obviously knew Harcourt or Riley personally. What's suspicious about that?"

"If he knew Harcourt that well, why didn't he know she was out ill?"

"He said he had come to see Riley, didn't he?"

"Yes, but remember, WCTS is supposed to have been a confidential program, and the room where the programming was taking place was supposed to have been off limits to unauthorized employees. If this Lakoff knew Riley well enough to barge in without knocking, he should have also known that Wayne York had reassigned her to another job and another desk late yesterday afternoon."

"Maybe he hadn't had a chance to talk with her."

Dana shrugged. "Maybe. We'll check it out."

"We will?" Gil asked.

"Yes. We're going to join Linda Riley for lunch and find out what she might have told Lakoff."

Gil thought about Dana's words as he picked up a tray and proceeded through the cafeteria line. "If you don't think he came by to see Harcourt or Riley, why did Lakoff come barging in?"

"He wanted to find out who we were and what we were doing."

"Just nosy?" Gil asked.

Dana shook her head. "I think someone sent him. As soon as Lakoff left this room, he hurried outside to make a call. I think that call was to report who and what he had seen. Employees are allowed to use company phones for personal calls. Privacy is the only logical explanation for using a phone outside the building."

Gil nodded. "That does seem to make his behavior suspect."

"He did tell the truth about one thing, however."

"What was that?" Gil asked.

"Well, after a couple of calls, I found out that five months ago, there was a computer banking mix-up that caused an error on Larry Lakoff's savings account. Somehow, the computer dropped a zero on a deposit he made."

"Five months ago? Wasn't that around the same time Datacomp got the WCTS software assignment?"

Dana smiled. "Yes. Good connection, Gil."

Gil smiled, feeling pleased for her small compliment. "How much of a deposit was involved?"

"Nine hundred dollars was credited to his account."

"But if nine hundred dollars was credited and a zero had been dropped, that means the deposit should have been nine thousand dollars."

Dana picked up a dish of peas and carrots for her tray. "Yes. And he's made four more nine-thousand-dollar deposits since. No apparent source. And the money was all in cash."

Gil whistled as he did a quick mental calculation. "That's a total of forty-five thousand dollars!"

Dana nodded. "Not exactly chicken feed. The nine-thousand-dollar increments are important, too. If he had deposited ten thousand, all sorts of people would have become interested."

"How do you mean?" Gil asked.

"Well, in order to trace drug money, large cash transactions are reported by banks to the authorities so drug-enforcement officers can investigate those who might be dealers. Apparently, Larry Lakoff knows ten thousand dollars is the reporting point, which is why he's made deposits of lesser amounts over several months."

"But you don't think he's involved in drugs?"

"No, I think he's involved in Harcourt's death and the infiltration of WCTS. Forty-five thousand dollars seems too large a payoff to an informant. I would say Larry Lakoff is not exactly a bit player in this little drama of ours."

"How do you think he's involved?"

"I'm not sure yet. I intend to find out, however."

Gil asked for some mashed potatoes from the server behind the buffet before turning back to Dana. "What ideas do you have?"

Dana put some baked whitefish with lemon sauce on her tray. "He could be providing access to the Datacomp facility."

"You think he might be letting someone into the computer room to make the changes? Maybe Kristin Harcourt walked in on them and that's why she was killed?"

Dana pursed her lips together in thought. "I don't think so. I found Harcourt's body in front of her terminal as entries were being made in a program flashing away on her screen. It looked a lot more like someone walked in on her than vice versa."

Gil picked up his plate of roast beef and set it on his tray, but his thoughts were on the scene Dana had just described of the murder. "What do you mean entries were being made—"

Dana put a cautioning hand on Gil's arm as some other people began to get close in the line. He understood that her touch meant he'd better hold his questions until later.

They took their trays and headed in the direction of the dining room separated into smoking and nonsmoking sections. "Do you know what Linda Riley looks like?" Gil asked as his eyes scanned the large numbers of people sitting at the tables.

"I see her," Dana said, nodding her head. She headed them in the direction of a corner table near a window in the nonsmoking section. As soon as Gil saw the lone woman sitting there, he could understand how Dana had recognized her.

She was exceedingly overweight, taking up nearly two of the seats at the small table. She looked up as they approached, shiny black curls surrounding a pink, smooth face. She watched them with dark eyes wedged within the ample folds of her puffy eyelids.

"May we share your table?" Dana asked.

The large woman gestured toward the empty chairs in way of invitation. Dana held out her hand.

"I'm Carmody. This is Lief."

"Riley," the woman said, giving Dana's hand a brief shake. "But then, since you're the new programmers in the special computer room, you knew my name already, didn't you?"

Dana watched the woman's dark, languid eyes, but they gave nothing away. "Did Wayne York mention us?"

Linda shook her head. "Not by name."

"Then how did you know who we were?" Gil asked.

Linda concentrated on buttering her corn, not looking at him. "There are lots of empty places in this section. I have to be the reason you picked this table."

Gil read Dana's nod at Linda's explanation and realized she was satisfied with it. He still felt confused, however.

"There aren't any completely free tables," Gil said. "Every one has at least one person sitting at it. Why should you think we purposely picked yours?"

Linda's eyes didn't waver. "People seek out others who resemble them when they're among strangers. There are at least three tables in this area alone that contain a man and woman of your approximate age and physical appearance. The natural thing for you to have done would have been to select one of those tables."

She paused for a moment to shake some salt over her cob of corn. "Now, if Ms. Carmody here had sat down by herself, I wouldn't have thought it unusual. Just like me, she carries around a physical handicap. Hers is a bad leg. Mine is two hundred extra pounds. And we're both female. All cloning attributes. But you are a male without any sign of a physical problem. Therefore, your presence at my table is...unusual."

Having said her piece, Linda attacked her buttered and salted corn on the cob with noisy relish.

Gil watched her, finding it curious he had never thought about the psychology of such a situation before. Dana had quietly begun to eat her lunch, and he followed her lead. She seemed to understand Linda Riley's explanation even before the woman gave it. Maybe being handicapped gave her the edge in understanding.

Dana felt Linda Riley's eyes studying her as she finished her lunch. When she finally sat back and looked directly at the woman, their eyes met in mutual appraisement.

"You're looking for something wrong, aren't you?" Linda asked.

Knowing the woman before her was no dummy, Dana had half expected the question. Still, it took her a moment to school her voice into nonchalance. "Why did you think so?"

Linda shrugged. "I knew something was wrong when Kristin kept me out of the computer room Monday morning. What's happened?"

Dana tried to select her words carefully. "We're here to check everything out now that the program is ready to go."

Linda cocked her head to one side. "Ready to go? Who told you the program was ready to go?"

Dana tried to keep her expression bland. "You mean it's not?"

"Not without a thorough testing," Linda said. "I told Kristin that. I wish for once she had listened to me."

Dana leaned across the table slightly, as though she was ready for a confidence. "Is Kristin hard to work with?"

Linda shrugged. "Give them a title of supervisor and selective deafness soon follows. The term 'subordinate' becomes synonymous with 'stupid.' They think somehow their supervising position gives them some divine intelligence the rest of us don't possess."

"You and Kristin were once colleagues?" Dana asked.

"Yeah," Linda said. "York came to us one day and asked us if we thought WCTS could be enhanced to perform more functions. We told him if he'd give us a set of parameters, we'd give it a try. He did, and after a couple of weeks, we told him the changes were feasible."

"Did both you and Kristin work on the basic WCTS and the enhancements?" Dana asked.

Linda looked at Dana a moment before answering. "I handled the enhancements. When York found out they were feasible, he turned around and promoted Kristin to supervisor and put her in charge of completing them. I was her 'staff.'"

From the FBI background investigative report, Dana knew the answer to the question she was about to ask, but she was curious how Linda would respond, so she asked it anyway. "Was Kristin promoted over you because she was more qualified?"

The expression didn't change in Linda's dark eyes. "I have a B.S. degree in Computer Science. Kristin took one night-school computer course at a community college. I'm thirty-three and I've been developing software for Data-comp seven years. Kristin is twenty-nine and has been with them a year and a half. I'm five-six and weigh three hundred and twenty pounds. Kristin is five-seven and weighs one hundred and twenty-five pounds. Of course that last, ah, qualification proved the most important to Wayne York."

Dana knew Linda's explanation dripped with intellectual sarcasm. "Do you resent Kristin's promotion?"

Linda reached for a handful of potato chips before answering. "Resentment doesn't change a thing. Kristin took her opportunity when it came, and she's worked long hours to try to stay on top of things."

"Was Larry happy for Kristin?" Dana asked.

Dana watched something like confusion pass through Linda's dark eyes. "You talking about Kristin's cousin, Larry Lakoff?"

Dana took the news with a straight face, even though learning Lakoff was Harcourt's cousin had come as a big surprise. That fact hadn't come out in the background report. Dana began to wonder what else had been missed. "Yes, that's the Larry I mean."

Linda shrugged. "I suppose he liked the idea of his cousin getting a plum assignment like WCTS. He came to work at Datacomp soon after her promotion. She helped him get the job. Said he was a distant cousin who she'd just met herself. She didn't get along with her mother, and I think she was looking for some family to love. We weren't supposed to discuss WCTS with anyone, of course, but I'm sure Kristin mentioned something to Larry about it. No doubt she regretted it later."

"Why do you say that?" Dana asked.

"Oh, he proved to be a real pest, hanging around the WCTS computer room. We finally had to lock the door to keep him out."

"You didn't normally lock the door?" Dana asked.

"No. Too much of a bother with one of us coming or going. We only resorted to it when both of us were going out. But WCTS was still secure. One of us was always there when the door was unlocked. Besides, nobody knew about the defense contract but York, Kristin, me and, unofficially, Larry. If we had made a big deal of locking the door, it would have drawn the attention we were trying to avoid."

"But you did eventually lock the door?" Dana said.

"Like I said, when Larry became too much of a pest."

"Did Larry ask questions about WCTS?" Dana asked.

Linda shook her head. "He said he didn't know anything about computers except for the menu prompts his job in procurement forced him to respond to."

"Then why was he in the WCTS room?" Dana asked.

Linda shrugged. "I think it was the idea there was something exciting going on that he wasn't supposed to know or talk about. His emotional growth was arrested somewhere in early adolescence."

"Do you get along with Larry?" Dana asked.

Linda looked at her strangely. "I hardly know him."

"Why did he come looking for you this morning?"

"Looking for me? You must be mistaken. He had to have been looking for Kristin."

"He didn't know his cousin was out ill?" Dana asked.

Linda frowned. "Well, yes. I told him yesterday when I was collecting my things after York reassigned me."

"Did you also tell Larry about your reassignment?"

"Yes. He noticed I was packing up a box and asked me where I was going."

"But you expected to move back," Dana said. "That's why you left so much of your stuff."

Linda shrugged. "All right. I thought I'd be coming back. As a matter of fact, I know I will. No matter what York says, I'm the one needed to test out WCTS, particularly since Kristin is obviously going to be out sick past our due date. Meaning no disrespect to you two, I know the software inside and out, and if there's a system malfunction, I could recognize, locate and correct it much faster."

Dana was beginning to see the eager gleam behind the practiced languid look in Linda Riley's eyes. But did Linda assume the uncaring facade to hide the hurt of disappointment or was it to hide something else? Dana couldn't decide about the programmer and that indecision felt very uncomfortable.

"I appreciate your offer to help, Linda. Hopefully, we won't be finding a system malfunction. It's been good to talk to you."

Dana got to her feet, and Gil rose with her, reaching over to carry her empty tray with his own.

"Something's wrong, isn't it?" Linda asked, suddenly leaning across the table toward Dana. "WCTS has failed, hasn't it?"

"Why would you say that, Linda?"

Linda's dark eyes studied Dana's face carefully, as though they were looking for some sign. "Something upset Kristin. I could hear it in her voice Monday morning when she told me to go back to my old desk and not come into the WCTS computer room for a while. It's why you've come early, isn't it? There's a bug or... something?"

Dana kept control over her expression. "We'll check everything out, Linda. Now I'm sure I don't have to caution you to be discreet about this conversation, do I?"

Dana smiled, then quickly limped away, leaning on her cane, Gil at her side, aware that Linda Riley still watched her with a disturbed frown on her face.

"She's worried, isn't she?" Gil asked.

Dana nodded. "But is it because something's wrong with WCTS, or is it because she thinks we've found something wrong with WCTS?"

"You mean she might be worried because a virus she's planted has been found?" Gil asked.

Dana nodded as she led the way out of the cafeteria. "It could be that. Or it could be she's just concerned that a project she's been working on has soured. Difficult to tell which at this point."

Gil shrugged. "Well, one thing is for sure. You were right about Larry Lakoff. He knew neither Kristin nor Linda was supposed to be in the WCTS computer room this morning. Do you think it's significant that he became an employee only after his cousin was assigned the WCTS project?"

"Yes, Gil, I do. And I'm concerned about his status as cousin to Kristin. As I told you before, we did background checks on Kristin, Linda and York before the WCTS project was awarded to Datacomp. None had other family members working at Datacomp then. I don't like the idea of this cousin who materialized.''

Gil reflected on their conversation with Linda. He knew the question he was about to ask might normally be indelicate, but since he was finding Dana's leg didn't bother him, he found he could ask his question easily. "You seem to understand Linda Riley better than I," he said. "Is it because, as she said, you have handicaps?"

Dana knew Gil was referring to Linda's deduction about their selecting her table. She felt rather good that Gil brought it up. People who could discuss another person's handicap so openly were generally undisturbed by it. She liked that quality in him.

"Gil, it's not personal experience. FBI psychological training discusses such phenomena. It stems from an innate need for acceptance. We all feel we'll be more readily accepted by those who resemble us than by those who don't. Special agents are exposed to such concepts."

"What about the not-so-special agents?" Gil asked.

Dana smiled. "All FBI agents are called 'special agents.' And much of our casework involves the psychodrama of interviewing techniques. We learn it in the classroom at Quantico."

"Quantico?" Gil repeated.

"Quantico, Virginia, where the FBI Academy is located. We receive fifteen weeks of basic training there."

"Basic training? Like a boot camp?" Gil asked.

Dana smiled. "Now that you mention it, I would say there are definite similarities. What did you think about Linda Riley's comments concerning WCTS?"

"I think she's a lot smarter than York led us to believe. Was that information she gave us about her education and background and that of Kristin's correct?"

Dana nodded. "It's obvious she's aware York's prejudice made him select Kristin over her. I'm beginning to wonder just how angry such a decision might have made her."

"Do you think she may have been lying when she said resentment didn't solve anything?" Gil asked.

"Not necessarily," Dana said. "She may not be wasting her time on resentment. She may be focusing it all on revenge."

Gil nodded as they approached the computer room. The locksmith was just finishing up. He demonstrated the new number-coded lock and Dana selected some random digits as their number code. As soon as the man had left she and Gil entered the room and locked it.

"How do you know you can trust that locksmith?" Gil asked.

Dana shrugged as she removed her tinted glasses to rub the small indentations they had made on either side of her nose. She had never worn glasses before and the pressure bothered her. "He's FBI. Don't worry. I'm not taking any chances on endangering my wizard."

She smiled up at him, and Gil found himself looking again into the clear gray of her eyes. His vague memories of Monday night drew into sharp focus. This was how he remembered her eyes, her face, the delicate bone structure beneath the porcelain whiteness of her skin. He ached to touch her again, to feel her touch him and not draw away.

Dana's eyes locked with Gil's, and what she saw in the liquid-gold light there caused her to draw a sharp breath. His eyes were caressing her face.

Dana stepped back, away from his hands, away from the look in his eyes. His hand shot out, circling her wrist in a warm embrace.

"Dana, I—"

A sudden whine of the telephone caused them both to jump apart. Dana stared at the instrument with a mixture of relief and regret. She extricated herself from Gil, and reached for the phone. After she identified herself, she just listened for several minutes.

Gil watched the rain in her eyes freeze. She mumbled something into the mouthpiece and replaced the receiver in the base.

Gil moved to her side and put his arm around her before he even realized what he was doing. "Dana, what is it?"

She looked up at him dully for a minute. Then as her vision cleared and she realized his arm was about her, she blinked and deliberately put on her glasses again, as though needing to reestablish some barrier between them. Her voice sounded strained as she slipped out of his encircling arm.

She exhaled before speaking. "I drove a blue MR2 off a cliff Monday night up in the Golden Gate National Recreation Area. It's been found."

Gil felt his heart begin to race as he clearly saw the small lines of fright circle about her mouth. "Dana, why is this car's discovery important?"

"Its location was accurately pinpointed by an anonymous caller. They found a note taped to the steering wheel."

Gil felt a sick foreboding. "What did this note say?"

Dana's voice was unsteady as she relayed the message. "It said, 'I'm waiting. If you want me, you'll have to come get me.'"

Chapter Ten

Gil wrapped his arms around her protectively. "Dana, tell me about Monday night."

Dana sighed in Gil's arms, feeling no desire to leave them. "I was being chased. I sent the car off a cliff, hoping my pursuers would think I had gone with it. They weren't fooled. Afterward, I was on foot, running away from them when I came across your Jeep."

Gil heard her words and wondered why he hadn't thought about how she had gotten into the park before now. Suddenly, he realized there were a lot of things he hadn't thought through until now. He decided he'd better make up for lost time. "Is this note from the men who chased you? Are they trying to tell you they know who you are?"

Dana felt the initial panic from the message easing as she considered its meaning. "He must know I'm FBI."

"How?" Gil asked.

"When Talbot came to your cabin, he must have been watching. Finding out Talbot's an agent wouldn't have been that difficult. But although he must realize I'm an agent, he can't know my name, otherwise he wouldn't have sent that note to try to flush me into the open."

"Him?" Gil asked. "You use that pronoun in its singular form. Who specifically are you talking about?"

Dana looked up at Gil's worried frown and wished now she had kept the news about the car and the note to herself. Gently, she eased herself out of his encircling arms. "I can handle it."

Gil took a gentle but firm hold of her arm again. "We're in this together, Dana. Tell me everything just as you'd want to be told."

Dana had to admit he had a point. She'd want to know what she was up against if she were in his shoes. She nodded in acquiescence as she extricated her hand from his.

"Okay, Gil. Here it is. The unadulterated story." She described the three men she had seen at Datacomp Monday night and the details of their chase.

Gil was quiet for several moments after she had finished, trying to contain a set of boiling emotions that were pressing to escape beneath the lid of his control. When he finally spoke, he found he had not been entirely successful.

"For God's sake, Dana, how could your superiors let you be exposed to such danger?"

Dana ground her teeth in growing anger. The old argument was back again. "I'm an FBI agent, damn it! This is my job."

Gil shook his head in frustration. "But this silver-haired man has seen you! You're a target!"

"He didn't get a good look at me. I'd be very surprised if he recognized me when we meet again."

"You'd be more than just very surprised, Dana. You'd be dead!"

Dana felt the blood rising in her neck. Her next words came through clenched teeth. "Damn it, why do you keep making me say it? I can defend myself! Besides, I'm the only one who can recognize this man. I have to take the chance."

Dana watched Gil's eyes flicker toward her leg brace and realized that perhaps she had played her part of the handicapped woman too well.

"Gil, you're going to have to trust me. I know what I'm doing."

He shook his head. He knew he wasn't getting through, but that didn't keep him from continuing to try. "Dana, this man is so unafraid, he's sending you notes."

Dana exhaled, trying to get her anger under control. "His note was a mistake."

Gil heard the new note in her voice. "What do you mean?"

"He would only have sent that note if he was worried about not being able to locate me. He wants me to actively seek him out so he can get a shot at me. By refusing to accept his challenge, I will force him to come after me more aggressively."

"I'm supposed to rejoice at this news?"

Dana felt new licks of irritation at the sarcasm in his tone. "You're supposed to be remembering that your job is computers and mine is protection."

He looked at her for a moment, feeling more than anxious for her safety now that he knew this silver-haired man stalked her. There was something about the way she had described him that told Gil Dana was frightened, too, no matter how much bravado she wore for his sake. He reached for her hand, trying to make contact.

"Dana, please. Get out of this. Let Talbot or Metcalf stay with me while I figure out what's happened to WCTS. For my sake, turn that lovely tail and run. Please."

Dana bit back the bitterness his words caused. "Gil, I asked you once to look past this outward form to the brains and determination contained within. I see now that I asked too much."

Gil felt her words like a slap.

She snatched her hand away and circled over to the computer terminal. "It's time to get back to work."

Gil nodded without speaking. He wanted her beside him, not cut off from his work, no matter how foolish she was.

He grabbed his tie and tried to straighten it when what he really wanted to grab and straighten out was Dana. "Okay, the checksum program should be complete. I'd like to compare the WCTS printout against the system design, line-by-line. You could help by reading the printout to me."

Dana nodded. "How long will this take?"

"Hours, probably. You'll have to sing out when you get tired."

She studied his crooked tie as he started shifting the printouts on his desk, and she felt her anger dissolving into a mushy lump in her chest. When he looked up, she was smiling. "What would you like to hear?"

Gil didn't miss the smile or her attempt to mend their communication break. He was finding her quick changes from anger to laughter both exasperating and endearing. He exhaled heavily. "Bach's Concerto No. 2 would be nice."

SPARR SAT BACK IN HIS chair, looking out the window, but not really paying attention to the muted lights of the overcast evening sky as Thiel gave his verbal report and Brine shifted restlessly in his chair. "So the MR2 was billed to an L. Sargentich at the FBI?"

"Right," Thiel said. "It was picked up at the San Francisco International Airport around five-fifteen Monday afternoon."

Sparr stroked a silver sideburn. "So she isn't local. That explains why she didn't know the area. And why I've never heard of her. Is this all your inside source could tell you, Thiel?"

"It's all he knows, and probably all he's going to know. When news of the car was released by park security, the FBI swarmed all over the place, told the local police to stay out of it."

Sparr nodded and moved forward in his chair. "I didn't think they'd want the regular police messing up their evidence. They're proud when it comes to their laboratory techniques.''

Thiel nervously stroked his well-trimmed beard. ''Are you sure this is what you want?''

Sparr's smooth face lifted into a small smile. ''They're not going to find anything in the car or the note to lead them to me. Even if she has the sense to hold back now, soon she'll see she has no choice but to come for me. And then—''

The telephone whined on Sparr's desk. He reached for it, answering on the first ring.

''It's after six and they're still there,'' Lakoff's raspy voice said into Sparr's ear without the preliminary of a hello.

''You're calling from the pay phone in front of Data-comp?''

''Yeah. I'm not going to be able to follow the woman. I promised Vogel I'd meet him. Things got left hanging Monday night, and Vogel thought he'd play it safe by not bringing the van by Datacomp last night. I've got things to do.''

''Stay there until I send Brine to relieve you. When you see a brown Chrysler LeBaron pull in the lot, you can leave.''

''Yeah, well, tell him to hurry. My time's expensive.''

Sparr heard the changed note in Lakoff's voice as well as his words. ''What is your problem?''

''Look, my deal is with Vogel. I don't work for you.''

Sparr leaned back in his chair, his right index finger pressing on his upper lip to relieve the sudden itching along his gums.

''Isn't your cut compensating you for your coopera-tion?''

Lakoff's voice was slightly sarcastic. ''For cooperation. Not for being set up as a patsy. As soon as I leave here to-night, Larry Lakoff is going to disappear.''

Sparr sat forward in his chair. ''What is this all about?''

"Don't play innocent with me," Lakoff said. "Vogel told me you killed Harcourt. Guess what cousin the cops are going to pick up?"

Sparr relaxed back into his chair now that he understood the situation. "Calm down. Leach killed Harcourt at Vogel's direction. So show your bad temper to Vogel, not me. Now, Brine will be there in forty minutes. Take off when you see him, not before."

Sparr slammed the phone down without waiting for a response. He looked over at the bald, mustard-skinned man. "You heard?"

Brine nodded as he removed the pistol from the holster strapped around his thick chest, releasing the magazine in a move that was designed to check to see if the clip was fully loaded. He looked satisfied as he shoved the clip back into position and replaced his pistol in its holster. "Has Lakoff lost his nerve?"

Sparr shrugged. "Vogel told him we killed Harcourt."

"Why?" Brine asked.

"Because Vogel's an unmarked poisonous snake. He'll lull Lakoff into a false sense of security just before he strikes."

Brine frowned. "And expect us to clean up the mess?"

Sparr shook his head. "I doubt Vogel thinks we'll even be around by then. I intend to surprise him, however. Now, I want you to follow the woman out of Datacomp. Let me know where she's staying. I'll have to arrange to get a look at her up close."

Brine got up and headed for the door.

"Where do you want me?" Thiel asked.

"Watch the rooms those FBI agents are in at the Holiday Inn," Sparr said. "You might pick up a lead to Webb or the woman."

"And if I find them?" Thiel asked.

"Then bring them to me."

"Undamaged?"

"At this point," Sparr said, "I'm not feeling too particular."

"I DON'T UNDERSTAND IT," Gil said.

"There's nothing here that shouldn't be, is there?" Dana asked, retrieving some of the printouts that had fallen on the floor.

"That isn't what's bothering me."

"What is?" she asked, straightening up with the newly folded printouts in her hands.

Gil realized she must be very tired. He sure was after all these hours of concentrated, detailed review. Still, she had endured the tedious work without a word of complaint. He turned back to his place in the voluminous stack of computer language and scratched at the stubble collecting on his chin. He'd worn a beard for so long that the sharp red whiskers were a novelty to his fingertips.

"Didn't York tell us WCTS was completed?" Gil asked.

"Yes. And Linda Riley said it was ready for testing. What's bothering you?"

"This program isn't finished. Look at this branch. And this one. They drop off into nowhere."

Dana leaned over Gil's shoulder, following his pointing fingers. As always, Gil detected her special hot-peppermint scent. It worked on him like an exciting, seductive perfume.

"Could they be the points of interface with other Defense Department systems?" Dana asked.

"No," Gil said, giving himself a mental shake. "Those points are elsewhere in the programming. See? Here and here and there."

"Is there a problem in the logic?" Dana asked.

"No, it's pretty straightforward. Why would Harcourt and Riley both claim WCTS was finished when it obviously isn't?"

Dana shook her head. "Doesn't make much sense."

Gil yawned and stretched. "Something's wrong, but I'm brain dead for the rest of tonight. It's almost eight. Let's get dinner."

Dana stood up, feeling a pinch of pain along her spine after the long hours of bending over the computer print-outs. "I need to stop by our new hotel to freshen up first."

Gil nodded as he followed Dana out of the computer room. "I see. We had to change hotels because that guy, Leach, found us at the Holiday Inn."

From the tone of Gil's voice, Dana could tell that Gil's concern over their safety, which had been effectively put aside over the past hours of concentrated work, was now once again in the fore. His next question was more pointed.

"What's going to happen to Leach's body?"

"His prison files indicate his next of kin—" Dana began.

"He was a convict?" Gil interrupted.

"An ex-convict," Dana said, and proceeded to give Gil Leach's background. "Anyway, as I was saying, his prison files show no living relatives. We're not releasing any information about his death to avoid spooking the others involved in this business."

"They've got to be wondering where he is," Gil said.

Dana nodded. "I hope it gives them sleepless nights."

"They'll still be around, though, won't they?"

Dana heard the new note in Gil's voice and turned to face him, ready for another fight. She could feel the sudden tightness and rigidity in her stance.

"Gil, I know they're after me because I can nail them to Harcourt's murder. But they didn't get a clear look at me. They know you're involved. That's how they tracked us to the Holiday Inn. But they don't know your new name or what you look like now. If we meet up with them, I can handle it."

Gil heard her tone challenging him to a rebuttal, but he'd learned verbal confrontations with Dana got him nowhere.

He fully intended to be ready to take action, no matter what she said. But he'd learned not to tell her. He sought a lighter tone.

"Well, since you got to pick the new hotel, I'm going to pick the restaurant. It serves real French food. You'll love it."

Dana looked dubious, as though she wasn't quite sure how to take his new noncombatant stand. "I don't know, Gil. I'm not generally one for dishes guaranteed to supply both heartburn and a few new pounds."

Gil turned off the light in the computer room and locked the door behind them. He casually draped his arm over her shoulders as they made their way down the hall, not feeling at all casual when the warmth and softness of her flesh invaded his senses. "Look, bodyguard, we've only got one life. And considering these men you describe who are after us, that life might be a short one. I'd like to get a few more hours of enjoyment out of it while I have a chance. Why don't you join me?"

Dana looked up at the invitation in his smile, enjoying the feel of his arm and thankful that for once they weren't arguing. Yet she knew she couldn't afford to indulge in the disturbing emotional response he invoked in her if she hoped to keep a clear mind.

With reluctance, she eased out from under his encircling arm. "I'm on duty, remember?"

Gil's head tilted in inquiry. "Surely not every minute?"

The last thing in the world Dana wanted was to set the situation's limits, but she knew she had to.

"Gil, if I let myself get…sidetracked, my guard will come down and we could find ourselves in serious trouble. I've got to keep my wits about me. Support me in this. I'm sure you understand why we need to… keep a distance."

His voice lost its earlier warmth. "Only too well."

Dana tried to swallow the thick lump collecting in her throat. A coldness was settling across her shoulders where his arm had been, and she felt a slight shiver. She knew he was disappointed at her decision, but it must stand. She must maintain her professionalism. As long as she was in Gil's company, she would have to be on guard against more than just the silver-haired man.

"SHE'S STAYING AT THE Hyatt Regency near Market. The man has an adjoining room," Brine said into the car phone.

"They're there now?" Sparr asked.

"No. They were up in their rooms for a few minutes and then left. I followed them to a restaurant off Shannon Alley. They're inside waiting to be seated now."

"Do you see Talbot or the one who was with him?"

"No. I'm their only tail."

"Good," Sparr said. "They must think their cover as new employees at Datacomp is going to keep them secure. Stay with them. Get a table and I'll join you in fifteen minutes."

DANA LOOKED ASKANCE at the entrance to the La Mere Duquesne Restaurant off shabby Shannon Alley, but was happily surprised at its gracious interior and the bevy of mouth-watering smells.

They were seated at a table for two, and Dana soon felt herself relaxing to the warmth and murmur of their fellow diners. When Gil ordered snails, however, her nose wrinkled in displeasure.

"All you really taste is the garlic and butter," he said, scooping one out of the shell and into his mouth, slurping it in front of her disapproving frown.

Her top lip curled. "If that's all you taste, why don't you just order garlic and butter and leave those little slimy things slithering on the ground?"

Gil smiled at her distaste. He felt good in her company, despite her attempts to keep a distance between them. "A New England–boiled fan, I see. Well, don't worry. It's never too late to educate a palate. Here's the wine list. Let's get a glass of the house Pinot chardonnay to go with the sword-fish.''

Dana shook her head. "I don't drink on assignment."

Gil smiled and put the wine list down. "Whatever you say, bodyguard. Do you drink when not on assignment?"

"Very seldom," Dana said. "I like being able to think clearly. Besides, I've read alcohol kills brain cells, and a long time ago, I realized I needed every one I've got."

He heard the small lightness she had allowed in her tone and took heart. "Well, what do you do for fun? Race cars? Hang glide?"

"I like a good workout or a good book."

Gil was clearly disappointed. "No, no. I didn't ask what do you do to keep mentally and physically in shape. I asked what do you do for *fun.*" He leaned forward and lightly circled her hand with his index finger, as though he was attempting to coax her. "Come on, Dana. This is polite conversation in a public restaurant. You're safe from murderers, and even from me, for the present."

Dana relaxed back in her chair, responding to the lightness in his voice and the flirtatious qualification in his words. "I'm part of an amateur theater group. We put on plays, mostly comedies. Oscar Wilde–type satires are our favorites. It's loads of fun."

Her smile was telling him just how much fun. She looked different somehow with that smile. Relaxed, approachable.

"An actress? Interesting. What got you started?"

"In a roundabout way, I suppose you could say my deaf mother."

"Your mother is deaf?" Gil repeated. "From an accident?"

Dana shook her head. "From birth. She's never heard sound. That's why I think she relies on expressive eye movements and other subtle body communication to add the tone and inflective meaning to her sign language. I must have picked those things up. I was selected for a lot of plays

because conveying emotions without words was something
didn't have to learn."

Gil had seen a softness smooth out her face as she spoke
of her mother. She did have an expressive face. Perhaps that
was one of the reasons she wore the tinted glasses—to mask
expressions that were too second nature to hide. "What is
she like, your mother?"

Dana smiled. "Loving, scolding, encouraging, overpro-
tecting. A good standard American issue of motherhood.
She accepted her deafness so matter-of-factly, it always
surprised me when others treated her as though she had a
handicap."

"And your dad?" Gil asked.

The smile never left her face. "Oh, he's basically off the
assembly line, too. Hardworking, sports loving and a bit too
uptight in his upbringing to express his feelings easily. I like
the way he still looks at my mother with love in his eyes."

Gil watched as Dana continued to smile over thoughts of
her parents. "Do you ever feel your handicap interferes with
your work?"

Dana frowned as the real handicap she associated with
herself, her small size in relation to the large responsibility
of her job, came forcibly to mind. She shook her head. "I
don't know, Gil. After seeing everything my mother could
do, more and more I think my true handicaps exist only in
my mind."

"You mean all the things you've convinced yourself you
can't do and therefore you never try?"

Dana felt surprised and pleased at his instant understanding. "You sound as though you've been through a bit
of it yourself."

"Who hasn't? There are lots of things I've told myself I'd
be lousy at, even though I've never tried them."

Dana let her eyes rest on the openness in Gil's face and
marveled at his ability to be so honest and at ease with himself after the recent devastating experiences in his profes-

sional and personal life. "What has kept you going these last six months, Gil?"

He shrugged. "Knowing I was innocent. You see, Dana, when you're innocent, you just can't believe the things that are happening to you are real. When suddenly, overnight, both Vanessa and my job disappeared, I didn't accept it. I kept thinking I'd wake up one day and everything would be back to normal."

Dana could understand Gil's negation of the truth. It was how she had felt right after John's death—that it just couldn't be true. "And when that day didn't come?" she asked.

"Well, then I told myself I just had to start again."

She heard the belief in his voice and was newly impressed. "I couldn't have remained so stable if I had lost my work, too."

Gil leaned across the table toward her, finally asking a question he had wanted to all day. "So it was your love you lost about a year ago?"

Dana's suddenly lowered head told Gil the memories could not yet be shared. He leaned back.

"I'm glad I seem to be projecting 'stability,' as you call it. But the man you're seeing now is a far improved one from the man you rescued on that cliff Monday night. You know why, don't you?"

Gil waited for her response, hoping she would give him the opening that would allow him to say what he wanted. But he was totally unprepared for the sudden jerk of her head and the fear in the sharp intake of her breath. "Dana, what's wrong?"

Her hand shot out to catch his arm as she whispered her warning. "We've been followed— No, don't turn around."

Gil wanted to turn around so badly, the strain of his resistance was giving him a stiff neck. He controlled himself, however, and continued to watch Dana as she slowly straightened up and removed her hand from his arm.

"Listen to me carefully, Gil. Continue looking at me and moving your mouth as though you're speaking. But don't make a sound. Periodically, I will appear to be responding, but my voice will not be audible, either. Do you understand what you are to do?"

"I think so, but—"

"No buts. I'll explain later. Begin now."

BRINE LEANED FORWARD. "You see them, Sparr? Two tables down on the left?"

Sparr followed Brine's directions to the bespectacled man and woman. "No one else has approached those two?"

"No one," Brine said.

"Do they know you've been following them?" Sparr asked as he lifted the water glass to his lips.

Brine stiffened. "You know me better than that, Sparr."

Sparr's eyes traveled to the brace on the woman's leg. "She's not one of the programmers on my list. We've nothing to fear from her scrutiny of the WCTS program."

"You want me to continue to follow them?" Brine asked.

Sparr nodded. "Yes. They may lead you to Webb and the woman. I've seen all I've come to see." He got to his feet and walked out of the restaurant.

DANA LIP-READ THE WORDS of the conversation between the two men, relieved they were deceived by Gil's and her altered appearances and frustrated she couldn't take the silver-haired man into custody.

But her training reminded her that the gesture would be foolish. Taking somebody into custody prematurely was not the FBI way. She had to locate the quarry and then carefully collect and document all the evidence needed for prosecution. So even though following him wasn't a current option, she knew she had another.

"It's okay, Gil. You can talk normally now."

Gil was instantly reassured. "You're smiling. What's up?"

"I've been lip-reading a conversation between two of our pursuers, and I've learned that although one followed us here, neither knows who we really are. They believe I'm the programmer and you're the FBI agent. So far, we're safe."

Gil nodded his understanding. "I assume you learned to lip-read from your deaf mother, too. Surprising how much more equipped for life some so-called handicapped people are. Did you learn anything else from the conversation?"

"Yes. The silver-haired man I told you about is called Sparr. He's gone now, but he picked up the water glass on the table opposite a bald man with dark, mustard-colored skin and light eyes who followed us. Sparr called him Brine. Now I've got to retrieve that water glass with Sparr's fingerprints on it, and I've got to move fast."

Her words shoved Gil's anxiety into high gear. "Dana, you're not—" he began, but she cut him off as she rose to her feet.

"Stay here." I'm going to pretend to visit the ladies' room so I can pass by the table. For your information, the bald man named Brine is sitting two tables in back of your left shoulder."

"Dana, I can't just sit here while you—"

"Don't call attention to yourself, Gil. If the food comes before I return, don't wait for me."

"Dana, what are you planning?"

"Trust me, Gil."

She didn't wait for him to respond. She was already limping away in the direction of Brine's table. As she approached it, she saw the waiter heading there, too. As soon as Brine told him he was the only one staying for dinner, the waiter was sure to remove the second place setting and the half-full water glass. It was going to be close. Dana picked up her gait.

The waiter got there first. His head bobbed up and down as he placed the second silverware setting and dinner plate onto his empty serving tray. Any moment now he would reach for the glass, perhaps smudging or even obliterating the precious fingerprints. Panic quickened her pace. She knew she would not get there in time. Then, unexpectedly, Brine repositioned himself in his chair, shoving his left foot slightly into the aisle. Dana literally stumbled forward into the presented opportunity.

It took only a second to thud the orthopedic shoe on the end of her right leg into the extended foot. "Oomph!" She exhaled as she lurched forward, bumping into the waiter, knocking over the sought-after glass of water, which splattered onto the two men and then plopped obediently into her open bag. She had closed that bag again and was propped up on her thick cane by the time the waiter and the bald man had even partly recovered.

"Oh, I'm so sorry," Dana said. "I tripped on something."

The waiter's face broke into a tolerant smile as his eyes took in Dana's braced leg. His accent sounded soft and French. "Not to worry, madam. I can make this table right again in the shortest of order. Are you not hurt?"

"No, no, the table broke my fall." She turned to Brine, donning her most flustered and contrite mask. "Are you all right? I think it was your foot I tripped over."

Out of the corner of her eye, Dana saw the waiter turn accusing eyes toward Brine, who mumbled something incoherent and glowered at Dana. He waved her away in irritation, but not suspicion. She had anticipated as much. This was not a trick she would have tried with Sparr, however. She proceeded to limp toward the ladies' room, the precious drinking glass safely in her possession.

GIL WATCHED EVERYTHING from his table, jumping to his feet and tearing off his glasses, ready for action as he saw

Dana stumble right into Brine's table. He knew she had instigated this diversionary move to obtain the drinking glass. He didn't know yet if she had been successful.

He continued his scrutiny until she started limping toward the ladies' room and he was satisfied she was okay. Then he collapsed back into his chair and replaced his tinted glasses on the bridge of his nose as he exhaled a clutched breath. His muscles were just starting to relax when the loud call came.

"Gilbert Webb! It is you!"

Gil's head jerked up as his eyes locked onto the very familiar face of the tall, beautiful blond woman with the bright blue eyes standing next to his table.

"Vanessa! My God, what are you doing here?" Gil stood up to face her, shock and excitement both vying for a foothold on his emotions.

"Having dinner," Vanessa said. "Imagine my surprise when I turned around and saw you. Only I almost didn't recognize you, Gilly. You must admit, you've gone through some changes. And from the cut of your threads, I'd say you've turned a prosperous corner."

Gilly. Her pet name for him. It brought back so many familiar memories. Yet, as Vanessa's eyes traveled over Gil, he was starting to feel strange. Many times over the past six months, he had dreamed of this reunion scene. He would be standing before her, vindicated of all wrong. She would be gazing into his eyes with just the expression of desire she wore now.

Except it wasn't happening that way. He had not been vindicated. She was not responding to his innocence. She was responding to the returned prosperity of his appearance. He studied her, trying to understand his feelings, but there didn't seem to be any. She was an external collection of beautiful form and feature, nothing more.

"Come on, Van. Your food's getting cold."

Vanessa gave her obviously irritated date, two tables away, a scathing look and then turned back to Gil.

Like an intimate caress, she laid a hand on Gil's shoulder, drawing closer to say her next words in a loverlike whisper. She obviously intended her date to suffer for daring to interrupt her conversation. Gil understood the action. He had been on the receiving end often enough.

"Call me, Gilly. You've been keeping out of touch too long. We've got much to catch up on."

Gil knew it was a ludicrous remark. Vanessa had been the one who refused to return the hundreds of messages he had left for her after the Computech data-base crash. Thinking he was washed-up, she had dumped him. Now that he looked prosperous again, she was obviously willing to forget the past as though it had never happened.

She moved back to her table in the assured manner of a woman intimately aware that every male eye in the room was watching. Gil saw this, too, believing that he might be seeing a lot of things for the first time. As he caught the look of Vanessa's escort, he read the jealousy and desperation and knew that, but for a chance of fate, that could be him.

Goodbye, Vanessa, he said to himself deliberately, knowing he had just read the last page of a story he hadn't enjoyed very much.

He was just easing back into his chair when suddenly a feeling of dread shook him. In his initial excitement at seeing Vanessa, he had totally forgotten Brine. He jerked around.

Brine's light, watchful eyes were staring straight at him as an ugly smile lifted his lips.

With a tardy, painful awareness, Gil sank into his chair, knowing that it was all over. His cover was blown.

Chapter Eleven

Dana stood at the edge of the room, witnessing the disaster taking place and knowing she was powerless to do anything about it.

From the moment the stunning blond woman yelled out Gil's name, Dana could see Brine's attention had been immediately engaged. Even across the room she had been able to hear some of Gil's and Vanessa's comments, although she had relied on lip-reading to follow the entire conversation. But with Brine's closer proximity, she was sure he had heard nearly everything.

And as soon as Brine reported back to Sparr that despite his new appearance, Gilbert Webb was the programmer at Datacomp, she had no doubt the silver-haired man would figure out who she was and wait to ambush them both. She had to act fast.

Dana started toward the public telephone in the back of the restaurant only to halt as she saw Brine rising from his chair. She ducked into the shadows as he stood and turned, confirming her worst fears. He was coming her way. He must be going to call Sparr. He must not be allowed to do so.

She looked about her. The area near the restrooms and telephone was deserted. With each of the man's footfalls, Dana's blood pumped excited and expectant.

She moved farther into the shadows as he approached the public telephone, circling her right hand firmly around her .38 Smith & Wesson, while her left hand still held her cane. He was less than three feet away when she suddenly stepped in front of him and pointed the gun dead center at his chest.

"FBI. You're under arrest. Stretch your hands above your head and face that wall."

Brine's small, light eyes squinted at her in amused disbelief as he stood his ground. "*You* going to make me?"

With all her might, Dana swung her cane against the back of his knee, reading with satisfaction the startled expression in his eyes and getting ready to pounce on him hard as he collapsed to the floor. She never got a chance. In absolute surprise, she watched Brine's mustard-tinged face go blank before her very eyes and the large man fall unconscious at her feet!

As soon as Gil saw Brine get up and head in the direction of where Dana had gone, he knew he had to do something. He couldn't just sit back and let Dana be taken unawares. So he went after Brine, following him from the dining room, waiting only until they reached the comparative darkness of the hallway.

His heart jumped into his throat as he caught sight of Dana on the other side of the man's huge frame. Brine was reaching into his pocket as he dropped to his knee. Gil didn't hesitate. One well-placed blow from the heavy steel platter Gil had borrowed from the waiter's counter and the unsuspecting Brine crumpled onto the thick carpet without a peep.

Gil saw Dana's surprised expression as she stood looking down at Brine. He felt immensely pleased. He had just proven the cowardly lion could roar, after all. That is until he saw her surprised expression turn into dismay.

"Gil, what have you done?" Dana sank to the floor, feeling for a pulse in Brine's neck as she slipped her gun into her shoulder bag.

Gil's eyes caught sight of the gun and realized Dana had been prepared for Brine. It irked him a bit that he didn't look so heroic after all, but he was determined to redeem himself.

"He was reaching for something in his back pocket, Dana. I couldn't take the chance he would harm you."

Dana didn't acknowledge Gil's explanation. She shot to her feet and grabbed for a nearby phone, punching in a number, speaking to Gil at the same time in clipped, authoritative tones. "Listen and do exactly as I say. Someone could be walking by here any second. Clean out his pockets. Then stand back and pretend you're a bystander. Let me do the talking. Got it?"

Gil nodded as he sank to his knee, finding himself reacting more to the tone of her voice than any words she spoke. He had expected surprise, thanks, a pat on the back—what the hell, anything except this impersonal, flat disappointment smashing out her words like overdone pancakes. It left him disoriented and just a little sore around his ego.

DANA IGNORED THE RAPPING at her hotel-room door for several moments as she continued counting off the number of her double-time sit-ups. When she reached one hundred, she reluctantly got up to answer the insistent caller. The last thing in the world she wanted was company, but she knew even before she checked the peephole who this would be, and there was no way he would be going away.

She let Talbot step inside, her nose telling her the bag he carried contained food. As she walked over to the chair to pick up a towel to wipe the perspiration from her leotard-clad body, she saw him lean against the door he had just closed and watch her as though he wasn't sure he shouldn't turn right around and go out again. Even his voice sounded tentative.

"I take it tonight's status call to Sargentich didn't go very well?"

Dana grabbed the towel and wiped off the excess moisture dripping from her forehead. The look she gave Talbot said more than any words.

He let out a low whistle that he managed to make sound just as precise and crisp as his words. "Well, that explains the steam dripping off your walls. You've obviously had a lot to blow off. What's wrong? I admit the methods might have been a little clumsy, but you've gotten Leach and Brine today, and you and Webb are okay. Wasn't he pleased?"

Dana couldn't seem to control the edge in her voice. "I'm not trying to please Sargentich."

She continued to wipe the perspiration from her bare arms, knowing Talbot's eyes studied her. "It's your own standard you're afraid of not meeting, isn't it? Both times, Webb gave you a hand, however unnecessary it may have been. But because he did, you're still not sure you could have done it on your own, are you?"

Talbot's assessment was too close to the truth for Dana's comfort. She said nothing.

"Why don't you tell Webb you can handle things, Dana?"

"I have told him. He doesn't listen. He just made things worse tonight by clobbering Brine and forcing us to take him out in an ambulance. I could have handcuffed him and gotten him out of there without arousing any attention if Webb had just left things to me."

Talbot's tone was crisp, uncompromising. "There was a knife in Brine's back pocket, Dana. The man was slipping his hand into that pocket. You had knocked him to his knees, but if—"

The frustration was a heavy lump in her throat now as the implication in Talbot's words hung in the air.

"I know, I know. Webb may have saved my life. But maybe I could have saved my own life. Besides, the fool could have been killed. If Brine had turned that knife on him..."

Talbot walked over to the corner of the room where two chairs were drawn up to a small, round table and set down his package. "Have something to eat, Carmody. There's a hamburger, French fries and a chocolate malt in the bag here. Certainly not health food, but maybe a sufficient dose of fat might help to insulate your spirits."

Dana shook her head and tried to soften her tone. She didn't mean to take out her frustration on her colleague and friend. "Thanks, but food just doesn't sound appealing at the moment."

Talbot nodded. "Webb told me he wasn't hungry, either. His face is almost as long as yours. Why don't you give the guy a break?"

Dana shook her head as she glanced over at the door between Gil's hotel room and hers. "Right now, the only break I'd like to give him is across his interfering neck."

"You mean that same interfering neck he stuck out to save your life tonight?" Talbot asked.

Dana looked at the feigned innocence on Talbot's face and shook her head. "All right. I should be grateful to him, but I'm not. So anything I'd say in the next few hours would probably just be sarcastic and inappropriate. Let me get a hot shower and a good sleep under my belt before I have to face Sir Galahad again. Besides, if I have to put that brace on again tonight, I'll scream."

Dana pointed at the leg brace sitting on top of the over-size dress and orthopedic shoes she had dumped unceremoniously on the floor as soon as she had arrived at the new hotel room.

Talbot walked over to the pile and picked up the brace. "It's an effective disguise. I almost didn't recognize you when I came by the restaurant tonight. Since this guy Sparr saw you, I understand why you need this stuff, but why do you feel it necessary to wear the disguise with Webb? Doesn't he know what you really look like?"

Dana shook her head. "He wasn't quite himself Monday night when we met. And his cabin was very dimly lit."

Talbot shrugged as he turned the brace over in his hands, studying it more closely. He reached into one of the metal bands and pulled out a slim, sharp knife, previously hidden from view.

"This isn't exactly Bureau issue. What's it for, Carmody?" he asked, holding up the knife.

Dana shrugged. "Hopefully just decoration. Still, Monday night, I would have given my eye teeth for a knife. Now I'm keeping one handy to play it safe."

Talbot nodded as he replaced the weapon in its hidden compartment within the brace. "You're also playing it a little tenser than I remember, Carmody. You've really put yourself on the line with this one, haven't you?"

Dana looked over at him and nodded wordlessly.

His puckered blue eyes studied her for a moment, and then he nonchalantly gave her shoulder a pat on his way to the door.

"The glass with Sparr's fingerprints is on its way to the lab. I called an old buddy. He said he'll have someone pick up the package at the airport and take it straight to him. If we get lucky, we might have some response by tomorrow afternoon."

Talbot's comment switched Dana's thoughts back to the case. "Have you learned anything about the other guy from the restaurant?"

Talbot shook his head. "Driver's license you took off him confirms his name is Brine, but I haven't been able to run him through NCIC yet because the computers are down. The CJIS computer system in Sacramento doesn't show a record."

Dana frowned. "Has he regained consciousness?"

"No. The doctor says he's got a concussion. Webb really whacked him hard. We've got him under a twenty-four-hour guard just in case. If he stays unconscious, that can work in our favor."

"You mean he won't be able to get a message to Sparr?"

"Exactly. So far, we've got him on charges of accessory to murder, resisting arrest and carrying two concealed weapons. To be honest, we'll never be able to make the accessory-to-murder charge stick since you didn't see him at the scene and we can't find Harcourt's body. The nurses' station at the hospital has been notified to contact us immediately if anyone inquires."

Dana nodded as she walked Talbot to the door. He must have read the expression on her face, because his next words were obviously meant to be encouraging.

"Don't worry, Carmody. The phone line into Brine's room is not only tapped, it's set up to register a busy in his ear no matter what number he tries. If he attempts to call out, we'll have a record of the number and a straight line to this Sparr character."

Dana nodded, but she still felt uneasy. "Did you find a car near the restaurant that fit the keys Webb took from his pocket?"

"A brown LeBaron. Like you suggested, I've left it in place with an agent watching. The DMV shows it's registered to Silver Security Systems. They're a company that specializes in circumventing industrial espionage."

Dana felt new interest. "Really? Can you get me a rundown on all the personnel at Silver Security?"

Talbot smiled. "Now how did I know you were going to ask for that? Don't worry, it's already in the works. I'll call you at Datacomp tomorrow. What else?"

"Learn anything more about Lakoff?"

"Soonest I'll have something is tomorrow."

"Did you tail him?"

Talbot nodded. "One of my men followed him from Datacomp just about ten minutes before you left the facility tonight. Lakoff drove into the city and parked in a garage two blocks off of Market. Unfortunately, my agent lost him there. Lakoff might have taken a taxi to wherever else he was going and used the closed parking structure as a decoy. His car is under surveillance. As of fifteen minutes ago, he hasn't returned to it.''

Dana nodded, feeling grim about their evening's efforts.

Talbot turned the knob on her door, his words echoing her thoughts. "I know. Things are sort of disjointed at the moment. Still, there's nothing more we can do tonight. Metcalf and I will be alternating watches, so there's no reason for you not to sleep straight through. There's a bolt on Webb's outside door, so no one can get in that way. The only path to him is through one of our adjoining rooms. See you tomorrow."

Dana said good-night, locking the door behind Talbot. Then she went over to her luggage and rummaged through her belongings looking for a bathrobe. She hadn't even bothered unpacking. Three hotels in less than two days was not conducive to a feeling of permanency.

She came across the can of gray hair-paint spray and tossed it on a chair. Her scalp itched from the spray-on dye coating her hair. Even if it meant having to respray her hair tomorrow, she was going to enjoy a shampoo tonight.

GIL CAME OUT OF HIS shower feeling even more keyed up than when he went in. He rubbed his hair and scalp so vigorously with a towel, he could hear the static charge. Nothing was right. Ever since he had crowned that guy in the restaurant, he sensed the new wall that had been erected between himself and Dana.

She had hurriedly made her call to Talbot and then explained to a very nervous restaurant manager that the unconscious man on his carpet was a diabetic friend of hers who had gone into shock.

It had involved some fast talking and good acting, but when she assured the manager she had already called an ambulance, the manager finally relaxed and left her in charge.

Gil had just wanted to handcuff Brine and drag him from the restaurant. But he realized after a while that Dana was doing the right thing. The man needed medical attention, and Dana didn't want to expose herself as an FBI agent in front of even more people than those that had already found out.

Still, the tension had positively sizzled as each moment more and more attention came their way from curious diners. After a very long thirty minutes, an ambulance did come by to pick up Brine, and Gil recognized Metcalf as one of the two blue-smocked attendants.

Then before Gil could get a word with Dana, Talbot had carted him off to yet another new hotel and had left him there with a dinner he couldn't swallow on top of a bellyful of anxiety.

He knew Talbot and Metcalf were occupying the adjoining room on his right and Dana was in the one on his left. He knew she was angry at his "interference." He was sure she'd come by and have it out with him. But as the minutes stretched into hours and she didn't show, he'd begun to realize she wasn't coming.

It made him mad. He could take anything but being ignored. If Dana chose not to come to him, he'd just go to her. That decided, he threw off his robe and yanked on a pair of jeans. He barely took time to zip up and throw his arm into a shirtsleeve before he was knocking on the connecting door.

"Dana, open up. I've got to talk to you."

Gil waited only as long as it took for him to slip his other arm through his shirtsleeve. When he hadn't gotten a response, he jiggled the door handle impatiently. He felt the unlocked door open in his hand and in surprise he stepped through into Dana's room.

The first thing he noticed from the minimal amount of light provided by a small table lamp was that she wasn't there. The noise of a hair dryer whirled away behind the closed door of the bathroom. He could see the pencil line of light seeping underneath its door. He decided to wait and headed for a chair.

Before he could sit down in the chair, however, he removed a can of hair-paint spray lying on the cushion. He fingered the can in his hand wondering how it got in Dana's room. He sat down, the can still in his hand, when suddenly the sound of the hair dryer stopped and the bathroom door swung wide open.

She strode quickly out into the darkened room, her long, exposed white legs limpless, braceless, her torso draped in a hotel bath towel. Gil watched her as she headed directly for her open suitcase to replace the hand-held hair dryer within its top compartment, while masses of beautiful light brown hair danced down her bare shoulders. He just stared at her, as though she was some hallucination he had had once and was experiencing again. Then, his eyes darted back to the can of gray hair paint in his hand and so many previous gaps in his understanding filled.

He'd been a fool. And she had helped to make him one.

Dana's mind was a million miles away as she went through the mechanics of replacing her hair dryer in her suitcase and popping a piece of peppermint into her mouth. Sparr would know Brine was following them, and his subsequent disappearance was bound to point directly to Gil and her. They were in a race against time now. Gil had to find out what had invaded the WCTS programming before Sparr discovered who they really were and took steps to permanently eliminate them from the picture.

She was still smarting from recent events. Faced now with just her conscience, she didn't know if she was more upset at Gil stepping in to help her against Brine or at his intimate conversation with his beautiful and obviously still interested fiancée.

Memories of Vanessa caressing Gil's shoulder in the center of the restaurant stirred a spate of unwelcome jealousy in Dana's heart. She looked down in dismay at the unattractive dress, hose, shoes and brace in a pile on the carpet. Given a choice of the woman they represented or the beautiful blonde in the restaurant, she had no doubt which one a man would pick. Her bare foot kicked the pile in irritation and dismay at the trap she had built around herself and at the all too recognizable yearnings that urged her to escape.

Still, she knew she was locked in now and nothing could be done. It was while she shook her head, telling herself to be sensible, that something flickered at the periphery of her vision and all thoughts but one instantly fled from her mind.

She was not alone.

She willed down a rising panic as she slowly, carefully made her way toward her shoulder bag on top of the dresser. She slipped her hand inside and brought out her gun, shielding the action with her body. Then she pivoted on her right heel, dropping to a crouched position as she swung the business end of her weapon to point at the dark shape. "Don't move or I'll shoot."

Gil's voice dripped with hurt and anger. "Go ahead, Dana. What's one more cheap shot?"

Dana exhaled a trapped breath as she dropped her gun hand and sank onto the carpet, able to concentrate only on the relief of finding out her intruder was Gil. Her backbone felt like jelly. "Damn it, Gil, didn't your mother ever teach you to knock?"

Gil got up from his chair and walked over to stand above her seated figure. He looked down into the clear gray of her eyes framed by the shining thickness of her cascading hair, and found himself caught in the conflicting emotions of anger and desire. It wasn't until he spoke that he realized the anger had won out.

"Yeah, my mother taught me to knock. She also taught me to tell the truth. You do know what the truth is, don't you?"

The angry sarcasm in Gil's tone finally penetrated Dana's initial relief and she looked up to see the fury on his face. It wasn't until that moment that she remembered not only was she not in her disguise, but also she was only half-clad in a towel. Feeling a bit chagrined, she pulled herself to her feet, fingering the ends of the towel to make sure they stretched as far as they could.

"I suppose I owe you an explanation," she said, trying to ignore the flash of well-developed chest muscles showing through his open shirt and the mass of red curls sinking deep below the waistband of his tight-fitting jeans.

Her nonchalant attitude flared Gil's anger anew as other deeper senses were reacting to the perfume of her freshly shampooed hair and the smell of the hot, sweet peppermint on her breath. He grabbed her arm and swung her back to face him.

"You *suppose* you owe me an explanation? Damn it, Dana, you've had me acting like an imbecile, thinking you were really handicapped, ready to punch out that stupid, prejudiced York, scared to death to let you out of my sight in case those madmen came for you. Do you know what you've put me through?"

The anger in his tone hit Dana like a slap across the face, but it was his grabbing her arm that shocked her the most. She tried to yank it away from his powerful grip, but Gil held on, pulling her closer, raking her with his penetrating gaze. His fingers felt like hot pokers stoking the deep, burning embers of emotion inside her into a blazing anger. Her words shot out like stinging sparks.

"Do I know what I've put *you* through? That's a laugh! Because of your inability to follow the simplest of directions, we're introducing our suspects to morticians and doctors instead of handcuffs. Damn it, Gil, where do you get off playing footsy with your fiancée in the middle of a crowded restaurant?''

Gil moved even closer, feeling the fight in her like a physical jolt to his senses, the flush in her face sizzling the marrow in his bones. "Footsy? Look who's talking about playing footsy! The consummate actress. And if you thought I had anything to do with my *ex*-fiancée opening her big mouth, you can add stupidity to your list of other sterling qualities, right under deception and mistrust! Damn it, I trusted you!''

Dana knew she hadn't meant to bring up his fiancée. She also knew she couldn't help feeling a strange relief at Gil's contemptuous reference to Vanessa's big mouth and his emphasis on her being his ex-fiancée. She felt caught in a confusing whirl of emotional inconsistencies, exploding inside her like bursting popcorn, fueled by the heat of hot, liquid gold in his eyes.

She shoved her free hand against his chest, trying to push him away, but finding the contact with his hard, burning flesh diluting all restraint, melting the very bones in her body. Her voice trembled, but she didn't seem to be able to do anything about it.

''What good did trusting you do? One, I told you to stay put. Two, I told you not to call attention to yourself. And three, I told you to let me handle things. In case you haven't checked your score recently, you're zero for three!''

Gil felt every cell in his body begin to burn as he wrapped his free arm around Dana, crushing her taut form against him. He felt the jolt of her muscles against his flesh and heard the sharp intake of her breath as their bodies met, but he also saw the clear gray of her eyes turning smoky with a smoldering desire. In exaltation, he knew it was her desire that prevented her from struggling against him, and his ache for her slashed deep inside him. He leaned toward her parted lips, knowing the intensity of his anger was anger no more, had never really been. His words dissolved into steam against her cheek. "Have you forgotten you also told me to stay away from you? I guess I've got nothing to lose by making it zero for four."

Dana couldn't have spoken, even if his lips weren't scorching hers, even if the breath hadn't been crushed out of her body by the force of his embrace. Because even if she had been free to speak, there were no words left as all thoughts were burned to a crisp by the sharp, sweet spasm of desire contracting against the base of her spine.

Gil gobbled up her peppermint-flavored mouth, thrilled to the uninhibited response of her lips, to her hands pressing him closer. Her body was giving him the message he craved, and he waited for no other. His arms scooped her up, and he carried her to the bed.

Dana was aware of his hands, his mouth, touching, caressing, exploring every quivering inch of her flesh as she kept trying to draw him closer, ever closer. She had no thoughts, only feelings, an intense heat generated by her contact with this man, setting her afire, growing hotter, consuming her body until, suddenly, it burned itself out and she fell back, gasping for breath.

Even after her breath stilled, it took a moment for her thoughts to return, to discover she was lying naked next to him, to feel shaken at the intensity of the feeling that had overcome her so thoroughly she could not even remember the logistics of how they had made it to the bed.

She knew she should be horrified, but she didn't feel horrified. She felt pleased and happy, emotions she had buried deep during the long year of her mourning. Now they had been shoveled out of the cold snow of her grief and warmed with new life. Gil had done that. She was glad it had been him.

Dana sighed, not wanting to think, content to drift, enjoying the warmth of his body and the clean scent of his skin mixed with the glow of their lovemaking. Her breath matched his, her heartbeat pulsed in unison with the vein in his resting wrist. She had only one desire—to once again hear the sound of his voice. "Gil . . . ?"

His response was thick and sweet in her ear, like melted marshmallow, repeating her thoughts as though they had been spoken aloud. "No, Dana, I'm not asleep. As a matter of fact, I've been lying here thinking I may never be able to sleep again as long as you're by my side. Still, it wouldn't be too high a price to pay."

He stroked the hollow between her breasts, luxuriating in the silky feel of her skin. She sighed as once again her thoughts diffused under his touch.

"You're lovely, Dana. At some level of consciousness, I've known since the moment you kissed me on that ledge of that cliff that I've wanted you. Even that crazy disguise you wore didn't stop my growing feelings for you. I understand now you altered your appearance as mine was altered to confuse Sparr. But why didn't you tell me?"

Dana knew there was no anger or hurt in his voice now, just a need to understand. She rolled over on her side to face him and to let her fingers play with the fiery mat of curls circling his chest.

"It seemed the right thing to do at the time, Gil. You see, at first, I didn't expect you to be taken in by the disguise. When you were, I began to think that perhaps it might be just as well."

His eyes looked deeply into hers, searching for the meaning behind her words. "You didn't want this to happen between us. Is it because you can't forget the lover you lost?"

Dana felt herself smiling at his words, knowing that in his arms she had not been able to even remember her own name, much less John's. It was another thing she was thankful for and she sighed with the pleasure of that awareness. "John was never between us."

Gil's voice sounded relieved and infinitely gentle as his hand stroked her hair. "Can you tell me about him now?"

Dana sighed anew at Gil's comforting tone and touch. Talking about John no longer seemed such a difficult thing. The hurt and grief floated through her mind like disembodied memories, not connected to pain. "We met at the FBI Academy. John was the type of individual born to be an agent. Smart, straight, physically strong. He was graduated top of the class."

"And you?" Gil asked.

"I had a struggle meeting the physical requirements. A real struggle. By the fourth week, I was spending all my free time working out in the gym, trying to build up my strength. Then John dropped by one night and after watching me fight to do even a couple of chin-ups, stepped in to give me a few pointers."

Dana shifted her weight to her elbow as she propped her head up to look at Gil. "He taught me how to employ leverage, diversion, surprise—all the things our normal training didn't cover. As the weeks went by, I continued to do the physical strengthening exercises, but it was because of his direction and encouragement that I really improved enough to pass."

"And you fell in love with this helpful classmate?" Gil asked, feeling strange little pangs of jealousy over Dana's memories of such a physically competent dead lover no matter how much he tried to be sensible about the matter.

Dana nodded, unaware of the emotional undercurrents in Gil's question. "Not at the Academy, of course. I had too much else on my mind. But later, when we found we had both gotten assigned to D.C., things started to come together for us, at least personally."

"But not professionally?" Gil asked, hearing the qualifying drop in her voice.

"Professionally, I was found physically wanting. My boss deliberately kept me away from the field assignments that might have proven dangerous. Again and again, he relegated me to paperwork.

"During that first year with John at my side and feeling the love growing between us, I didn't actively fight my boss's lack of belief in my physical abilities, despite how his attitude grated on my pride. Like a soothing narcotic, John's love dulled my sense of disquiet. And in the deep chasms of my soul, I kept remembering my physical difficulties at the Academy and wondered if my boss was right. Then John was killed on assignment."

Gil knew there were pieces missing in this picture. He tried to get Dana to fill them in. "You told me once that you weren't there when he needed you. Were you supposed to be?"

Dana frowned. "I should have been, Gil. I would have been if my boss didn't think my small stature and minimal muscle development qualified me just for paperwork."

Gil heard the pain in her voice and wished there was something he could do to take it away. "Your boss has put you on this assignment. I'd hardly call what you've been involved in since Monday night 'paperwork.'"

Dana sighed. "Yes, this is a real assignment, but don't let it fool you. It's my first one since I became an agent. You've no idea how hard I've fought for this chance to prove myself, Gil. I've got to show I can handle myself."

Gil thought he was finally beginning to understand why his attempts to help her had not been well received. She had needed to stand on her own two feet, and he had been constantly scooting a chair into the back of her knees. "I made a mistake when I knocked out Brine. You needed to take him into custody by yourself, didn't you?"

Dana nodded. "I needed to try. Remember what we talked about in the restaurant? How our handicaps are really in our heads? Well, tonight I've come to realize the real physical handicap I've been carrying around the last two years was not really in the mind of my boss, but in my own mind. I allowed him to talk me out of 'dangerous' assignments because, deep down, I was afraid he might be right about my ability to perform.''

''Are you still afraid?''

''No. This assignment has taught me that I had been letting myself give less by not really fighting for the opportunity to do more.''

Gil smiled. ''So I'm forgiven for helping tonight?''

Dana shook her head. ''You don't get off that easy, Gil. Heaven knows I have more than a passing acquaintance with this strong, marvelous body of yours, and it's obviously more than physically capable, but an FBI agent is not just muscles. He or she is distinguished by brains fine-tuned through solid training. You don't have that training. One wrong move tonight and you could have gotten yourself killed.''

Gil studied her worriedly. ''But if Brine had gotten to his knife . . . ?''

Dana smiled as she patted the end of his nose with her index finger. ''He thought he was facing a small, handicapped woman. I knew he would probably resist arrest because he underestimated me. Frankly, I was counting on it. But he wasn't counting on my ability to block and retaliate. Surprise is a dynamite weapon, Gil. Worth a ton of muscles.''

Gil nodded. ''Still, it makes things hard for me, Dana. A man likes to think he's needed. Here I'm captivated by a lovely lady who first met me when I was staggering drunk. Now I find that all the 'help' I've been trying to give her since has really been a hindrance. Doesn't prop up the old male ego too much.''

Dana studied the discomfort on his handsome face and felt a strange, sore little tightening in her chest. ''You're my wizard, remember? Frankly, the success of this entire case rests in your hands. You carry a burden I couldn't hope to lift.''

Gil ran his finger down the smoothness of her cheek. Her clear gray eyes looked singed with concern for his feelings. Her caring filled his heart with a taste even sweeter than her kisses. He cradled her head in the hollow of his neck, knowing he couldn't keep the thickness from his voice.

"Doesn't sound too heroic."

She settled her body against the broad expanse of his chest. "There are a lot of ways to be heroic, Gil. As far as I'm concerned, your shining armor was dazzling when you stood up for me with York."

He just stroked her hair for a few moments, finding he had no adequate words to offer. Despite her assurances, he felt the frustration of his earlier futile efforts. She might not expect better of him, but he expected it of himself. Being of real help had never seemed so important as it did now.

He knew where his feelings were taking him, but he knew it was a ride he could not hope to share with her unless his prospects changed. Suddenly he found the importance of their success on this assignment even more crucial than it had been but an hour before. He had to come through for her. For both of them.

"What will happen to Brine?"

Dana wondered at the new tone of businesslike resolve in Gil's voice, but didn't let it sidetrack her answer. "When he regains consciousness, we have a couple of things to hold him on, at least until the doctor releases him and he makes bail."

Gil's tone was worried. "And if he calls Sparr?"

"Actually, in a way I hope he does call from the hospital. We'll trace the call and find Sparr that way."

"And if he doesn't call Sparr, but makes bail instead?"

Dana's lips tightened. "Then he'll be so bugged, he'll swoon if he gets near a Raid can. And as soon as he contacts Sparr, Talbot and Metcalf will close in and pick them both up."

Gil wrapped his arms around her very tightly. His voice sounded a little desperate. "They've got to pick up Sparr, Dana. Brine knows who I am. It isn't going to take much of a leap of imagination to figure out your appearance has been altered, too, and who you are behind those enormous glasses and underneath that gray hair paint."

"Yes, thanks to Vanessa," Dana agreed. "What an unlucky break. There are more than forty-two hundred restaurants in San Francisco and to paraphrase Bogart, out of all those gin joints in all the world, she had to walk into ours."

"I'm afraid it was a bit more than an unlucky break, Dana."

She heard the new discomfort in Gil's voice and looked up to see the frown on his face. "What do you mean?"

"I mean the restaurant was one of our favorites. It wasn't so unusual to find her there. I just didn't think when I picked it. What a rotten impression I'm making on you."

Dana snuggled into the warmth of his arms. "On the contrary. From the first, you've left me with much too good an impression."

He nuzzled her ear, happy at least for her words. "Is that why you let me believe in your disguise?"

Dana nodded. "I knew my reactions to you could interfere with my job. Keeping you at a distance seemed to be the thing to do."

"And now?" he asked.

She turned in his arms to smile up at him as her finger rose to trace the fullness of his lips. "Now I don't want you a centimeter farther away from where you are."

He gave her a satisfied squeeze, made even warmer by the smile that traveled from his lips to his eyes.

"Dana, my love, that's what I wanted to hear."

She told herself to take his endearment lightly. Many people bantered around the word *love* without thinking anything serious.

He didn't give her much time to dwell on what he had meant by it. His hands and body moved to caress her again, this time beginning deliciously slow and sensual, rubbing gently against her senses to rekindle the fire he knew waited within the glowing embers deep inside her.

"THEY'RE GONE," Thiel said as he walked into Sparr's office at CustomKey. Sparr descended into his desk chair with the controlled grace that approximated slow motion.

"What do you mean, 'gone'?"

Thiel exhaled an exasperated breath. "The FBI agents are no longer at the Holiday Inn. The desk clerk still shows they're occupying the same adjoining rooms on the fifth floor, but when I couldn't find the green Olds in the parking garage, I let myself back into the rooms. They're cleaned out."

Sparr's index finger pressed into his upper lip angrily. "Damn it, it's her. She must have found Leach there and figured we'd be watching. They've slipped out on us."

"What do you want me to do?" Thiel asked.

"Nothing now. Vogel returned to his office a while ago. There was some kind of trouble earlier tonight when his programmer went back into WCTS. I'll find out about it tomorrow morning early and tell you if anything needs to be done."

"Did Brine have anything to report?"

"Nothing further or he would have called. I've seen the programmer the FBI sent. She's nothing to worry about. Neither is the male agent with her."

"Where is the woman FBI agent?" Thiel asked.

Sparr's finger rubbed his upper lip with a vengeance. "I don't know, but I'll bet she's got Webb with her. We've got to get this WCTS thing settled before he can get to it. I feel her presence. Tonight I found myself studying the faces of the women on the street when I walked to my car, almost believing I would see her."

Sparr got up and went over to the window to watch the blackness of night as he spread his palms upon the glass. "She's close. Only just out of reach. But I can feel her getting closer. Soon I'll have her within my hands. These two hands."

Sparr's hard fingers squeaked against the glass as they curled into two massive fists.

Chapter Twelve

Gil watched Dana as she stabbed at her pink grapefruit in the hotel coffee shop the next morning. She was back in full disguise, complete with large tinted glasses. But the image of her that materialized inside him was, as always, the truer picture—the warm, exciting woman who had made such hot love to him throughout the night until even the ends of his hair felt singed.

Now as she concentrated so intently on carving out the sections of the pink flesh and laying them side by side on her plate, he found himself wondering what she could be thinking.

The way she stacked them so carefully, he knew it wasn't really the fruit that was claiming her attention. She was a million miles away, organizing some other pieces of information. Gil reached into his pocket and pulled out some change.

"A penny for your thoughts," he said as he laid a coin next to her plate.

Dana looked up as her mind sped back from the mental storage cabinet it had been rummaging through. She felt a small smile curving her mouth as her eyes took in Gil's freshly shaved face and slightly crooked tie. She doubted if he'd ever really be able to get his tie straight, and that small imperfection set off a sweet and endearing sigh inside her heart.

She removed her obscuring glasses and set them on the top of her head. "Are you trying to bribe a federal agent?"

Gil's eyes lit in good humor from her returning tease. "Only if it works."

Dana speared one of the slices of grapefruit from her plate, popped it into her mouth and rolled it around her tongue seductively before swallowing it. "This agent isn't open to bribes." She licked the bare fork suggestively, her lips curling into a mischievous smile as her eyes turned seductively smoky. "At least not monetary ones."

Gil rubbed his suddenly sweaty palms against his slacks as he took two quick breaths. "Don't do this to me, Dana. Not after kicking me out of your nice warm bed at 4:00 a.m. and telling me to return to my own cold one so as not to shock Talbot and Metcalf. If challenged, I'm not above picking you up and carrying you back to one of those beds right now."

Dana blinked at him, just a little surprised at the effect of her teasing and not too sure his warning wasn't serious. Its intensity hit her on several levels, all exciting. Still, she knew this was no time to get carried away, no matter how delightfully provocative the literal images of that possibility were proving to be.

She replaced her glasses across the bridge of her nose and straightened up into a more businesslike posture. "Okay. I'll give you your money's worth."

Before she told him, however, Gil noticed her light, teasing smile was replaced with a frown.

"Talbot ran a check on Larry Lakoff. This morning he knocked on my door to give me a fax that had come into the office from Columbia, South Carolina, the home town of Kristin Harcourt's second cousins, the Lakoffs."

"Well, don't stop now," Gil said. "What did the fax say?"

"It said that Larry Lakoff died of an untreated case of blood poisoning just about a year ago."

Gil frowned. "But if the real Larry Lakoff is dead, then how could the one we met pass as her cousin?"

Dana rubbed an itchy nose. "Remember Linda told us Kristin said she'd just met Larry for the first time? Well, I think he must have just dropped in on her and told her he was her cousin she'd never seen. Since Harcourt was happy to meet someone calling himself family, she mustn't have asked too many questions."

"If the guy isn't her cousin, who is he?"

"Good question. Another good question is, why is he pretending to be Kristin Harcourt's cousin? Was it so she would help him get a job at Datacomp? And if so, has he been the one who has been infiltrating WCTS?"

Gil was still frowning. "Didn't Linda Riley tell us Lakoff knew nothing about computers?"

Dana nodded. "She's right. From everything in his schooling and experience, Larry Lakoff knew nothing about computers. But we don't know about the man impersonating him, do we?"

Gil nodded. "How are you going to find out who he is?"

"We're going to pick him up. Talbot had a tail on him when he left Datacomp last night, but he parked his car in a San Francisco garage and never returned to it. He didn't go back to his apartment, either. If he shows up at Datacomp today, there are a couple of agents standing by to take him into custody."

"If he shows up? You don't sound like you think he will."

Dana shook her head. "No, I think he's been warned off or scared off. He looked very uncomfortable when he confronted us in the WCTS room. His nerves were definitely showing."

Gil considered her words. "You know, for a moment I could have sworn I recognized him from somewhere."

Dana's interest was instantly piqued. "Really? Can you remember where?"

Gil shook his head. "No. That's why I didn't mention it earlier. All I know is he's no one I ever met before, but he seems to be someone I've seen before. You understand the difference?"

Dana nodded. "Try to concentrate, Gil. This could be very important. Try to picture where it was you've seen his face."

Gil did try, but ended up scratching his head. "It's no use, Dana. The specifics are just not coming through. It was such a fleeting impression that, at the time, I thought it might have been because I had seen his face earlier in the hall or walking into Datacomp. That might still be the case."

Dana looked disappointed. Gil hated to see her that way and decided there was something he could contribute that might help. "Something he said yesterday could be important in determining his identity, however."

Her eyes lit up in new interest. "What was it?"

Gil sat back, feeling himself on firm ground now. "Remember when he was complaining about computer errors and how they would be compounded if computers were eventually put in charge?"

"Yes, that sounds familiar."

"Well, he said something that struck me as odd at the time. He indicated when the day came that computers took over, human programming would probably be wiped out in 'one big global reformat.'"

Dana dissected the words, trying to find the significance that Gil had found. After a moment she shook her head in defeat. "It sounds all right to me. If you reformat a hard disk, you lose all the programming that existed there. Obviously, he was viewing the globe as analogous to a hard disk and, with a bit of imaginative license, seeing computers committing a reformatting error that wiped out all traces of humankind. Actually, it sounds rather clever and sophisticated when you think about it.''

Gil looked at her intently, smiling. It was his look that finally brought the truth of the matter to her attention.

She leaned toward him, excited. "But, of course! It is clever and sophisticated! Much too sophisticated to have been thought of by someone without a very good understanding of computers! Gil, I see. Whoever this guy really is, he's someone who knows computers, no matter how much of an act he's put on to the contrary!''

Her face was glowing with discovery. She was so lovely, Gil just wanted to scoop her up into his arms and kiss her. He actually found himself leaning across the table with the intent of at least giving her a kiss when suddenly she jumped up.

"Come on, Gil. We haven't a minute to lose. If Lakoff's impersonator is the one who's gotten into WCTS, we've got to find out what he's done.''

VOGEL'S VOICE WHINED OVER the phone line into Sparr's ear. "Leach still hasn't contacted me. You told me he would. What the hell's going on?''

Sparr recognized the unreasoning panic in the man's voice. In his present state, he wasn't any good to anyone and was quite possibly becoming a danger. "Get a grip, Vogel, and for once try to use your head. If Leach had talked, the Feds would be swarming over CustomKey right now.''

The other end of the line was quiet for a long moment. Sparr waited while Vogel made an attempt to steady his nerves. "Why haven't I heard from him then?''

"Take it as good news. The Feds are very proper in their procedures. If they charge somebody, they read him his rights. Leach would have been on the phone to you for a lawyer.''

"So where is he?'' Vogel asked.

Sparr stroked a silver sideburn. "Frankly, I don't know. And at the moment, I don't care. Forget him. Tell me about this mess your programmer found last night that has interfered with your making it to the bank this morning for my bonus and also made you postpone your flight out until tomorrow morning."

Vogel gasped. "How can you know about all that?"

Sparr's voice was as coolly controlled as always. "I'm not interested in your questions, Vogel, only your answers."

Vogel's voice sounded somewhat strangled when he finally found breath enough to speak. "When the Harcourt woman busted in on the WCTS file Monday night, something happened to the programming."

"She interfered with the new programming?" Sparr asked.

"No. We checked the parts of our installation and they worked fine. But it didn't occur to us at the time to check the basic WCTS program. I was sort of eager to get out of the area quickly when Leach came back with the news he had killed the Harcourt woman. As soon as I called you, my programmer and I were out of there."

"And so what did you find last night when you accessed WCTS again?" Sparr asked.

Vogel's exhaled breath blew irritatingly through the phone receiver. "Harcourt's overtyping caused some peripheral programming to be lost. Several branches disappeared."

"You mean WCTS is no longer ready to go?"

Vogel's tone trembled. "No, no, it's okay. My programmer had a copy of what was lost and typed it back in. It's just that it took most of the night, and now we'll need tonight to verify our alterations haven't affected the basic program. And . . ." Vogel's voice faded away.

"And what?" Sparr prompted.

Vogel's voice ascended into new realms of panic. "What if the FBI programmer noticed the missing branches? What if she sees the changes?"

Sparr sat back in his chair. "It would take a very competent programmer several days to work her way to WCTS peripheral branching. I'm not even sure this woman FBI programmer is marginally competent. You've probably replaced the missing programming in time. Worry more about having my money for me tonight, Vogel."

Sparr dropped the telephone into its base, far more irritated at earlier news than the latest Vogel had to offer.

He got up to pace around his desk as his left hand found a pocket in his pearl gray suit pants while his right hand adjusted the already impeccably straight charcoal tie resting against his light silver shirt. In the privacy of his own office, an uncharacteristically deep frown dug straight canals into the normally smooth flow of his forehead.

Where was Brine? He wasn't answering his car phone or the one in his apartment. The Hyatt Regency where his quarry had a room claimed no one by the name of Brine was registered. Sparr wouldn't have thought it necessary for Brine to have taken a room under another name, but he might have. Just to be safe.

And Brine was a man known for playing it safe. That's why his not calling in this morning was bothering Sparr. He might have thought it unnecessary since they had seen each other at the restaurant the night before and he didn't have anything additional to report. He might have, but Sparr doubted it.

As Sparr circled his desk for the third time, a new possibility worked its way up into his thoughts. Had Brine been picked up?

It was an interesting thought and perhaps the logical explanation. Still, if Brine had been picked up, that meant the FBI woman had been the one who picked him up. There was only one reason she would have done it and that was if Brine had learned something.

A new excitement coursed through Sparr's veins. This could be what he had been waiting for. If Brine knew something, Sparr was sure he could depend on his employee to find a way to tell him. For the first time in hours, the silver-haired man smiled.

"THIS IS CRAZY, impossible," Gil said from in front of his computer terminal.

Dana immediately left her terminal to walk over to Gil's so she wouldn't have to raise her voice. "What is it?"

"The checksum formula I loaded in yesterday."

"It isn't adding up?" Dana asked.

"No, it's not. Still, that's not the craziest part."

"What is?"

He turned to her, his glasses pushed back on his head, his hazel eyes alight as he slipped his arm around her waist, not wanting to miss any opportunity to touch her. She felt warm and enticing and he found he had to concentrate even to remember what he was about to say. "Remember those three branches I pointed out to you yesterday? The ones that hadn't been completed?"

Dana raised a hand to finger his hair, surprised at its feather softness. She knew she was enjoying this new closeness between them in ways she couldn't yet even define, and she assiduously refused to think about its unsuitability. "What's happened to them?" she asked.

"They're completed now. Somehow, overnight, someone has completed them."

Dana found his words disturbing. "But, Gil, nobody got in here last night. I verified the lock on the door wasn't compromised. In addition, I set up two hidden recorders to switch on at the slightest sound. I checked their tapes first thing. They're blank."

Gil was shaking his head. "I believe you, but I also have to believe my eyes. And there's something else you should know. Whoever put those branches in last night had to have already known the correct programming. Even to type in that much stuff would have taken several hours. To have

tried to write it first would have taken days, even for someone knowing what they were doing.''

Dana bit her lip as she looked about the room. ''Someone is getting into the WCTS programming data base without gaining access to this room. It's the only possible
explanation.''

Gil nodded at her observation and gave her hand a quick
squeeze as his arm slipped from around her waist. ''I don't
know how it would be possible, but I agree it seems a way's
been found. Can you get me another minicomputer?''

''What are you going to do?''

Gil smiled. ''Let's just say I think it's time we see what
happens when WCTS gets transferred out of this one.''

Dana reached for the telephone. ''I'll call Talbot right
now.''

''YOU WANT AN ELECTRICIAN sent to Datacomp to check the
circuits?''

''As soon as you can arrange it, Talbot,'' Dana said.

''Has Webb uncovered something?''

Dana glanced over at Gil, his head now bent over the
WCTS system configuration printout, already lost again in
its intricate mysteries. She was finding herself unable to take
her eyes from his well-developed forearms flexing quite
nonchalantly as he rolled up his sleeves. An appreciative
smile curled her lips as she remembered the exquisite pressure from those muscles as they caressed her body the night
before.

''Carmody? I asked if Webb had uncovered something?''

Dana deliberately pivoted so that her view was of one of
the blank walls. She gave herself a mental shake and a professional scolding, but inside her chest her unrepentant heart
skipped happily.

''I think it's more like he's confirmed something has been
going on,'' she said in a controlled voice. ''Until now, all

we've had was Kristin Harcourt's word. Now he's found proof WCTS is being invaded. Only questions that remain are why and how."

"And the how is what you want the electrician to verify?"

"Yes. The data base was gotten into last night and the room was secure. There must be a tap into the computer somewhere. I want all of these cables checked, even if it means ripping up the floor. Webb also needs a second minicomputer."

"All right. The electrician and additional minicomputer will be there this afternoon. By the way the guy calling himself Lakoff has disappeared. His apartment is cleaned out."

"You haven't found out who he really is?"

"We're dusting his place for prints now. And speaking of fingerprints, that reminds me. I found out Brine's driver's license thumbprint and his real thumbprint don't match."

Dana blinked at the message in Talbot's words. "You mean he's carrying a false identification?"

"Only explanation. I've put a rush on getting a correct identification on him from the fingerprint lab."

"Has he regained consciousness yet?" Dana asked.

"No."

She heard the uneasiness in Talbot's normally crisp enunciation. "Is everything all right?"

"Honestly, Carmody, I don't know. The X rays confirm Brine has a concussion, but the doctor believes he should have come to by now."

"What is the doctor doing?"

"She's adopted a wait-and-see attitude. If Brine still hasn't regained consciousness by late this afternoon, she'll have him taken back for a more complete set of X rays to try to uncover an injury they missed the first time."

Dana felt uneasy at Brine's condition. She wanted him to regain consciousness and lead them to Sparr so both men could stand trial for their sins. She didn't want to dwell on the possibility that Brine might die, helped along by her hand.

"Talbot, I know I've kept you and your squad hopping, but have you found out any more about Silver Security Systems or the personnel at CustomKey?"

"Silver Security has been difficult. Although it has a major office in San Francisco, I found it's headquartered in Europe. I've got more on CustomKey, however. It seems its elaborate series of corporate overlays is basically camouflage. Its San Francisco manager, Irwin Vogel, the one I told you about earlier, is also its sole owner of all preferred stock."

"You mean Vogel is financing CustomKey himself?"

"You've got it. He used to be a quite wealthy man until about eighteen months ago when the bottom fell out of some overseas investments. It looks like he's thrown all his remaining eggs into this CustomKey basket. Starting a new business is not exactly consistent with his investment background, but apparently he must believe he has an eventual winner to have taken such a step."

"You said 'eventual winner.' Isn't CustomKey doing well?"

"Not well enough to keep up with expenses. Vogel buys his keyboard components from a manufacturing firm in Taiwan. Then he has them shipped to his San Francisco address, where they are assembled into their custom configurations."

Dana shook her head. "Wait a minute. Are you saying Vogel is using his ultraexpensive offices to assemble keyboards?"

"Not just to assemble, but also to store and ship. The Market Street address is also listed as his warehouse."

Dana shook her head, feeling confused. "With the high leasing costs for that piece of real estate, I'd say CustomKey may have one of the most expensive warehouses in the country. Something feels strange here.''

"Maybe Vogel's trying to maintain complete control over the operation by having everything in one place," Talbot said. "He's had a slick, one-page feature description printed up, but he's failed to do any media advertising. It looks as though he relies on the personal visits of a very small sales force to push the product."

Dana's brow continued to wear a frown. "That doesn't sound like very good business savvy to me. He needs advertising to develop a sufficient demand for his product to cover his basic operating costs."

"Maybe that's why CustomKey has yet to squeeze into the black," Talbot said. "Still, no matter how lousy a businessman he is, that doesn't make him a crook. And it doesn't tie him into this case. Remember, his products are hardware. He has nothing to do with a software application like WCTS."

"I suppose," Dana said, but she still felt something about CustomKey wasn't right. She thanked Talbot for the update, then hung up and returned to Gil's side. She found him busily scribbling notes on the system configuration.

"How's it going?" she asked.

He looked up at her when she spoke, and she could tell his mind had been a million miles away. "Hmm?"

Dana smiled and was rewarded by a return smile dazzling enough to put a glow on her toenails. "You just concentrate on being a wizard and I'll go back to my terminal and watch."

She did watch for the next hour as Gil began to enter a new program into WCTS. Its language and intent eluded her, but she could see Gil was constructing it outside of the basic WCTS framework. She was just about to get up and go over to ask what he was doing when a knock came on the door. Instantly, she jumped to her feet and approached the door cautiously, her hand wrapped securely around the gun in her shoulder bag.

In relief, she opened the door to admit the delivery of the second minicomputer, followed by an electrician who had spoken the magic word, *Talbot,* as he passed through. She pried Gil away from his terminal to give the workman a chance to check the cabling and set the new minicomputer in place. Gil participated in the hookup of the new unit and before the electrician had completed his check of both units, Gil was back at work at his terminal.

"You're clean, Carmody," the electrician said as he gathered his tools.

"You're sure there's no way a cable could be in the floor?"

"You can dig up the floor, but you won't find any lead-ins to this cabling or the processors. Look closely and you'll see the container for both the minis is elevated from the floor by wheels. Only way somebody can get into either of these machines is if they use a terminal hardwired to it."

Dana relocked the door behind the electrician. She felt anything but relieved at his findings. She went back to her monitor to watch Gil complete his programming, while her mind fought with the inconsistencies of what could not be, but was.

"YOU WERE RIGHT, SPARR. Brine's been taken," Thiel said as he lowered himself into a side chair in Sparr's office at CustomKey.

"What did you learn?"

"Well, it seems a man answering to Brine's description was taken ill last night at La Mere Duquesne Restaurant and rushed to a hospital by ambulance. Except when I checked, no hospital in San Francisco has any record of anyone by the name of Brine being admitted."

"How about anyone from the La Mere Duquesne Restaurant?"

"I checked," Thiel said. "Nobody."

Sparr began to rub his index finger across his upper lip. "What about the car Brine was driving?"

"It was still sitting in front of the restaurant with a parking ticket on it. I called our contact over at the precinct and arranged for the LeBaron to be taken to the police impound lot. He'll be able to release it to us and get rid of all the paperwork by tonight. Do you think the Feds spotted it?"

Sparr shook his head. "I don't know. Still, we can't take a chance. It's the one thing leading to the firm. Which ambulance company took Brine away?"

"Nobody knew. Some woman claimed he had a diabetic attack and called 911."

Sparr sprang to his feet so quickly and silently that Thiel flinched. The silver-haired man's black eyes shone. "Some woman! Damn it, we know what woman!"

"Yes," Thiel said. "Two paramedics came rolling in a stretcher a few minutes later. The woman left as soon as Brine was taken away. That's all the manager knew."

Sparr paced the room like a wild, caged cat for a moment before he suddenly just stopped and molded his body so perfectly back into his chair that he seemed to become a part of it. "He saw her, Thiel. He saw the FBI woman and she took him out. I still don't know how. Brine was one of the best. Yet she took him out and then coolly called the ambulance and had him taken away."

"You think he really was able to recognize her?" Thiel asked.

"It would be the only reason she would have risked picking him up. Remember, Brine was sitting behind the wheel when she ran past the delivery truck Monday night on the way to her car. Out of all of us, Brine got the best look at her. Damn. She must have walked into that restaurant soon after I left. I probably just missed her."

"So what are we going to do?"

Sparr paused to consider the options. "Brine must be hurt. That explains why he has been tardy in contacting us. No doubt the woman had him admitted to a hospital under a false name."

"You want me to try to track him down?" Thiel asked.

Sparr shook his head. "The FBI may be waiting for just such an inquiry. You'd only succeed in leading them back here to me."

"What are we going to do about Brine?" Thiel asked.

"Nothing. He's not going to talk. He'll get word to us if he can. If he can't..." Sparr shrugged much as anyone might over spilled milk. "Everyone is expendable at some point, Thiel. Meanwhile, Vogel has scheduled his programmer to run the final tests on WCTS tonight. I think you and I should be there to make sure Vogel has our promised bonus."

"And after he's paid it?" Brine asked.

"Well, then we won't need him, will we?" Sparr said.

Thiel was still frowning. "Won't the FBI halt the delivery of WCTS until it can be fully checked out?"

"I doubt they'll be able to. Remember, York has a lot to lose if WCTS isn't in place Monday morning. There's no way that FBI programmer they've sent is going to be able to detect the parasite, and without proof of infiltration, York and his Pentagon contacts will make sure WCTS is sent on its way. From the beginning our only worry has been Gilbert Webb gaining access to WCTS and, fortunately, the FBI was too stupid to use him."

"Even though the FBI agent saw the Harcourt woman's dead body?"

Sparr shrugged. "Don't worry, Thiel, York will demand proof, and proof is the one thing she doesn't have."

"She's got Leach and now Brine," Thiel said.

"Leach is dead," Sparr said.

"How do you know?" Thiel asked.

"Because the FBI can't hold someone incommunicado. They would have had to charge or release him by now, and either way, we would have heard. Since we haven't, I've given you the only possible explanation."

"And Brine?"

"If Brine isn't dead, too, he'll be in touch soon, no matter what they try to charge him with, which can't be a whole lot. Think about it, Thiel. What does the FBI have? One of their agents says she saw a dead woman, but there's no trace of the body or foul play."

"And the guard?" Thiel said.

"The evidence left behind at the Harcourt woman's address all points to their going off together. The FBI programmer can't find a virus in the WCTS program. Even if the female FBI agent's superiors believe her about Harcourt's death, there isn't a whole lot they can do about it. There's no evidence."

Thiel nodded knowingly. "What about the FBI agent?"

Sparr felt the sharp conflict of the need for a speedy departure and the desire to take care of unfinished business. As always when in conflict, his logic ruled.

"Our flight leaves tonight and Vogel's setup is just too sweet a deal to jeopardize."

"It doesn't matter she can identify us?" Thiel asked.

"The bodies of Harcourt and the guard are at the bottom of the bay. We'll be out of her reach in a country without extradition. Besides, with the amount of money we can be expecting soon, we'll be able to go anywhere and change our identities to anyone we want."

Thiel looked surprised. "You're willing to forget her?"

Sparr wore the look of the hungry cheetah waiting in the brush. "You know me better than that, Thiel. But once in South America, I can put out the special kind of contract on our elusive lady that will pay her back in full for all the trouble she's caused. With that to look forward to, I can wait."

Chapter Thirteen

Dana got up from her position in front of the terminal to answer the telephone, aware from the intensity of Gil's expression that he had not even heard it. She identified herself and then straightened up as she heard Sargentich's voice.

"You've been keeping Talbot's squad so busy, they've delegated investigating Silver Security to me."

"Did you find out anything?"

"Are you sitting down?" Sargentich asked.

Dana decided that question coming from her boss probably was a strong hint she should be. She pulled up a chair. "What's up?"

"Silver Security is a privately owned Swiss firm with offices in Europe, America and South America. It's been employed by several companies working on sensitive products or processes to 'protect' them from the industrial spies of competitors. The authorities believe Silver Security has included sabotage and even murder under its charge of 'protection.' Interpol has had it on its suspicious-dealings list for years, but no proof has ever been compiled to charge individuals in the company."

"Well, I admit that's enlightening news, but I think I could have accepted the information standing up," Dana said.

"How about if I tell you the president of Silver Security in this country is one Nigel Sparr?"

Dana gasped at the news, very glad now she was sitting down. Her thoughts spun and when she found her voice again, it had risen high with her excitement. "What else do you know about him?"

"Very little, Carmody."

"But I don't understand, Lew. He's our man. Surely by now the lab has lifted his fingerprints from the glass I messengered and taken a sample of saliva from the rim?"

"Yes, the lab got a DNA print from the saliva. But you know such results are only helpful in identification if we can match them later at the scene of a crime."

"All right. What about his fingerprints?" Dana asked.

"We ran the laser light over the surface and picked up two right thumbs and an index fingerprint. The two thumbprints were from two different people."

Dana raked her mind coming up with the only possible answer. "Of course, they would be. The waiter probably handled the glass when the table was set. All we need is to get his fingerprints so we'll know which one was Sparr's. Is there a problem?"

"In a manner of speaking. The fingerprint on Nigel Sparr's California driver's license doesn't match either of the fingerprints we lifted off the glass."

Dana shook her head, as though she could roll her mental marbles back into the right logic holes. "I don't understand. How can they not match?"

"Nothing matches, Carmody. Not the Swiss passport, the Swiss driver's license nor the California driver's license that were faxed to us this morning. You understand? Not the pictures, not the prints. The identification lab has it all, and the experts are telling me that these are three different men. You've described Sparr as forty, approximately six-four with a full head of silver hair and black eyes. That's the description of the three IDs, but the pictures are of different men."

"Could you have the wrong licenses? Are there just several men all with the same name of Nigel Sparr?"

"No, everything was double-checked. The pictures and fingerprints don't match, but the thread of identity runs through them all. There's only one Nigel Sparr involved, I'm sure. Only one who is president of Silver Security. Only one with a Swiss passport in that name. Only one listed as a San Francisco resident, although the city address given by the person taking out the license is bogus, too. Not an easy thing to do since they ask for proof of address, but not impossible to forge if you're clever and motivated."

"He's certainly that," Dana said, shaking her head. "You know what I think this man has done, Lew? I think he's paid other people of similar build and coloring to take out these driver licenses for him and even pose for his passport. He doesn't want to be fingerprinted or identified in any way. Could it be he's afraid such identification will tie him in to some earlier crime?"

"Bingo, Carmody. The one match we have for one of the thumbprints on that glass is from an unsolved, six-year-old case involving the execution-style death of an FBI agent investigating a Florida murder, also still unsolved. If that print is from this man Sparr, then it's our first real lead in the case."

On some level, Dana wasn't surprised at the news. From the moment she had glimpsed the silver-haired man, she had sensed the danger he represented. Still, news he had been involved in the death of an FBI agent jolted her thoughts. "I'll have Talbot fingerprint the waiter at La Mere Duquesne first thing tomorrow so we can rule him out."

"In the meantime, watch out, Carmody. We have nothing on this guy Brine you picked up. His driver's-license picture is also close but just like Sparr's, it's not really him. Wherever these two have slithered up from, they're being extremely careful not to leave a trail."

Dana got a sudden chill. She found herself looking over at Gil for warmth. Seeing him there, working away diligently was immediately comforting and helped to clear her thoughts. "Lew, will you do me a favor?"

"What is it?" Sargentich asked.

"Talbot did a rundown on CustomKey's financial status, but now I'm curious whether they've included a security-company expense in their quarterly filings for estimated income tax. Could you give the IRS a call?"

"I see," Sargentich said. "You think if they have, it would have been Silver Security?"

"Exactly."

"Okay. But you've told me CustomKey just sells keyboards. What would they need a security company for, and what interest would they have in a Defense Department software application?"

"Good questions all, Lew. Wish I had some good answers. All I know is that something doesn't feel right about CustomKey."

Lew's tone didn't sound convinced. "You've admitted the only lead you have to them was the Cadillac that chased you Monday night, and it was reported stolen the previous weekend."

"Yes," Dana admitted. "Still CustomKey deals with computers and I can't help shake the thought that there is a connection. I think we should take the time to thoroughly check it out."

"Time is a resource we're running out of, Carmody. It's nine o'clock here. York has told his uncle, Colonel Ramsey, that WCTS will be set up with a datalink Friday to transmit its program directly to the Defense Department computers so that it will be up and ready for interface programming Monday morning."

"But tomorrow is Friday," Dana said.

"I'm glad you're keeping track of the passing days."

Dana felt the panic drilling a hole into her stomach lining as she checked her watch. "But, Lew, it's already six o'clock here. We know something is wrong with WCTS. Someone got into it last night after we left."

"How?"

"We're not sure."

"Has Webb identified a virus or anything that will interfere with the program's performance?"

"Well, no—"

"Carmody, listen. You've got to find out whatever is wrong with WCTS tonight. If you try to hold up its data-link delivery to the Defense Department without concrete evidence, York will scream bloody murder and rake us over the coals. If you don't find anything and WCTS is delivered and later found to be defective, then York will still rake us over the coals because he contacted us at the first indication of trouble and we failed to locate it. You can bet he's going to make sure he's not going to be the loser in this."

Dana felt a sour taste on her tongue. "This isn't right, Lew. We've got to be given enough time to do our jobs right."

"Carmody, those words echo out of the mouth of every employee in every industry in America today. You want to estimate your chances of finding a willing ear to listen to your lament?"

Dana exhaled heavily, knowing she didn't have an adequate reply and wondering what one would be.

"Listen, Carmody, you do your best in the time you've got and you've got to make your best count. Remember, York will demand tangible proof if you try to hold up the WCTS delivery past tomorrow. Be sure you have it."

The dial tone echoed in her ear along with Lew's last words. Tangible proof. Something she could hold on to, sink her teeth into, lift up for everyone to see. And so little time left. Dear God, where was it?

She looked over at the back of Gil's head, as he intently studied the monitor before him. His broad, straight shoulders looked tired and sore from so many hours in front of the screen. She knew he was working as fast as he could. Lunch had been a cold sandwich and two cups of coffee, handed to him over his protests, consumed without thought as he continued working on the program. They had barely exchanged a dozen words since.

Suddenly her heart squeezed in pain as she began to question her decision that had dragged Gil into this mess, risking his remaining reputation and even his life. She had had no right. He had shown her at dinner the night before what a fighter he was. He believed in himself and his ability to bounce back from adversity. He would have done just fine without her interference, her arrogance that made her think she was the only one who could offer him a second chance.

He didn't need people giving him chances. He was a man who would make his own chances, one who would never give up. Why had she involved him in this? She wished to God she could turn back the clock again to Monday night and run past the gray Jeep on the cliff ledge.

No. She couldn't wish that, no matter how hard she wanted to. If she hadn't stopped, last night never would have happened. And last night was important not only in closing the door to her pain, but also in opening new doors to her heart. Besides, she knew if Gil couldn't find the problem in WCTS, nobody could. He was the best. She owed it to her country to recruit him. She could only pray she hadn't given him an impossible task.

Squaring her shoulders, Dana strode resolutely back to her own position on the other side of the room to watch the steady stream of data across the screen.

Over the next couple of hours it mesmerized her, however, and she felt her attention drifting. When she suddenly felt the hand on her shoulder, she whipped around, shoving her hand inside her shoulder bag, reaching for her gun.

"Dana, it's all right," Gil said. He knelt down beside her and gently brought her cheek to rest against his own.

Dana gulped down her fright, exhaling a jagged breath. "Sorry. Just a few taut nerves. I'm fine now. What's up?"

"I've found something."

Her pulse quickened as she noticed the new gleam in his eye and lightness of his tone. Her heart beating wildly in her chest, Dana jumped to her feet. "The virus?"

He gave her a quick hug, not able to suppress his own excitement. Then he sat down in her chair, his fingers flying across the keys. The previously hidden file emerged slowly on the screen, reluctantly, as though it was still trying to hide.

Gil watched Dana's eyes search through the code, knowing the evil of its message and intent would not be easy for her to see. He decided not to waste her time and began to explain. "This has been a very difficult virus to locate, Dana."

"What do you mean?"

"Its invasion was subtle. It entered the program in an inactive state. Since it wasn't replicating, affecting the program's operation or causing damage to the data base, it's been easy to overlook. I think the best way I can describe it is by saying it's more like a parasite that is dormant within the body of the WCTS program."

"A dormant parasite?"

Gil circled his arm about her waist. "I believe the protozoa that causes malaria has dormant and active phases. It enters the human body in an active phase, reproducing and traveling throughout it, lodging even within the walls of the tiny capillaries in the earlobes, where it becomes dormant. The medicines used to treat the disease and the body's natural defenses are too large to follow the protozoa into those capillaries, which is why all the symptoms of malaria return when the next cycle of reproduction begins.''

Dana tried to follow the implications of Gil's words. ''Are you saying this . . . parasite in the WCTS program is behaving like the malaria protozoa does in the human body?''

Gil nodded. ''The analogy is close. The hidden WCTS parasite will also erupt out of its dormancy without warning at its prescribed time.''

''Prescribed time?''

''Yes, Dana. Like the malaria protozoa, the WCTS parasite has a specific site in the program where it lies dormant. You see, just as every human body has earlobes, every software application has a time-keeping routine geared to the computer's internal clock. That's where this parasite heads for and nestles in undisturbed, undisturbing and nearly undetectable until its programmed time.''

Dana's eyes traveled from the screen to Gil's face. ''You mean it's scheduled to become active at a future date?''

He nodded. ''Two things activate it. If its host program is hooked up with another data system, the parasite replicates itself and sends the twin program on to infect the other system. In that way, all software systems interacting with WCTS will eventually carry the parasite and pass it on.''

Dana nodded. ''That's why you wanted the second mini? To see if this parasite would infect another data system?''

Gil gave her waist a squeeze. ''Actually, I wanted it for something else, but using it to transmit data to the WCTS program did help me to isolate the parasite and see it in action when it replicated and traveled to the new computer system.''

''You said there were two things that activated the parasite. What's the second?''

''A predetermined time. The WCTS parasite is a time bomb ready to explode in whatever computer system it inhabits. It will stop the various transactions of the infected systems when triggered by their internal clocks on a certain date, at a certain time.''

"Can it be overridden?"

Gil exhaled heavily. "I've tried. But I've found once it has infected a system, any attempt to remove or alter the parasite destroys the program it's in. When I was finally able to isolate it, I tried to change and then remove it. That activated its powerful reformatting program. It wiped away every byte of software in a fraction of a second."

"Is WCTS gone?"

"No. The WCTS data I transferred to the new mini is. The old mini still has the infected program. But before anything is transferred to the Defense Department, a clean WCTS program, one free of the parasite, will have to be entered into a new computer."

Dana gasped as the full implication of Gil's words finally sank in. "My God, Gil. Monday morning, this infected WCTS system is scheduled to be interacting with the Defense Department's entire array of computer systems. If they were all wiped clean, we would be left without even a rudimentary missile-warning system or the capability to retaliate. As a nation, we'd be a sitting duck. And we'd be that way for a long time while the whole defense network was rebuilt. That is, if an unfriendly country didn't find out first and decided to get rid of us while it could."

Gil nodded. "Yes, I figured that might be the setup. Do you think the computer experts at the Defense Department would have been able to locate the parasite before they hooked WCTS up to the other systems?"

Dana licked her dry lips. "I can't know for sure, but I very much doubt it. They've developed a lot of scanning programs for viruses, but since this parasite is already in WCTS, it would look like part of the program. Your checksum test showed that. The existence of the parasite would only become detectable after it entered another system—and by then, it would be too late."

Dana began to pace, finding the harder she tried to digest the information, the more mental heartburn it generated. "Extortion or sabotage, Gil. Maybe both. Whoever has introduced this parasite into WCTS is either ready to extort from the government whatever price he cares to name, or to sell the date and time of our expected paralyzed state to an enemy."

Gil got up to stand by her side, taking her suddenly cold hand into his. "It's all right, Dana. We've discovered it in time. WCTS's delivery date will have to be postponed, but when it's finally delivered, it will be without any devastating parasites."

Dana looked up into his reassuring smile, realizing he had not considered other possibilities that had presented themselves to her.

"Gil, WCTS isn't the only software program being purchased by the Defense Department. I know of at least two others that have been integrated recently, and I'm sure there have been more. In addition, there are numerous other software applications being bought by the various branches of government from low-bid contractors in the private sector. What if the WCTS invasion is not an isolated incident? What if this parasite has been passed through other programs?"

Her words brought an immediate frown to Gil's face as the possibilities presented themselves all too vividly. "Damn, you're right, Dana. The time bomb might already be set in place. For God's sake, is there someone you can call and warn?"

Dana exhaled heavily. "If it's already in place, a warning wouldn't be of any help now. We've got to find the people in back of this parasite, Gil. It's only from them we can learn if they've invaded any other software."

"You mean Sparr?"

Dana nodded. "And the person who's hired him. We've found out Sparr heads Silver Security, a company that offers its services to protect against industrial espionage."

"So Sparr isn't the only one involved."

The glimmer of an idea was flashing in Dana's brain. "Can you tell when the parasite program was completed?"

"Not exactly. Still, whoever did it would have had to have waited until WCTS was completed, and we know that was last Friday."

Dana nodded. "We also know Harcourt noticed the data shadows on her screen Sunday. How long would it have taken to install the parasite?"

"Just a few days for someone who knew what he was doing."

"Or nights. Remember, whoever completed the three missing branches of WCTS did so last night. Gil, whoever is getting into the WCTS data base is doing so after hours. Is there any reason you can think of that they might need to get into the program to make any more changes?"

Gil thought about her question before he ventured his opinion. "Since they completed the three missing branches last night, they might want to run some tests before WCTS is sent to the Defense Department."

"Well, if they're going to run tests before the system is sent, tonight must be the night. Let's sign off the system and turn off the lights."

"You mean wait until someone breaks in to use the system? I thought you said they were doing it without getting into this room?"

"That's what I said, all right. However, I always try to keep an open mind."

He gave her shoulder a squeeze as he sat down at her terminal. Before signing off, however, he took a few minutes to type in a brief program. She watched him, but found he went too quickly for her to grasp the program's purpose. Then he turned off her monitor.

"Clear your screen, but leave your monitor on," Dana said. "We'll need something to see by when we switch off the lights.

Gil nodded as he logged off the WCTS program from his terminal and then moved to the light switch, turning off the ceiling fluorescents and encasing the room in darkness.

They pulled a couple of chairs into a dark corner and settled down to wait. Dana offered Gil a peppermint candy, and they each savored a piece as his steady, strong arm found its way around her shoulders and she leaned against him, relaxing into the drawing heat of his body.

Illuminated only by the rectangular beam of light from the blank screen, the details of the room slipped away and Dana got the strange sensation of having traveled back to a time when cave dwellers huddled next to their mates in the darkness, focusing on a portal of light from the outside, a light that could be darkened at any moment by the hungry outline of some primeval beast. Only she knew it would be a modern electronic beast invading this portal of light, and somehow, it seemed even more deadly.

The small shiver occasioned by her imagination caused Dana to instinctively snuggle up closer to Gil, and he responded by wrapping his other arm around her. It felt good to be this excited when she was close to someone, knowing they would share whatever dangers were to come. The blood coursed happily through her arteries, bringing a bubbling well-being to all her cells, as though they had been infused with a magnum of champagne.

"I don't know if you realize how special your success is, Gil. I don't believe there's another computer programmer who could have found that parasite in the small amount of time you've had. I'll admit to you now there was a moment today when I didn't think even you'd be able to do it, when I was beginning to regret having dragged you into this mess."

His hand stroked her cheek. "Don't ever have regrets, Dana. No matter what happens. Since you took me into your arms Monday night, I've never been happier."

Gil's lips brushed the side of her cheek, warm and tender before they worked their way slowly and seductively to cover her mouth. Dana closed her eyes as his hands pulled her to him and she found herself melting into the welcoming heat of his body.

It was the sudden squeak that broke them instantly apart, the soft, unmistakable squeak of an infrequently used hinge scraping across Dana's nerves like a rusty hacksaw. Her eyes flew open to stare at the door to the hallway as she instantly pushed away from Gil and jumped to her feet. But it wasn't that door that was opening.

Chapter Fourteen

Gil's attention immediately switched from the hallway door to the second squeaky-hinge sound coming distinctly from the other side of the room. He leaned over to whisper in Dana's ear. "It's coming from the left."

She turned her head just in time to see the dark silhouette of a head and shoulders coming through the emergency-exit door. Dana froze in surprise. How could somebody use that door to get in? It was an interesting question, but another far more important one soon claimed her attention. Who was invading the WCTS computer room?

Her eyes strained in the darkness. At first all she could make out was that the person was large. Then as the figure turned to secure the door, Dana knew immediately who it was.

Linda Riley walked directly toward the light of the computer monitor, unaware of Gil and Dana's presence in the dark corner. She passed by Kristin Harcourt's lighted monitor and headed straight for her old terminal, leaning over to turn on its screen. Then she pulled out the chair and sat down, resting her fingers for a moment over the keyboard. Wisps of her dark hair were caught in the monitor's light as the back of her head was silhouetted against the screen.

Gil started forward, but Dana pulled him back. She wanted to see what Riley would do.

Linda accessed WCTS easily and then began flipping through the file. Soon she was talking out loud to the file as if it was a favorite offspring.

"You're looking good to me, baby. We'll give you a tough problem to solve and watch how well you do. Now, let's see. Something I've already worked out an answer to." She reached for one of her documentation binders and flipped through the pages for a minute. "Okay, let's try this one."

She entered in a large set of figures and then gave a command for WCTS to process. Without only a few seconds, the answer was flashing on her screen. Linda leaned over to give the monitor a big hug. "You did it, baby! See, there's nothing wrong with you. I knew it."

Dana leaned over to whisper in Gil's ear. "Get the lights."

Dana felt more than saw Gil's nod as he moved swiftly to the light switch. She stepped forward in the couple of seconds it took to brightly light the room.

Dana watched Riley spin around in her chair, the documentation book in her lap dropping noisily to the floor as she stared at Gil in fright. Her mouth fell open as her dark eyes then bounced from Dana to Gil. Her voice was barely a squeak. "What are you doing here?"

Dana limped forward, studying the woman's unveiled stupefaction every step of the way. "No, Linda, that's our question. We're the ones owed an explanation."

Riley raised a shaking hand to her forehead, shoving back the hair that had rushed forward in her wild turn of a moment before. Her voice was still far too high. "I didn't expect to find anyone here. You scared me."

Dana kept her voice hard, uncompromising. "That wasn't the answer we were looking for, Linda. Try again."

Riley looked around the room for a moment, as though she was looking for a door to escape through. The changing expression on her face told Dana she hadn't found one. Suddenly, her shoulders slumped and she sighed heavily.

"I know I shouldn't have done this, but I just couldn't help it. WCTS is more mine than it ever was Kristin's. Even its basic program was my idea. The first time I told him about it, he wouldn't listen. So I told Kristin about it and got her to approach him."

"Him?" Dana repeated.

"York, of course."

"Of course," Dana said. "And he listened to Kristin?"

"Yeah. Same idea, just a different source. Made all the difference."

Dana saw the sharp, bright pain in the woman's dark eyes. She knew the emotion was real. "Why did you come here tonight, Linda?"

The woman's head pivoted questioningly. "Why, to check WCTS out, of course. To find the problem."

Dana saw the edges of confusion lace Riley's eyes. She moved forward to get closer to those eyes, so expressive now where they had been so guarded at lunch the day before. She stopped just a foot away to look down into the round face. "To find the problem, or to be sure the problem couldn't be found?"

Riley's pupils expanded to fill her entire eye sockets. "What are you talking about?"

Dana continued to study the woman's eyes. "How do you know there's a problem with WCTS?"

"I told you. Kristin wouldn't let me stick around Monday. And then she mysteriously disappeared and you two show up. I'm not dumb, no matter how I look."

There was a world of hurt in Riley's tone, but Dana put aside her reactions to it as she pressed on in her questions. "What do you mean Kristin 'mysteriously disappeared'?"

Riley's eyebrows shoved together in a frown. "I've called her two nights in a row. If she were really home with the flu, she would have answered. You've got her stashed away somewhere, haven't you?''

"Why were you trying to reach Kristin?"

The woman shrugged. "I thought I could get her to tell me what she had found wrong. I..." Riley's voice faded away as her head sank to her chest.

Dana knew she had to keep on with her questions. "Why is finding out what is wrong with WCTS so important to you, Linda?"

When the woman raised her large head, Dana saw the tears swimming through her dark eyes. "You won't understand this, but I'm proud of what I do. It's not even important anymore if no one knows it's me that's doing it. But it is important to me to know I've done it right."

Dana did understand, both the words and the naked, exposed pain on Riley's face. "Linda, are you telling me the truth?"

A thin, fierce rim of pride circled the sad, dark pools floating in Riley's eyes. "I've been called a lot of lousy things in my life, but a liar has never been one of them. But you go ahead and think what you like. I don't care."

And at that moment, Dana was firmly convinced Riley didn't. She gave her a moment to compose herself before asking her next question. "Is tonight the first night you've come into the WCTS computer room?"

The woman nodded as she took a tissue from her pocket.

"How did you manage to come through the emergency-exit door since it has no lever or handle to allow it to be pulled open?"

When Riley looked up, Dana could see the moisture in her eyes. "I used a heavy, industrial-sized, magnetized handle. It adhered to the metal door with enough strength to allow me to pull it open."

Dana limped over to the door and pressed the metal bar to open it. She stepped out briefly into the cool April night air and felt for the magnetized handle. When she found it, she also found it took all her strength to remove it from the door. She stepped back inside and the door closed behind her.

Holding the handle in her hand, she limped back to where Linda Riley sat. "What released the latch from the outside and prevented the alarm from going off when that door was opened?"

Riley's head came up. "I just accessed the security program in the master computer and switched off the spring on the electronic latches and the emergency-door alarm programs. Piece of cake."

Dana and Gil exchanged glances, as if each was thinking that such a possibility was so simple, they should have thought of it. Dana looked back down at Linda Riley, feeling a string of emotions ranging from mild pity to deep respect. She dropped the magnetized handle onto the table and exhaled as she made a sudden decision.

"Leave through the hallway door, Linda. Get to a terminal where you can access the master computer again and reactivate the electronic latches and emergency-exit door-alarm programs. Then call us on this extension and let it ring once to let us know the system's back on-line."

Riley looked a little stunned by Dana's words. "Then what? Am I supposed to come back here?"

Dana began limping toward the door to unlock it so the woman could pass through. "Then go home, Linda."

Riley got to her feet, looking at both Gil and Dana in continuing surprise as she slowly made her way to the door. "You're not going to report me for breaking in tonight?"

Dana stood rather stiffly next to the now-open door. The same stiffness saturated her tone. "I think the less said about tonight the better. We'll be in touch about WCTS."

Riley was almost through the door when she stopped and turned to face Dana. She looked at Dana a moment, then mumbled a small thank-you before passing through to the hallway. Dana closed the door behind her and locked it. She turned back to Gil.

"You believe her, don't you?" he asked. "That's why you decided to give her a break and let her go."

Dana nodded. "She's been kicked a lot. I didn't see any reason for us to add another boot mark. Besides, she carries too much pride in her work to be responsible for infecting it with the kind of parasite you've found. Don't you think so?"

Gil logged off Riley's terminal and turned off the monitor. Then he smiled at Dana as he came to put an arm around her shoulders. "Yes, I believe her, although I admit I didn't want to at first. Life would have been so much easier if she had turned out to have been the one. Still, I'm glad you let her go."

Dana nodded as she circled her arm about his, enjoying the excitement of his touch and the gentleness she found in his heart. "Doesn't look like we're going to get an easy break on this one."

He gave her forehead a fleeting kiss as he repositioned her glasses on the top of her head. "Ironic, isn't it? We put a new lock on the front door and yet ignore the back. Well, at least now we know how our computer infiltrator got in."

"Do we?" Dana asked as she repositioned his glasses as he had hers.

Gil's unveiled hazel eyes gave her a questioning look. "If Linda Riley could figure out how to inactivate the electronic latch and alarm, someone else could. Doesn't that explain how they got in?"

Dana scratched her sprayed hair. "It doesn't explain why the tapes set to activate at any sound didn't record someone in the room."

Gil frowned at Dana's words, having momentarily forgotten about the recorders. "Is there any way they could have malfunctioned?"

Dana shrugged as she considered his words. "One maybe, but not both. Besides, I checked them out last night and this morning. They were operating perfectly."

"Well, what's the answer?"

"I don't know. What do you say we turn off the lights again and resume our orchestra seats. Maybe we still have a chance to be an audience for the upcoming WCTS penetration performance, that is, if our Miss Riley's unscheduled appearance on stage hasn't scared them off."

As though on cue, the telephone rang once and then stopped. "That's her signal the alarms are back on. Flip the light switch, will you, Gil?"

Gil was already halfway there. As soon as the room was in virtual darkness again, except for the light from Kristin's monitor, he joined Dana, once again sitting side-by-side in the dark corner of the WCTS computer room.

"We may have a while to wait," Dana said.

His arm circled her shoulders once again, bringing her close to him. "It could be all night for all I care," he said as his lips once again sought the softness of hers.

"IT WAS THE RILEY WOMAN who must have been running the check program through WCTS," Thiel said as he lifted himself up into the back of the beige delivery van. "When I went around to check, I saw her leave through Datacomp's front entrance and drive away in her car."

Thiel's words did not reassure Sparr. "How did she get into the WCTS computer room? I would have thought the FBI programmer and agent would have arranged for a new lock."

"They didn't even lock the door when I walked in on them Wednesday," the man known as Lakoff said as he sat in front of the monitor hooked up to his own CustomKey keyboard sitting on a table in the van.

Sparr looked over at the thin, dark-haired man, so covered with nervous perspiration his thin shirt was soaked through in the comparatively cool temperature of the van. "All right, maybe it was just the Riley woman. Try it again," he said.

Vogel came to his feet, rising from the padded bench seat lining one wall of the van. "Now wait a minute, Sparr. I'm in charge here."

Sparr's dark eyes bored into Vogel's heavy face. The force of the look alone sent Vogel spiraling back onto his seat. "The only thing you're in charge of, Vogel, is running the portable generator. I think our programmer is ready for some juice. Turn it back on."

Vogel nervously leaned across the seat to throw the switch on the noisy generator that instantly sprang to life. Lakoff positioned his fingers over the keys and began to type in the jerky rhythm of one who used a computer keyboard frequently, but had never learned to touch-type.

"I'm in," he said. "I've accessed the WCTS program. I'll run a few check programs, similar to what the Riley woman was doing, but focused on using the time components built into WCTS. That should tell us if our little parasite will lay dormant through the Pentagon's normal program runs. Shouldn't take more than fifteen to twenty minutes to be sure."

All eyes in the darkened van sought the light of the computer monitor and its changing displays.

GIL HAD ALMOST FORGOTTEN where he was with Dana's soft lips melting so enticingly into his own until her excited, albeit breathy words brought him crashing back into stark reality.

"Gil, Kristen's monitor! Something's happening!"

Gil turned to stare at the screen's quickly changing data as Dana jumped out of his arms. Then he quickly followed her as she rushed over to stand in front of the monitor. He watched, fascinated, as the WCTS software not only flashed onto the monitor but as letters and symbols requiring programs to be run magically appeared.

Dana voiced his own unspoken question. "I don't understand. How are those commands being entered, Gil?"

"Just as though someone was sitting here at this position and typing away," Gil said. "Except someone isn't. Dana, this is fascinating."

Dana's voice all of a sudden sounded very strange. "That's what it was doing that night."

Gil turned to look at her staring eyes and the unnatural expression on her face. "Dana? What is it? What night are you talking about?"

Dana blinked as though she had been in a momentary trance. "Monday night, Gil. When I walked in and found Kristin sitting at this position. The screen looked like this one does now—like someone was sitting in front of these keys and typing away."

Gil nodded. "Yes, I remember when you mentioned that just before we were to meet Riley for lunch yesterday. I thought the description strange. I remember I was going to ask you more about it when some people came within hearing distance and I had to drop it."

"Can you explain it?" Dana asked.

"All I can tell you is that someone is somehow bypassing this keyboard and using this terminal to gain access to the minicomputer to make changes to WCTS."

"But, Gil, isn't that impossible?" Dana asked.

Gil exhaled and shook his head. "I would have said yes until I saw this. I'm afraid it's hard to argue with what's happening right in front of you."

"Can you stop what they're doing now?" Dana asked.

Gil sat down in front of the rapidly changing monitor display and rubbed his hands, as though they needed additional circulation for the attempt. "Actually, I have a little surprise for our invisible visitor here."

"A surprise?" Dana asked.

"Yes. A little program of my own to unleash."

His fingers depressed the control and then the Z key to activate his program, but he was diverted as he saw the result on the screen before him.

"Look, Dana. The Z I typed came out looking like a shadow compared to the other figures and text being entered on the screen. A data shadow, Dana. Isn't that what Kristin said she saw on her screen?"

Dana nodded, but she felt confused. "Yes. If there was other data being entered somehow from somewhere else, I can see how Kristin's entries would mix with them like shadows. But there must be something wrong with your keyboard. I couldn't hear the click when you pressed the keys."

"It's okay, Dana. You're not supposed to hear them. This is a QuietKey keyboard. Not bad once you get used to it. Cuts down on an office's ambient-noise level considerably."

"A QuietKey keyboard?" Dana stared at the label on the keyboard, seeing above it the larger product designation of CustomKey for the first time. Several pieces of information came at her at that moment and congealed into a very strong suspicion. The black Cadillac had been owned by CustomKey. This was one of the keyboards in their QuietKey line. Could it be coincidence? "I wonder," she said aloud.

"You wonder what?" Gil asked.

Dana didn't hear Gil's question. She was too busy rummaging through her shoulder bag, trying to locate the electronic sweep device. She finally succeeded and pulled it out, passing it over the QuietKey keyboard as Gil sat staring at her. Each letter or number flashing on the screen registered as an active transmission.

"Gil, the keyboard. It's the bug!"

Gil blinked at her. "What?"

Dana was still staring at the blips the device was picking up from the transmissions through the keyboard. "All the safety precautions taken with the metal shielding, all the double checks with passwords and door locks—no wonder none of it worked! They had the transmission mode right here. See, Gil? Look at the pulses registering as active transmissions through this keyboard."

"Dana, are you saying someone's using this keyboard to gain access to the WCTS software in the minicomputer?"

"Yes, Gil! I bet it's a duplicate keyboard—one that communicates with this one like a Siamese twin. Ingenious, isn't it? These keys on this board are both senders and receivers to its twin. At the moment they're acting as receivers, transmitting information into the minicomputer being typed on another CustomKey keyboard equipped with a similar set of sending and receiving keys."

"Another keyboard?" Gil said. "Dana, I've never heard of anything like you're describing."

"Neither have I. It's got to be a new technology, spawned, if I'm not mistaken, by the makers of CustomKey computer keyboards."

Gil felt a noxious balloon beginning to expand in the pit of his stomach. "CustomKey? Dana, how sure are you the people of CustomKey are in back of this infiltration?"

But Dana hadn't heard his question as she was trying to put other facts into place. "They've got to be close by. I don't think this type of sophisticated transmission could be too reliable from too great a distance."

Dana knew she did not have a moment to waste. She ran to the phone and grabbed it, punching in Talbot's number as fast as her fingers would move.

"Talbot, it's Dana. I've found how they're doing it! It's the keyboard, CustomKey's keyboard, that is the access to the WCTS software. You understand? They're getting in through the keyboard."

"Carmody, slow down," Talbot said. "I don't understand. What's all this about a keyboard? Has someone broken in?"

Dana took a deep breath, attempting to put a halt to her racing thoughts. "They didn't need to get into the WCTS computer room. Everything being typed on a CustomKey keyboard in this room was transmitting to them at an off-site receiving station. And the off-site station can transmit data from its electronic tie-in through this same CustomKey keyboard into any computer it's connected to."

Talbot's precise whistle echoed in Dana's ear. "Dear God, Carmody, how did you find out?"

"They're transmitting right now. Webb and I are watching everything they're doing on the monitor. They've got to be close by, Talbot, maybe in some temporary structure or even a mobile unit.... No, wait a minute. The beige delivery van I saw Monday night. I bet they're set up inside it!"

"You might be right, Dana. It could be parked on some side street around there and nobody would have given it a second thought."

"Talbot, we can take them now. We know what they've been doing and the way they've been doing it. If we can catch them in the act, we'll have everything we need for prosecution. How fast can you get here with backup?"

"Thirty minutes, Carmody. Except there's a problem."

Dana felt a small twinge up the back of her spine. "What problem?"

"Well, you launched into your discovery so fast, I didn't have a chance to tell you. I was just about to call. Apparently, Brine has been playing possum with us. He wasn't unconscious for nearly as long as we thought. He was just waiting for an opportunity."

"Talbot, what are you saying?"

"He escaped from the hospital, Carmody, about twenty minutes ago. He took a nurse hostage when she came in to change his IV. He stole his guard's gun, then knocked his hostage down in the parking lot after he got the keys to her car. I've alerted the local authorities and have half my squad out looking for him."

Dana's previous small twinge was now gyrating up her spine like a washing machine struggling with an uneven load in the spin cycle. She grabbed hold of the small table edge with one hand as the other squeezed the telephone receiver in an effort to maintain her control. Still, she was surprised her voice didn't quiver when she responded. "He may head for CustomKey or Silver Security."

"I've got agents waiting if he does. Don't worry, Carmody. We'll get him. Now you sit tight and we'll be there soon."

Dana hung up the phone and turned to Gil. Gil had heard her side of the conversation and had seen how very white her face had become. Without further hesitation, he circled his arm about her and drew her to him, needing to feel the beat of her heart.

"Brine escaped?" he asked.

Dana felt Gil's warmth seep in to steady her nerves. She related Talbot's side of the conversation and felt a release of a lot of tension with the ability to share these things with Gil. When she finally stepped out of his arms, the relief of her unburdened thoughts proved short-lived as she saw the look on his face.

It was full of shock and anger, emotions she couldn't believe had materialized from just learning about Brine's escape. Then she knew. Something else had happened to Gil. Something her own concerns had blinded her to until now.

"Gil? What is it?"

Gil felt her light eyes caressing his face, smoothing out the lines of disillusionment he knew had dug their way around his eyes and mouth. A feeling of déjà vu came over him as he remembered how her eyes had touched him in this soft, searching way on Monday night and overcome his hesitancy to discuss the loss of his fiancée and job. And now those same subjects were coming up again. He took a deep breath in preparation for what he was to say.

"Dana, I had one of CustomKey's computer keyboards at Computech. I had begun using it just two weeks before the data loss."

He watched the shock hit her face and then gradually turn into the light of discovery. "Gil, these people getting into WCTS to plant their sabotage, they must be the same ones who destroyed the new-product date base at Computech!"

Her excitement flowed through her hands as she grabbed Gil's arms. He felt the pressure, hard and firm like the determination in her voice. "All we have to do is trace the keyboard transmissions to them and we've got the people who framed you. Gil, you understand, don't you? Soon we're going to know who they are!"

Gil felt his breath catch as he watched her lovely face aglow with her enthusiasm to right the wrongs done to him. He raised his hand to run the back of his fingers gently across her flushed cheek, but found his hand was shaking so badly from the intensity of his feelings for her that he had to drop it again to his side.

It took him a moment to steady his voice for what he had to say. "I already know who they are, Dana."

Chapter Fifteen

Dana felt the astonishment freeze the expression on her face. "You know, Gil?"

"Yes, Dana. It was just about seven months ago that Vanessa presented me with the gift of the QuietKey keyboard."

Dana was sure she had heard wrong. "Your ex-fiancée gave you the keyboard that was used to destroy your career?"

Gil exhaled and nodded. But the information was still causing Dana to frown. "This doesn't make sense, Gil. I saw Vanessa in the restaurant with you. I lip-read the words she said. She didn't act like somebody who had set you up. There was nothing in her words or mannerisms that spoke of animosity. Quite the contrary."

Gil detected the jealousy in Dana's last words and smiled, curiously reassured of her interest and finding it took a lot of bite out of the betrayal he had been feeling. He slipped his hand into hers, luxuriating in the softness of her skin next to his.

"Vanessa told me it was her father's idea. It could be she wasn't in on it. He'd gone into a new business, and she said I'd be doing him a favor by trying out one of his new products and letting him know what I thought. I'd met her father a few times, and I can tell you I wasn't impressed. But for her..."

As Gil's voice faded, Dana found Vanessa's beautiful blond hair and blue eyes flashing vividly into mind. Yes, she could imagine that for her, most men would do almost anything. Then Dana's mind played back Gil's recent words, and she found other matters claiming her attention.

"You said the keyboard was from her father's new business?"

Gil nodded. "CustomKey. Her father is the founder and president, Irwin Vogel."

The words swirling around in Dana's mind found their way to her lips. "Of course, CustomKey. It all ties in. Vanessa got you to use the keyboard at Computech. No doubt the bogus cousin, Larry Lakoff, was the one instrumental in getting Kristin Harcourt to use this CustomKey keyboard here. Gifts from the Greeks."

"Gifts from the Greeks?"

"The Trojan horse, Gil. Or in this case, two Trojan horses. One you carried unwittingly within the walls of Computech's new-product data base. This second one, Kristin Harcourt unknowingly let into WCTS data base. I wonder how many more are out there."

Gil shrugged. "Well, at least this one is just about to frustrate the hell out of whoever is using it for destruction."

Dana turned back to the screen at Gil's words. For a moment, nothing seemed to have changed. Then all of a sudden, lines of data began to black out and then blink on as others blacked out. "What's happening?" she asked.

"Oh, just a little program I thought might come in handy when next the WCTS program was invaded. This ought to keep them tearing their hair out until Talbot and his troops get here."

Dana smiled up into Gil's eyes. "You really are a wizard, aren't you?"

He kissed her nose as he hugged her to him. "As long as you think so."

IRWIN VOGEL JUMPED TO HIS feet as he glared over the programmer's shoulder. "What in the hell is happening?"

The thin young man at the keyboard was sweating even more profusely as his fingers flew over the keys. "I don't know! This is crazy! These damn rows are blinking on and off like Christmas-tree lights!"

Sparr watched the monitor with growing unease. "Are you telling me there's something wrong with your *perfect* parasite?"

At the deadly calm in Sparr's voice, Vogel began to sweat. He looked at the silver-haired man nervously and then back down at the man sitting before the keys. "What's wrong, damn it? You didn't have this type of problem at Compu-tech."

"I don't know, Irwin. Maybe it's just a failing monitor. Help me hook up that new one sitting over in the corner."

Sparr watched the two men struggle to coordinate their efforts to replace the monitor. After a couple of minutes, despite their clumsy efforts, they succeeded. But soon it was evident the new monitor wasn't helping.

The programmer's voice was almost in awe. "I've never seen anything like it. There's absolutely no pattern to it. Lines just fade away and then come back at different intervals."

Vogel's voice reflected all the strain that had swelled up in the man. "Damn it, fix this. We've got billions of dollars riding on this deal. Fix the damn thing!"

Sparr watched the programmer continuing to press keys in a frantic attempt to stop the blinking of the rows. The minutes ticked by—fifteen, twenty—and then he slumped back and just watched the blinking screen as though he had been caught in a hypnotic trance. When he finally made his proclamation, Sparr knew what he would say.

DANA STOOD BESIDE GIL AS she watched the frantic entries filling the screen. "Whoever it is must be getting the feeling he's losing. What if he gives up and leaves?"

Gil nodded. "It's possible. However, I judge the worth of a programmer by how long he stays with a task. For someone who designed that devastating parasite program, I think he should at least stick with this problem for an hour or so."

Dana heard Gil's words but knew he might be reading too much of his own determination into the mind of this other programmer. She couldn't take the chance that this frustrated programmer might quit before Talbot and his agents arrived. She made the only decision possible under the circumstances.

"I've got to try to locate them before the others arrive," Dana said as she reached into her ever-present shoulder bag to reassure herself of her gun's location. "The savings in time could make all the difference."

"Dana, you can't go out there alone. They might spot you."

"Don't worry, I'll be careful, Gil. But I can't risk the chance of losing them now. I know they're close by. I just want to be sure I keep an eye on them until backup comes."

"Well, there's nothing more I can do here," Gil said as he tried to straighten his tie, not quite succeeding. "I'm ready."

Dana shook her head as his intent became clear, both warming and chilling her heart. "Absolutely not. You stay here and wait for Talbot. Or my return, whichever comes first."

Gil took a hold of her arm. "Dana, please. You can't expect me to just sit here and wait while you're out there facing who knows what. I know you can handle yourself, but—"

"And I know you can handle yourself, too. But you're untrained, Gil. You're the programmer and I'm the agent, so stay here and make sure you're locked in nice and safe."

Dana could tell her words hadn't made much of a dent in Gil's resolve to help. She raised her hand to his cheek and stroked it gently. "Gil, if I'm worried about your being hurt, I could make a mistake and get hurt myself. For my sake, you must remain here. You must. And that is an order."

His eyes read the worry in her face and he found himself nodding only to relieve it. "All right, bodyguard." He walked with her quietly to the door, but just before she passed through, he pulled her to him and kissed her hot and hard. "I love you, Dana."

Dana was still feeling Gil's kiss and hearing his words branding her heart as she walked out the door, a part of her wishing she had never left his arms. But the other part of her knew her job required her best, and her best was what she would give.

The security guard gave her a cursory glance and then redirected his attention back to the ball game blasting from his portable TV set.

As she limped through the glass doors, a cold blast of night air rushed into her lungs. She shivered as she peered out to the main road leading into the Datacomp facility, faintly lit by the building's lights. It was empty. The only vehicle in the parking lot was a small, beat-up Datsun, probably belonging to the security guard.

She decided to circle the building to see if there was a smaller road or two around back, reasoning that if she was going to use a delivery van to do some industrial snooping, she would park it in the most out-of-way spot she could find. Once out of the guard's sight, she held her cane up high and began to run, attempting to keep pace with her sense of racing time.

Rain sprinkled on her face as a strong breeze ripped cold and wet through her light clothing. Dana picked up her pace as she circled the building, feeling her muscles warming to the movement and knowing such movement was all that was keeping her from freezing. When she reached the back of the building, she paused and stared into the black night as her warmed breath emitted short puffs of steam into the chilling air.

Vaguely, she could distinguish the outline of a large vacant lot, polka-dotted with tufts of nondescript vegetation. But she could see no farther. The strong westerly wind kept a battalion of dark and heavy clouds marching across the sky.

Then while her eyes were focused straight ahead, the clouds parted just long enough for the light from a half moon to circle the delivery truck parked along a side road about thirty feet away. Dana couldn't make out any detail, but she was sure it was a light color. She could also see the strip of light escaping from its slightly ajar door at the back. Her heart began to race as she drew the gun out from her shoulder bag and closed the distance.

The wind whistled past her ears as the sky darkened in ominous prophecy. Just as she made it to the front of the van, Dana gasped in surprise as a crack of lightning flashed right in front of her. Her eyes opened wide as it lit the beige van and the silver Mercedes that had been pulled off to the side of the road screened by a row of thick pine trees. And another car. A small dark car. Was it just pulling up? Or did its appearance of movement come from the shadows of swaying trees?

Too late. The lightning passed and the night turned black once more. It was decision time. Should she head for cover to wait for Talbot and the others, or should she try to get closer and discover how many they were up against and how well they were armed? Her training provided the answer.

Slowly, carefully, she felt her way to the back doors of the van, flattening her body against its metal side, her fingers sliding across its cold, slick surface. She was thankful for the comforting darkness that gave her cover, for the whistling wind that muffled the sound of her shoes on the loose gravel.

Closer and closer, she approached the small sliver of light at the back door. She was just at the corner of the van when she began to hear the voices coming from inside.

"IT'S NO USE, IRWIN. The program's not responding. It's caught in some weird loop that's causing this blinking thing. I don't understand it at all. I can't even shut off WCTS."

Vogel's voice was loud and shrill as he turned on the dark-haired man sitting in front of the keyboard. "What are you saying?"

The programmer turned to him with slumped, bony shoulders, his raspy voice full of frustration. "What do you think I'm saying? It's over. When they turn the terminals on tomorrow, they're going to see this. York can't transfer this...this garbage to the Defense Department. I don't care how mediocre the FBI programmer is. She can't miss this."

Sparr watched as Vogel's face became redder with each word out of the programmer's mouth. When the large man finally spoke, he was so angry he sputtered. "'I'm the best,' you said. 'Trust me,' you said, 'I can fix the keyboards. I can fix the program with a parasite.' You imbecile! Do you know the money I've wasted on your empty promises?"

The pimpled face of the programmer turned beet red in frustration. "It should work! I know it should work!"

Vogel wasn't listening. With a vicious cuff of his hand, he knocked the young man to his knees beside the chair in front of the computer monitor. "I'll kill you for this!"

Sparr stepped in front of the large man. "You've lost, Vogel. Accept it like a man and hand over my money."

Sparr watched several expressions cross Vogel's face, all predictable. "I'm not getting my payoff. Why should you get yours?"

"Because, Vogel, my payment is not predicated on your success. I provided security. I intend to get paid for my services."

Vogel's eyes darted nervously from Thiel to Sparr. "I don't have it with me," he said, running the back of his hand over the moisture collecting on his upper lip. "I'll have to get it."

Sparr nodded to Thiel, and the big blond man began searching Vogel's pockets over the immediate loud protests of the angry man. Thiel ended up unbuckling a thick money belt from around Vogel's waist and, after a brief scrutiny of its contents, nodded back to Sparr. "Half a million in cash."

Vogel's voice shook as with one hand he reached for the money belt while the other dived into his back pocket to emerge with a small gun. "You can't take that. Give it back or I'll shoot."

He barely had time to get the words out when one of Thiel's powerful hands grabbed his thick neck while the other swatted the gun from his hand as though it were a toy. Sparr nodded again, and the big blond man smiled as his powerful hand closed tighter and tighter around Vogel's throat. A strangled gasp was the last sound out of Vogel's mouth before he collapsed onto the floor of the van.

It was in the following instant of quiet while all three men were staring at the dead one on the van floor that the shouted warning flew in from the open door.

"Dana! Behind you!"

Dana knew instantly it was Gil's voice coming from behind her. In pure reflex, she dropped to her knees and spun around. On some level, she recognized that he had once again ignored her orders and followed her. But she had no time to dwell on the ramifications. She felt the bullet shear off the wayward strands of hair at the top of her head as she let loose her cane and raised her gun to return fire. She didn't have to consciously think of the direction. Hours of practice on the shooting range took over to focus her aim.

The two loud retorts of her gun deafened her ears. Yet an instant later, she heard the heavy thud of the falling body and knew she had hit her mark dead center.

It had all happened so fast, a momentary shock swept in to dull her brain. She walked on wooden legs to the fallen figure, reaching him just at the same moment that she felt Gil grab her in a hug that was so forceful, it knocked her glasses back onto her nose.

She reached out her free hand to grab him as the door to the back of the van opened wide. Her first thought was to raise her gun, but before she could whip it from around her back, she felt it ripped out of her hand. As she looked up to see Sparr's and Thiel's drawn weapons, she realized it didn't matter. She wouldn't have even had time to get off a shot.

"Drop the gun," Sparr said.

Dana was about to answer she didn't have it when suddenly she heard the gun dropping by her feet and the import of Gil's action finally registered. He had taken the gun from her so that Sparr would still think that it was he who was the FBI agent and she the programmer. For whatever it might buy them, the masquerade was still on. She gave Gil's arm a quick squeeze to tell him she understood.

She didn't have time to feel angry or happy that Gil had gone against her specific instruction and followed her. Yes, he had just saved her life, but in doing so, he had put his own in mortal danger, and that knowledge was burning into her heart like a hot coal.

As she looked at the two men before them now, she knew the odds of either her or Gil getting out of this alive were too slim to contemplate.

"Are there others around?" Thiel asked.

Sparr's head shook. "No, they would have yelled out 'FBI' and have us surrounded by now if there were. Fools that they are, these two are alone."

Thiel jumped down from the back of the van and walked over to them, shining a light on the dead man at their feet. He pushed Dana and Gil back and kept them there with the threat of his gun before taking a good look at the fallen man. "Damn, it's Brine. What goes on? He disappears for a day, and the next thing we know, he's shot to death right next to the van. I don't like this, Sparr."

Dana didn't think Sparr looked as though he liked it, either, yet his voice was deadly calm, that same deadly calm she had overheard only moments before as he told Vogel he intended to get his money. "Get these two into the van. Maybe they've got some answers."

Thiel yanked her away from Gil and then poked her in the back with his gun as an incentive to move. She limped over to where she had dropped her cane, intending to pick it up as a possible future weapon, but Thiel shoved her past it and ripped her shoulder bag from her arm, throwing it down on the ground and out of her reach. With exaggerated feebleness she dragged her body along as her racing mind searched frantically for a means of escape.

On command, Gil leapt agilely into the back of the van, but Dana knew she couldn't do the same, not if she hoped to maintain her projected weakness. As soon as she feigned her climbing difficulty with her braced leg, Gil started forward to help, but Sparr used his gun to wave him back. "Get her up here, Thiel."

Dana felt herself grabbed from behind, lifted and thrown into the van like a sack of potatoes. Instinctively, she curled up as her leg brace screeched loudly along the metal floor like some tortured thing, until her body crashed against a side panel and came to an unceremonious halt, draped over something still warm but dreadfully still.

In a flash of understanding, she now understood the uneasy quiet that had followed Vogel's desperate demand for his money's return. The man had been murdered. She wanted to gasp for the breath just knocked out of her lungs, to push away from the loathsome corpse she was jammed up against, but with everything she had she forced herself to go limp, to lie still, to keep her eyes shut and to barely breathe at all.

For all the evenness in Sparr's voice, his displeasure was evident. "Damn it, Thiel. It was the woman I wanted to interrogate. When you beat up a woman, even if she won't talk, a man will always spill his guts to get you to stop. She's no good to me passed out."

"Don't worry," Thiel said. "I'll rouse her."

Dana heard and felt the vibration of Thiel's heavy boots as they came toward her. She felt Vogel's body being pushed aside. She knew that whatever the man planned wouldn't be pleasant and braced herself, but the sudden, vicious kick to her side forced an uncontrollable gasp from deep inside her lungs.

Fortunately for her, Gil lurched at Thiel, yelling a particularly filthy and derogatory expression at the same moment the man's boot was connecting with her flesh. He caught the blond, bearded man's arm and attention just at the right moment to mask Thiel and Sparr hearing her outcry. Unfortunately, from the following unmistakable sounds, Dana realized it had also earned Gil the next kicks.

Thiel's tone smarted worse than the blow he had administered to her ribs. "Let's forget the woman. She's out cold anyway. Besides, I'd rather concentrate on him. He's just inspired me for the task."

Dana risked opening her eyes a little to see what was going on. Her heart gave a painful lurch when she saw Gil doubled over and kneeling on the metal floor, his suit coat pulled down over his arms to inhibit his ability to fight back. A sharp, acrid anger coated her tongue. She watched these evil men with new bitterness as Sparr stood in back of Gil with a gun pointed at his head and Thiel stood before him, his gun at his side as his other fist balled in anticipation of inflicting further pain on his helpless victim.

"Tie his hands first," Sparr said.

Slowly, unobtrusively, as their attention was diverted, Dana slid her hand down her leg toward her brace. However, she hesitated for an instant in surprise as she saw the pimple-faced man she knew as Lakoff suddenly materialize from out of the shadowed corner holding some cord out to Thiel. Since Gil's and her capture, she had forgotten all about his being in the van.

His voice was shaking almost as badly as the rest of him. Dana got the distinct impression he had been cowering there in hope he would be forgotten.

"Look, Sparr. I know you did to Vogel what you had to do. I mean, the scum bumbled Harcourt's death and was trying to cheat you. But I don't want to stand around and watch you and Thiel kill these two. Man, I don't have the stomach for it."

Thiel grabbed the cord from the programmer's hands, yanking Gil's suit coat off him as he went about the business of tying his hands. Sparr turned slightly toward the shaking Lakoff.

"You don't have the stomach for it? I find your squeamishness a bit unconvincing from someone who planned to ruin his father's company and shove his country into an imminent nuclear attack. Or is it you just can't face your victims when the time comes? Afraid of the blood, Lionel?"

At Sparr's mention of the name Lionel, Dana saw Gil's bent head jerk in the direction of the young man. His voice sounded not just surprised, but incredulous. "You're Lionel Cobb's son?"

"How do you know about my father?"

Sparr's powerful hand closed over Lionel's face and shoved him down, knocking his head against the floor with a sharp whack. Dana saw the young man's head roll to one side. He was either unconscious or dead.

"Boneless little twit." Sparr turned his attention back to Gil, who Thiel had yanked back to his feet now that his hands were tied in back of him.

As always, Sparr's voice was deadly calm. "It isn't the question I had planned to start out with, but I admit my curiosity has been aroused. How do you know about Lionel Cobb?"

Dana thought Gil's next words had a surprising ring of truth, considering what a big lie they were. "We've kept a complete file on Computech ever since the new-product data base crashed. Cobb's filed a big tax loss. Some of us at the Bureau thought he was pulling a fast one and claiming destruction of programs that never really existed in an attempt to defraud the IRS. None of us figured his own vindictive kid was in back of it."

For just a moment, Dana thought Sparr might swallow Gil's lie, but then so fast she barely saw the movement, the silver-haired man's gun hand came swinging down across the side of Gil's head, digging a vicious gash on his temple, sending his glasses spinning across the floor and knocking Gil once again to his knees.

"Wrong answer," Sparr said. "The IRS has its own set of investigators. The last thing the FBI would do is get involved in a case not within its jurisdiction. I've carefully studied all the criminal investigative procedures of every standard and quasi-law enforcement agency in this country. You're not going to be able to lie to me, so you'd better stop trying."

Dana felt the pain in her head, just as though it had been she instead of Gil who had been hurt. She was sick and furious, but she fought down the emotions, knowing they would only blur her effectiveness. Her hand had worked its way to the top of her brace. She stretched her fingers inside, straining them to reach the knife, praying she would get it in time.

Thiel's left hand had grabbed hold of Gil's shirt and torn it open as he pulled him back to his feet. Dana watched the blond man slip his gun into the holster on the side of his right hip as he sought to free his hand to rip the rest of Gil's shirt away. Then he held Gil propped up and stationary as he used his right hand to mercilessly punch Gil in the stomach. "You were asked a question, FBI man. You'd better answer it."

Dana bit her tongue as she heard Gil coughing in pain and gasping for breath. With racing heart, she slipped the knife out of the brace and grasped it firmly within her right palm. She knew Thiel sounded as though he really didn't care if Gil answered anything. He only wanted an excuse to hit him again. Her muscles tensed as she scooted her body around in preparation.

Thiel was reaching back, ready to land another blow at Gil's stomach when Sparr suddenly held up his hand. With a slight frown on his forehead, he studied Gil's bared chest. "Wait. Pull him up straighter so I can see him better."

Thiel yanked a barely conscious Gil to his feet as Sparr circled to his side to get a better look. Dana saw the blood spilling from Gil's temple onto the red stubble of his beard and the exposed fiery curls of his chest. She was already on her knees, the adrenaline shooting through her arteries.

Sparr stopped circling as Gil once more fell to his knees. "Look at the color of the hair on his body and his face. It's red."

Thiel sounded neither impressed nor enlightened. "So it's red. What's the big deal?"

Sparr's voice was no longer calm. "Don't you see? The darker hair on his head isn't his true color. No wonder he knows about Lionel Cobb. This is Gilbert Webb! His appearance was changed to fool us, but it's got to be him. And if he's Webb that means—"

Sparr never finished his sentence. He didn't have to. Dana had seen the truth flashing in his surprised eyes as they flipped to where she had lain on the floor a mere second before, the barrel of his gun following in a trailing arc. Only she was no longer there.

Because by then, she had sprung up and was plunging a sharp knife between Thiel's shoulder blades, directly into his black heart. As the knife hit home, Thiel collapsed against Dana, crashing them both to the floor. Dana grabbed for Thiel's holstered gun.

"Don't do it," Sparr warned in his deadly calm voice.

Dana's hand stopped in midair as she looked up into the steady barrel of Sparr's gun, three fourths of her body pinned beneath Thiel's heavy bulk. She was trapped.

Sparr's black eyes gleamed. "So we finally meet. An auspicious moment. You can't know how pleased this makes me."

Dana's heart hammered her chest wall while she struggled to imbue her voice with a calm she was far from feeling. "You'll forgive me if I fail to rise to the occasion?"

Sparr's eyebrows rose. "And a sense of humor, too. What a worthy adversary you've proved to be. There you were, parading right before my eyes while I've searched for you in corners. Yes, a very worthy adversary. I'm almost sorry the game is over.''

Dana braced for a final desperate grab for Thiel's gun. ''The game's not over yet, Sparr.''

''It is for you, FBI agent.''

Sparr's finger curled around the trigger.

GIL WAS WOOZY AND SICK from the blows he had taken. With every ounce of determination, he was trying not to black out, to concentrate on what was being said.

As Sparr's last words burned in his ears, desperation swelled inside his chest and he did the only thing he could think of to stop Sparr completing his action. Summoning all his strength, Gil lunged sideways into the silver-haired man with a force all the more potent because it was fed by his desperation. The last thing he felt was the vicious blow of Sparr's gun across the side of his head as the man's ugly, surprised oath spat in his ear.

Dana's hand tore around Thiel's corpse. With one last yank, she freed Thiel's gun and raised it in Sparr's direction.

In that split second she looked up to locate her target, Dana saw Sparr down on one knee, his placid expression changed into unmasked fury as he shifted his gun's direction to Gil's fallen frame. Dana didn't have time to think or aim. She fired. And fired.

The first bullet tore a hole in Sparr's shoulder, turning his muscles to lead. The second went through his ear, the force of its velocity shoving his head against the side of the van. Neither did his gun hand lower nor did his open, staring eyes blink as his stiff, dead body collapsed onto the van's floor.

Dana didn't wait for Sparr to fall, nor did she give him a second thought after he had. With strength she didn't know she possessed, she kicked Thiel's corpse off her and scrambled across the floor to Gil's side.

Gently, she laid his bleeding head in her lap, babbling in relief as she felt the pulse in his neck, in shock as she saw the two open wounds on his head, in dread as she found his face so stark white, so quiet.

"Gil, please don't die. You'll take me with you if you do. Damn it! If only this one time, you must follow my instructions! You must!"

She pressed her fingers against his bleeding head wounds to stop the flow. It seemed like years before she heard Talbot call out. She answered him, barely aware of what she said. He opened the door to the back of the van and whistled when he saw the bodies everywhere. She saw his expression change from surprise to concern as he caught sight of her holding Gil. He yelled to someone behind him and then jumped up into the van.

"An ambulance is on the way, Carmody. How is he?"

Her voice broke on a choked sob. "I don't know. Dear God, I don't know."

Chapter Sixteen

Gil woke to see Dana's white and worried face hovering above him in the lurching ambulance. Strands of her gray-streaked hair were sticking out in all directions. Her flowered fifties dress was torn, and it was missing a collar button. She had dried smudges of blood mixed with tears running across her cheeks, but the strength of her hand in his told him she was all right. He thought she was the most beautiful sight he had ever seen and told her so.

Or at least he tried to. But the thick blackness was closing his eyes again and weighing down his tongue and he was no longer able to fight against it.

"YOU DID A GOOD JOB, Carmody," Lew Sargentich said to Dana as she paced the hospital's waiting room.

Dana turned to him, surprised at his unexpected presence and at the lack of emotion she felt to a compliment she had once thought she needed. "What are you doing here, Lew?"

He strode over to her with a small smile on his face. "Get serious, Carmody. One of my agents breaks what is proving to be the most important case of the decade—and also manages to close the books on another three-year-old murder case—and you ask me why I'm here to share in her glory?"

Dana nodded dumbly. Each hour that had passed without word on Gil's condition drove new pain into her heart.

Lew's voice was surprisingly gentle as he laid a hand on her arm. "Webb's got a good chance, Carmody. Hospital records show his vital signs were steady when they brought him in. A brain-injury specialist arrived during the night to take over the case. I have it on good authority this delay is just the normal rigmarole associated with running him through the million or so X rays that always get ordered in cases of head injuries."

In surprise, Dana looked up into the bespectacled blue eyes that watched her. "He's out of surgery?" Dana asked.

"Has been in recovery for the last hour," Lew said. "Don't worry. They're watching him carefully. And if a miracle is required, one will be performed. I told the doctor if Webb didn't pull through, I'd arrange it with a friend at the IRS to have the doctor audited—for the last seven years."

Dana watched Lew's unchanging expression, hearing the good-natured joke in his words, but not knowing how to react. Finally, to her own absolute amazement, she heard a chuckle in her throat.

"Lew, this is a side of you I've never seen."

"Well, as they say, turnabout is fair play. Over the last few days, you've shown me a side of you I've never seen. Not that I'm disappointed to learn of it, mind you. As a matter of fact, after we get this amazing programmer of yours fixed up, I have some suggestions for—"

Lew halted in midsentence as a haggard-looking, blue-smocked doctor approached. Dana immediately turned in his direction, no longer able to concentrate on anything but this man's next words.

"It's okay, Lew, he's going to be fine. Surgery went well. All our X rays show no threat from internal bleeding. He'll probably sleep for another six or seven hours. Do I have to stay at his bedside or may I go home now?"

Dana's relief flowed through her in a welcome gush. But even it did not stop the curious look she gave Lew at the doctor's addressing him by his first name or asking his permission to go home. Lew gave her a small smile in return.

"Special Agent Dana Carmody, I'd like you to meet my brother-in-law, Dr. Greg Swanson, your Mr. Webb's specialist."

Dana turned back to Dr. Swanson to express her thanks, but he stopped her with a halting gesture of his hand. "Some brother-in-law, waking me up in the middle of the night, threatening to sic the IRS on me if I don't come down and perform a miracle on some genius he's damaged on assignment."

So Lew's threat hadn't been a joke! Dana felt amazed at the lengths her boss had taken to see that Gil received the best of care. She was more than touched as she gave his arm a quick squeeze before turning back to Dr. Swanson's amused smile. "May I see him?"

Dr. Swanson shook his head. "No. He'll be in intensive care for at least another hour. Go home. You look dreadful. Get some rest and some makeup and come back in six hours. I'll be back in seven. Good night."

As Dr. Swanson walked away, Lew took hold of Dana's arm. "You heard the doctor. Come on. I'll drive you back to the hotel. It will give us a chance to talk about some things, Carmody. While you've been standing your vigil here, Talbot has been wrapping up a few things I think you should know about."

To GIL IT SEEMED as though he had been out for just an instant when next he opened his eyes and found Dana smiling above him. Only as his thoughts cleared, he realized much more than an instant had passed. The stationary bed beneath his body was one indication. The changes in her appearance were another.

She was dressed in a dark blue business suit, her porcelain skin washed of blood and tears. A beautiful cascade of light brown locks framed her face and, although her spring-rain eyes were obviously weary, the look they held promised sunny skies for a lifetime.

"You look wonderful."

Dana sat on the edge of his bed, shaking her head. "I'm not sure I believe you anymore, Mr. Gilbert Webb. The last time you told me how good I looked, I caught a glimpse of myself in an ambulance mirror and nearly fainted in fright."

Gil chuckled as he reached for her hand and brought it to his chest. "I didn't know if you had even heard me. All I knew was that I woke up and you were alive."

Dana felt her heart squeeze at the simple sincerity in his words and leaned down to brush his lips with hers, carefully inserting her free hand behind his neck so as not to disturb the liberally applied bandages around his head.

From the startled look in his eyes, she realized he was only just becoming aware of them. He released her hand so he might use his two to explore the extent of the wrappings.

"I feel like a mummy. What did they have to perform, a lobotomy?"

She smiled as she leaned back, happy for the strength and humor coming through in his voice. "Not quite, Gil. But you do have two very mean wounds there. They just wanted to ensure all that brain power you've got stored up didn't come pouring out of the wrong orifice."

Gil tried to sit up as a dull headache throbbed and other more unpleasant thoughts started to return. "How long have I been out?"

"About twelve hours."

"What happened, Dana? The last thing I remember was lunging at Sparr and getting whacked on the head for my trouble."

She smiled at him as her finger brushed the porcupine red stubble on his chin. "Your trouble saved my life. You got his attention long enough to give me a shot at him." She went on to describe what he had missed in the van.

Gil's voice sounded light and relieved. "So both Thiel and Sparr are dead?"

"Yes. Talbot was late getting to us because of heavy traffic on the Golden Gate. And if it hadn't been for you, Gil, he would have been too late. I owe you my life."

Gil captured her caressing fingers within the warmth of his two hands and kissed them. "You know I'd do anything for you."

She laid her head on his chest and sighed as he stroked her hair. "Except follow my instructions, of course."

There were many things he wanted to say then, but he didn't because he had a life to rebuild first. Thinking about the first steps of such a rebuilding process brought new questions to mind.

"Did Lionel Cobb's son survive?"

Dana raised her head. "Yes. Sparr knocked him out, but now he's very awake and very talkative. Talbot took his deposition. He's admitted to approaching Vogel a little over a year ago and presenting him with his scheme of computer infiltration. Having experienced recent financial setbacks, Vogel saw Lionel, Jr.'s plan as a way to make a killing, so he set up CustomKey and got the ball rolling."

Gil was shaking his head. "He's a brilliant kid, Dana. I remember his dad telling me that so many times, but I didn't realize how brilliant until I uncovered that parasite he designed."

Dana nodded. "And don't forget about the keyboard transmitters. He designed and installed those, too. Our electronics lab is learning a few tricks from taking them apart, I can tell you."

"Such a waste of brain power. Why did he do it, Dana?"

She heard the bafflement in Gil's voice and recognized its similarity to her own only a few hours before as Lew had given her the story. She now related it to Gil.

"These kinds of things are complicated and not really subject to simple answers, but I think at the crux of the matter is Lionel, Jr.'s long-standing resentment of his father. The way he tells it, no matter how good he did in school or how well behaved everyone said he was, his father just shrugged and told him he could do better. Lionel learned he could get much more of a rise and attention out of his father if he misbehaved. Apparently, the boy preferred emotional verbal blasts to stoic indifference.''

"He misbehaved to get his father's attention?" Gil asked.

Dana nodded. "Unending, destructive pranks followed through his high school and college years, escalating in sophistication and culminating in the use of his parasite against his father's business-computer programs. Since his father had banned him from Computech's offices, Lionel, Jr. had Vogel plant his vehicle of destruction through his daughter's gift to you.''

Gil shook his head. "Hard to believe a son could harbor such ill feelings toward his father. I knew they didn't get along, of course. Lionel never even let the kid come out of his room on the two or three occasions when he threw parties for the employees at his home. You know, now that I think about it, I realize I must have seen a picture of Lionel, Jr. on the mantel on one of those visits. That's why there was something familiar about his face.''

"Yes," Dana said. "And it was during those visits to Cobb's home that Lionel, Jr. watched you from a peephole he had made in the floor of his upstairs bedroom. He knew what you looked like, Gil. That was the reason Sparr directed him to take a good look at you in the WCTS computer room on Wednesday. But fortunately, he didn't recognize your changed appearance.''

"What was the impetus for infecting WCTS with his parasite?''

"Purely financial, Gil. Vogel and Lionel, Jr. figured that after the parasite inactivated the U.S. defense system, if the government wouldn't pay to keep the country's helpless position secret, someone else would pay to learn of it. They had the world to market their information to, and not a scruple standing in their way.''

"What's happening to WCTS?"

"I've told York that if he gets a new minicomputer and gives Linda Riley a permanent promotion as supervisor, the FBI will convince the Defense Department to hold the contract open until she can enter a clean program and save his hide. He came across subdued but agreeable. Of course, I didn't give him a whole lot of choice."

Gil stroked Dana's hand, warmed anew by her act of kindness toward Riley. He exhaled a weary breath. "I feel sorry for Lionel, Sr. now. I wonder how he'll feel when he finds out it was his own son who sabotaged his company."

Dana's voice was cold. "Don't feel sorry for him, Gil. He's been told, and you know what his first question was?"

Gil looked up at her in surprise at the vehemence in her tone. "What, Dana?"

Dana pushed the words out through closed teeth. "He asked my boss if that meant he *had* to give you back your stock and the money he received from the sale of your possessions."

"What?"

"Gil, Lew and I think Lionel Cobb knew all along that it was his son who crashed his data base. Lionel, Jr. claims he told his father he did it, although he kept the method secret. He wanted his father to know because he figured that way the pain would be greatest."

Gil shook his head, trying hard to understand such a father-son relationship so alien to the loving one he had known. "Maybe Lionel, Sr. just couldn't accept it."

Dana didn't feel so charitable. "Gil, I'm not so sure. I now think he had an ulterior motive in making you the fall guy. Your stock represented forty percent of the company's total. He had sold off all but about twelve percent of his original fifty-one percent. With your forty back in his hands, he regained controlling interest in a company that he felt slipping through his fingers."

Gil sat up straighter as he heard the news. "Dana, is that really true? Had he been selling off his stock?"

"Yes, Gil. To cover some bad stock-market investments. When he talked to you about selling the company, what he didn't tell you was that it was already almost a fait accompli. But once he got your stock back in his hot little hands, he's done an about-face and, for the last six months, has been busy with expansion."

Gil's mouth had contorted into an angry frown. "How could he do that to me, Dana? We've worked together, been friends for years. He stole my reputation, my very livelihood."

Dana nodded gravely. "Maybe what we're now seeing in the father is what has made the son the way he is."

Gil inhaled as his lips drew into a firm line. "I'll take him to court, Dana. Not because the money is all that important, but because he falsely sullied my good name for lousy greed. He'll feel my wrath in the place dearest to him—his pocketbook."

Dana saw the disillusionment in Gil's eyes and felt a small pinch in her heart. "I'm so sorry, Gil."

He shook his head. "Don't be, Dana. I've been a fool to pick such a man as a friend and business associate. Just like I was a fool to pick Vanessa as a fiancée. In so many parts of my life, I've shown an uncanny lack of good judgment."

Dana slipped her warm hand into his. "I believe in your judgment, Gil. I believe in you."

The warmth of her words reached inside him, softening the hard knot of resentment that had begun to form. He felt the tension dissipate as his eyes took in the trusting look on her lovely face.

"Are you aware that you have this endearing trait of making me believe the world is a sweet, sane place despite all evidence to the contrary?"

In answer, she smiled and leaned over to kiss him gently, leaving a delicious aftertaste of hot peppermint in her wake.

"How would you like to work for the Bureau full-time?"

Gil looked at her in surprise. "Seriously?"

Dana nodded. "Sargentich wants you to head up a new computer squad, working as both an investigator and staff trainer. He's told me your first assignment will be to go through the Defense Department's software with your magic wand and discover if we've any more parasites lurking about."

Gil's smile told Dana just how pleased he was with the offer. "Is this your doing?"

She shook her head. "No. My boss knows a great programmer when he sees one. Your identification of the WCTS parasite bowled him over. He responds to talent, and he's responding to yours. It's a good job, Gil. And there's a pride working for the Bureau I don't think exists anywhere else."

He smiled at the sincerity in her words. "And when am I supposed to be starting this new assignment?"

"As soon as they release you from the hospital. The doctor said that should be in a few days. But I've told Sargentich you won't be able to start for at least a month."

Gil heard her words in surprise. "A month? Why so long?"

Dana smiled as she straightened up and stretched leisurely, as though she was just discussing the weather. "Well, I want a little honeymoon before we both have to start back to work again."

Gil's eyes lit up as her words sank in. Before she knew it, he had leaned across the bed and grabbed her wrists, his voice an excited whisper. "Dana, darling, did you just propose to me?"

She smiled over at him as her gray eyes danced. "We're already in a hospital, so getting the blood tests should be a breeze."

Gil felt his heart begin to twist in his chest. "Oh, Dana." Tenderly, he gathered her in his arms, resting her cheek against his, stroking her soft hair. "I want to marry you. I want nothing more. I wanted to ask you since Wednesday night after we made love. But I can't. I've got nothing to offer you right now. Not even the money for a honeymoon."

Even more than his words, his tone told her of the ache they carried. She sat back on the bed so that she could see his eyes and so he could see the message in hers. "You'll have money again soon. What does it matter if I pay for the honeymoon?"

He shook his head. "Dana, it'll be a long time before I can get back on my feet financially. I know you've got your own job and your own money, and I'm proud you do. But for me to use your money for our honeymoon, well, it makes me feel so..."

His voice trailed off, but she read the message in his words. "Okay, Gil. I know a cozy little cabin up in Marin County that will do fine for two people so much in love they're not going to see anything else but each other anyway."

He gathered her back in his arms. "Dana, my cabin is a dump."

"Gil, give me a month with you there and I promise even you won't care."

She felt him exhale in surrender. "I love you, Dana. For the sweetness in your soul. For the way you always turn the impossible into an exciting reality. Okay, I'm putty in your hands. I want you too much to refuse. There's just one condition I'll insist on."

She smiled. "Name it."

"That the first night we find a rainstorm and visit a very special cliff up in the Golden Gate National Recreation Area."

Dana straightened to see his face. "Gil, you're sentimental."

A devilish gleam came into his golden eyes. "Maybe. Or maybe I just want to give you a taste for what that night would have been like if I had been sober when you kissed me."

Dana found herself smiling clear through to her heart as little licks of excitement danced down her nerves. "Are you saying I'll be lucky if we make it back to the cabin?"

He wrapped his arms around her, hugging her to his chest. "I'm saying you'll be lucky if we make it back to the Jeep."

He kissed her then, and on his lips she tasted the promise of their future—loving, exciting and only just beginning.

Jingle Bells, Wedding Bells

The joy of Christmas and the magic of marriage await you in this special collection of four heart-warming love stories.

All I Want for Christmas
Nora Roberts

Jack's Ornament
Myrna Temte

A Very Merry-Step Christmas
Barbara Boswell

The Forever Gift
Elizabeth August

Published: November 1995

Price: £4.99

SILHOUETTE